THE GIRL OF THE LAKE

Also by BILL ROORBACH

FICTION

The Remedy for Love

Life Among Giants

The Smallest Color

Big Bend

NONFICTION

Temple Stream

A Place on Water
(with Robert Kimber and Wesley McNair)

Into Woods

Summers with Juliet

INSTRUCTION

Writing Life Stories

Contemporary Creative Nonfiction: The Art of Truth

THE GIRL OF THE LAKE

STORIES

BILL ROORBACH

ALGONQUIN BOOKS
OF CHAPEL HILL
2017

Published by
ALGONQUIN BOOKS OF CHAPEL HILL
Post Office Box 2225
Chapel Hill, North Carolina 27515-2225

a division of
WORKMAN PUBLISHING
225 Varick Street
New York, New York 10014

Printed in the United States of America.
Published simultaneously in Canada by Thomas Allen & Son Limited.
Design by Steve Godwin.

LIBRARY OF CONGRESS CATALOGING-IN-PUBLICATION DATA
Names: Roorbach, Bill, author.
Title: The girl of the lake : stories / by Bill Roorbach.
Description: First edition. | Chapel Hill, North Carolina : Algonquin Books of Chapel Hill, 2017.
Identifiers: LCCN 2016053907 | ISBN 9781616203320
Subjects: LCSH: Interpersonal relations—Fiction. | United States—Social life and customs—21st century—Fiction. | LCGFT: Short stories.
Classification: LCC PS3568.O6345 A6 2017 | DDC 813/.54—dc23
LC record available at https://lccn.loc.gov/2016053907

10 9 8 7 6 5 4 3 2 1
First Edition

For Jim Harrison

Contents

THE GIRL OF THE LAKE

Harbinger Hall

BOBBY MULLENDORE WAS SICK of sixth grade, especially without his best friend Jack B., plus it was spring. Painstakingly, key by key, a hard jab on each with his index fingers, he typed a missive in the exact language of the carbon copy Jack had given him as a good-bye treasure just this past fall, only adjusting the dates, and dropping in his own name:

> Dear Mrs. Applegate: Due to a career emergency, we are moving as of 16 April 1963. Robert will attend his last class this Friday, April 13. He will start school in Asheville, North Carolina, a week hence. Please accept my apologies for this short notice. It could not be helped, and we regret it.

After twenty focused, difficult minutes, after typing the *Sincerely yours* one letter at a time, Bobby pulled the curled paper from the Royal Standard, flattened it carefully, and signed his mother's name.

That afternoon at two fifteen, moving against the tide of the other kids leaving class, Bobby made his way to Mrs. Applegate's desk. She was searching through a low drawer, sat up straight when he made a noise, looked surprised. And she just started talking, as she could do:

"Robert! Well. Your homework is better the last few weeks. Your hands are much cleaner, too!"

Bobby made no response, just handed her the letter.

"Oh my!" said Mrs. Applegate.

"Yip," Bobby said.

The next day, Mrs. Applegate sprang a surprise, just as she had for Jack's departure: "Bobby Mullendore," she announced, "is moving."

MONDAY, BOBBY WORE THE same old clothes, but with the addition of one Sears Roebuck watch, a reviled Christmas present, strapped self-consciously to his wrist. Mom saw it and smiled inwardly but still visibly, knew in her Mom way not to say anything. Bobby walked to the bus stop clutching his lunch, stood there a minute in case Mom should look down the road, then leapt into the woods. Ancient Mr. Green stopped the old yellow beast, might have even honked (he didn't like to miss a kid), but a couple of Bobby's former classmates yelled out, "Moved! Moved!"

Bobby could hear Mr. Green croak, "Bobby moved?"

"Moved!" the kids cried.

Mr. Green: "Well okay, then!" The bus roared off, wouldn't stop there again.

Bobby crossed Wahackme Road, trotted down to Dogwood Lane, ducked past Mrs. Smith's, trotted down past the PRIVATE LANE sign, remembered to breathe, trotted along the high stone wall in front of the Schraeder's house, then into the pine forest along the needle-soft path that would bring him to the old stone stable where he and Jack B. had found wondrous things: cigarette butts, beer bottles, a big-girl's bra, a pair of tightie-whities with Brent Lovelace's camp tags sewn in.

The stable was on the D'Arcy estate, Bobby knew, the centerpiece of which was a stone mansion five minutes on foot from the stable through well-kept forest on a wide bridle path. *From another era*, as

Bobby's dad phrased it. Jack B. and Bobby had often slipped up to the house at dusk to look in the windows, saw nothing but a maid once in uniform, and another time a small party—old people having dinner on the great stone patio. Jack B. had had the *tuff* idea of blowing squeals through long grasses, which they did. On the stone porch the party went silent in the night. The old people rose. "Now what's that?" one said. And another: "That's some sort of crane." "Rare, I should think," and pretty soon they'd left their desserts and come tottering across the lawn to investigate.

Bobby and Jack B. giggled back into the woods, blew parting calls all the way down the bridle path, luring the old folks on, then silence: the birds had flown. "Scared them off," the one voice said. "Quite sure these are cranes," said the other. The little knot of nine or ten old folks huddled there in the woods where any ogre might get them. "A harbinger, I should think," that third voice said.

And then for months and months Bobby and Jack B. whispered those phrases under Mrs. Applegate's nose: "Rare, I should think!" Stifled giggles. "A harbinger, I should think!" Gales of laughter, reprimands. The "I should think" became part of the comedy repertoire of the whole sixth grade: "Sloppy Joes for lunch, *I should think*!" The boys didn't know what a harbinger was, and didn't look it up, but Jack B. used the word to name the estate.

Bobby spent his first day of freedom in the abandoned stables of Harbinger Hall, inspecting every corner of the place, looking out every bubbled window, finding astonishing things to discuss in a possible letter to Jack B: six old horseshoes, a 1903 penny, a pair of girl's underpants with two curled red hairs more or less *pasted* inside (Brent Lovelace's girl Jenny Oswest had the reddest hair), rotting tack, the skeleton of a cat. He ate his lunch exactly at twelve fifteen at a desklike shelf in the groom's quarters, no awful pressure to trade his Ring Dings for egg salad.

"FUNNIEST THING," HIS MOM said at dinner (fish sticks and tartar sauce). "I saw Mrs. Crawford at the A&P, and she said she'd heard we'd *moved*!"

"Empty-headed woman," Bobby's dad said.

Bobby hadn't thought till that moment that there was any possible flaw in his plan. But the train of conversation chugged quickly away from Mrs. Crawford (Benny C.'s mom) to a "communication" problem at Dad's company in New York and then to a similar problem at Mom's garden club. Bobby felt the safety of his plan settle in around him.

THE NEXT MONDAY, BOBBY stepped off the bridle path exactly where he'd stepped off each day the previous week, trotted into the forest on his recon trail till the mansion came into view. Now it was tree to tree, the Nazis in there holding Jack B., dark day, about to storm, and the microfilm in Bobby's pocket in direst danger of getting wet in the rain and fizzing to deadly acid: he had to make the stone entryway where he'd brazenly hidden his G.I. poncho on Friday's mission, a note to Jack B. folded inside it. Was Jack dead? Had Jack been able to decipher the encrypted message? The line of azaleas hid a machine-gun emplacement.

Bobby crawled on his belly in a stone-lined drainage ditch, then to the driveway portico and the grand entryway, breathing hard. His carbine, a polished stick, turned into a Luger lifted from a Nazi corpse. He tucked the weapon into his pants for the climb chink-to-chink up the stone wall of the entryway, a good twelve feet high. Bobby put his face in the void where the poncho would be. He held on to the rock crevices, muscles quivering with the effort. No poncho.

He climbed back down, pulled the heavy Luger from his pants, let it turn into a machine gun to be held with two hands. Who could have taken his poncho? The game had turned ninety degrees toward the real, and his fear turned with it. He flopped to his belly in the fine gravel of the drive, crawled the width of the great entryway, hidden only by the lip of the single marble step. Next corner of the house he peered around, peered into a study, saw the back of an old man writing at a desk! Writing orders to send Jack B. to the firing squad! Bobby stood, aimed his machine gun.

Exactly then Bobby heard two sudden steps in the gravel. An enormous hand grabbed his neck, another the belt of his pants, and someone lifted him off the ground. The game was over. This was one hundred percent real. Heavy foreign accent, however, very like that of the Nazis on TV, saying, "Vat does this mean!"

"I'm just a neighbor kid!"

"You are spyink!"

"I live over there!" Trying to point.

The man pulled Bobby up the step by the collar and belt, across the marble and through one set of massive oaken doors, then through a second set and into an expansive marble foyer. Bobby's heart fluttered in his chest. He began to thrash, but the man just yanked him off his feet by the belt again, let him kick in the air.

The maid appeared, the very one, appeared on the great marble stair that rose straight ahead. She said, "Oh, is this the person who's been . . . "

"The same," said Bobby's captor.

"I'll get Hilyard."

And too soon a door opened and a butler came into the great foyer, an unmistakable *butler* in actual tails, carrying the poncho in front of him. He said, "This is . . . yours?"

"It's just my raincoat," Bobby said.

The butler produced the note to Jack B., read: "Attack-way 0900 hours-ay, illkay allway?" Then, translating: "Free you through back wall—stand clear for dynamite?"

"It's just a game."

"Use acid on maid's face?"

"I'm sorry," Bobby Mullendore said. He would not cry.

"What do you think, Dort? Shall we bother Mr. D'Arcy?" Hilyard said the master's name in three distinct syllables like letters: *D.R.C.* He turned on heel. The hand at Bobby's neck squeezed harder, urged him to follow. Prisoner and guards walked about a mile down a corridor of heavy doors to an elaborately arched stone doorway. The butler gave the gentlest knock. After a long, silent wait the thick door opened slowly.

"My," said Mr. D'Arcy. He was the man Bobby had seen at his desk, the one Bobby had been about to machine gun through the great windows. He was way older than Grandfather, and more frail. He did not look kind.

"A game, he says," said the butler.

"And what game was this?" Mr. D'Arcy said.

"War?" Bobby said helpfully. "World War Two?"

"Do you call that a war?" Mr. D'Arcy said.

With the old man's slow smile, Dort let go of Bobby's neck, retreated silently down the hall. The butler lingered, but at a subtle nod from his master, sighed and padded off.

"Your name?" Mr. D'Arcy said.

"Bobby."

"Come in, then, Robert," Mr. D'Arcy said. "I've been expecting you." He shuffled forward, impatiently waving for Bobby to keep up, as if Bobby were having a problem sustaining the old man's tortoise pace. Bobby scoped the surroundings. The room was all dark wood. Books reached to the ceiling in dark bindings. The tall windows were filled with plants—some of them trees, really, growing in enormous earthen pots and pushing the dark, heavy curtains aside in their battle for sunlight. The floor was heavy reddish flagstone. A dozen tall floor lamps lit the whole warmly. The fireplace, set with a fire unlit, was tall as Mrs. Applegate—she could put her whole desk in there and stand behind it and her head wouldn't even be up the chimney! The brightest spot in the room was Mr. D'Arcy's desk, piled with books and papers and rubber stamps and a heavy old phone, all of it lit by two golden lamps. A tall accounting book lay open, a fountain pen uncapped upon it, work interrupted. Mr. D'Arcy straightaway recapped the pen, placed it in its golden holder. Bobby wasn't scared at all, he told himself, something about all the books and lamps.

Mr. D'Arcy smelled of cologne, looked warmly stuffed—taxidermy in corduroy. He was carefully shaved, hair neatly trimmed, none of Grandpa's long ear hairs and nose hairs, hair dyed black, it looked like, and shot through with white strands, all damply combed. The spotted hands had a little shake to them like conducting their own small orchestra. The face, when Mr. D'Arcy finally looked at Bobby, was large and serious, spots and lines, yet something kindly in there, something soulful and sad inside the hardness of the eyes.

"You want to play war?" Mr. D'Arcy said abruptly. And he marched around his desk to the bookcases, reached for a book, pulled at its spine, and a section of the bookcase slowly swung out into the room, a secret door straight from monster movies.

"Tuff," said Bobby.

"Tough?" said Mr. D'Arcy.

"Cool," said Bobby.

"Ah," said Mr. D'Arcy.

In the new room there was just darkness until Mr. D'Arcy found the switch on the table lamp. When he closed the bookshelf door, the lamp was the only light. He said, "Our map room." No windows, no door visible at all, but a fresh breeze coming from somewhere. Two walls were all big cabinets, narrow drawers. The other two walls offered complicated banks of roll-down maps. Mr. D'Arcy shuffled around the room, turned the switches on a dozen lamps, gradually lit a stately oaken table the size of two Ping-Pong tables pushed end to end. A colorful map almost as long and wide as the table was already rolled out and weighted at its four corners with stout pyramids of iron.

What land did the old map show? Bobby bent to it with sharp eyes. It was like a painting, cracked and crinkled, hugely detailed, the lakes showing waves, the mountains green with white peaks, cities with ornate buildings, the borders with other countries orange and forbidding. The very lettering was foreign. Bobby had studied and imitated ancient Egyptian hieroglyphs, knew the word *cuneiform*. But he didn't know this alphabet.

Mr. D'Arcy let him look a while. "Now tell me Robert, to begin the game: what country is represented here?"

Bobby pored over the map, leaning into it, followed a great river with his finger. "I can't read the names," he said. The lines of latitude curved narrower and narrower to the top of the map where they nearly closed, forming a circle, and North was clearly enough delineated. Just off the thick paper, then, was the North Pole, correct?

Mr. D'Arcy said, "Of course you can't read it. The alphabet is Cyrillic. That is your second clue."

Make-believe? Was it a map of, like, Cyrillia? Bobby didn't chance the answer. He kept up his close inspection, a creepy feeling tickling its way up his neck, walked slowly around the table away from the old man, examining the map all the while.

Mr. D'Arcy said, "One last, big clue: it is a country now part of the Soviet Union."

"Russia!" Bobby said. Goosebumps rose on his arms.

"You are correct. Now. To make things easier, let us find a similar map marked in English." Mr. D'Arcy shuffled to a bank of tall tubes, knocked on the correct one. Bobby helped him lift it—very heavy—and helped lug it to the table, and there they pulled it out, unrolled it over the first map, weighted it carefully flat with the iron pyramids.

"Russia!" Bobby said again. He recognized it now. He'd been hiding under his desk with the rest of his class for years in case these monsters dropped the atom bomb!

Mr. D'Arcy didn't look like a spy. He only looked amused. He said, "Relics, these old campaign maps. I buy them at auction. What I paid for this would build a carriage house and two barns plus horses to fill a stable. But see how beautifully made. It shows the Russia of the tsars, and comes from one of their palaces. Now. Here's our game. Let us call it 'Russian Revolution.' All right? And we are tsarists. Yes?" Mr. D'Arcy opened a drawer in the table, struggled to produce from it an ornate leather box, opened this carefully with both hands, tilted it to show Bobby what was inside: figurines—a dozen large handfuls of tiny metal people, nicely painted.

"We live over here." Mr. D'Arcy walked around to Bobby's side of the table very slowly, carrying the box of people. He placed it carefully atop the map, put a precise finger on St. Petersburg. "But it is summer now, so we are down here at our dacha, our summer cottage that is, just south of the great new city. The year is 1905."

Bobby had his eyes on the figurines. Each was about one inch tall and there were hundreds, all seemingly different.

"Yes? Let's put some players on the board. First, we'll need a nobleman." Mr. D'Arcy fished in the pile of little people, found a proud fellow dressed in a smart military-looking uniform. This he placed at the dacha. He said, "Our nobleman's name, as our little game begins, is Count Darlotsoff. He is twenty-three years old—quite young to be running an estate, don't you think? Quite young to be father of three children. But such was the time and place.

"Now, let us represent young Count Darlotsoff's family." Mr. D'Arcy emptied the leather box into the North Sea, shuffled a handful of people up next to Sweden, indicated with a quavering hand that Bobby should pick out the players as they were named. "Father, or the Old Count," he said solemnly.

Bobby picked out a fat fellow in jacket and medals, put him near Count Darlotsoff.

"Now, Mother, or the Old Countess."

And Bobby picked an overweight little thing in a gown painted red.

"Uncanny choices," Mr. D'Arcy said.

Soon there was a crowd on the map in the area of the dacha, Count Darlotsoff's relatives: his beautiful wife (a redhead like Jenny Oswest), their three children, her two sisters, their husbands, their six and eight children respectively, dozens of servants, two old aunts. The dacha was not a cottage at all, as Mr. D'Arcy described it, but several mansions surrounded by a dozen fine barns, huge fields. "The trees there," Mr. D'Arcy said. "They were as big as our elms here in Connecticut—very large trees they were, Russian maples, I should say, in rows both sides of the lane. One looked down over long lawns to . . . what shall we call them? To *terraced* ponds, and past these one glimpsed the homes of the peasants, the Old Count's *people*, as he called them, 'My *people*,' which he said as he might say 'My *cattle*,' people, as it happened, who were being stirred up by thinkers from St. Petersburg's universities."

The Old Count's son, whom Mr. D'Arcy called the Young Count, was one of the troublesome thinkers. He'd taken the new philosophies deeply to heart, finding them humane, at least in theory, moderate and achievable. The serfs had been freed long before, in the year 1860, but freed only to economic slavery. The thinkers rose up with ideas to solve these problems: constitutional monarchy, social democracy, anarchism, nihilism, Bolshevism, Menshevism, land reform. The peasants began to covet the fields they worked.

Mr. D'Arcy gave Bobby a long look. "These are things we can talk about in the future, you and I, should you be inclined."

Bobby nodded noncommittally, offered a polite smile.

Mr. D'Arcy fingered the figurine of the Old Count. "Him exactly," he said. And then: "But I'm afraid our game starts with the violent death of this man, and with the revision, I should say, of the Young Count's idealism." The Old Count, it seemed, had cut off all but the most rudimentary foodstuffs to his peasants after the uprisings of 1905. He made hunting illegal, fenced off the ponds, saw trespassers and poachers hung. Mr. D'Arcy pointed at various places on the map as if the very neighborhoods and shop fronts and carriages were pictured there. The Neva blacksmith, he explained, Iosif Vladimirovich Alyoishin, became enraged when his dog was run over by the mounted escorts of the Old Count's party, which had come into St. Petersburg to meet with the hated tsar. Iosif, a reader and declaimer of poetry, educated by the decrees of the Edict of Emancipation, eloquent far beyond his station, ran after the carriages, caught up with them at the Neva River Market, demanded restitution.

"And what do you think the Old Count said to kindly Iosif, Robert? Did he say he was sorry? Did he send a servant down next day with one of his *two hundred forty-six* dogs? No. The Old Count said this: 'Well, blacksmith, call on butcher Evanitsky! You and your brothers won't need your meat ration this month!'"

Iosif forgot himself and leapt, pulled the Old Count out of his saddle onto the cobblestones. And that might have been that, with Iosif hanged shortly, but the crowd surged in. There was no time for rope, no guns, none of that—the peasants pulled up cobblestones and bashed noble brains, carried the bodies through the market square, hung twelve of them on the iron spikes of the fence around the old church. The priest burst out, aghast, held his hands up for quiet, said: "You have proved to God that you are serfs always!"

Soon he was hanging from the fence himself.

Mr. D'Arcy gazed at the Old Count's figurine a long time, said, "I'm glad you've picked him out—you've a marvelous eye—let us bury him.

We'll need a graveyard before we're through, I should say! Let us put our cemetery somewhere beautiful, somewhere we won't have to move it, here in Sweden, perhaps."

Bobby flew the remains of the Old Count to Sweden with a slow, solemn hand, lay the fat little figurine on its back. In the ornate box of people he'd seen a priest, so he picked that figure out too, flew it slowly to Sweden, visibly pleasing Mr. D'Arcy, then found eleven nobles one at a time, flew them to Sweden, too.

Bobby said, "The tsar is like the king?"

"Bigger than a king! And his work of repression—repression is a holding down by force—the repression in those years was bloody, inhuman. All of life became so. Murder poured from the palace. The Young Count prevented what he could on his own lands through acts of kindness, but saw Iosif to the gallows, saw half the peasant men of the county hung, as well, for merely having been in the square. Then history moved forward. You'll want to pick out some babies there, and more children, and some teens, and some young adults. Six in ten must be buried. Disease, largely, but common accidents as well."

Bobby counted out a dozen babies and young children and youths and maidens, flew them solemnly to the growing pile in Sweden. Mr. D'Arcy stood as if at a funeral, watched each flight to heaven solemnly, none of the familiar adult hurrying or condescension when it came to make-believe.

When all the dead were safely buried, he said, "World War I broke out in 1914. The Young Count was less young now. His politics, which had formerly urged him toward an enlightened aristocracy, urged him now toward an unpopular parliamentarianism in which a monarch might have some role, however ceremonial. I hope you are following some of this, Robert. Good, good—smart boy—we'll fill in the gaps presently—we have years to come in our friendship!"

Bobby grinned. He wasn't having trouble following Mr. D'Arcy—

there was the map in front of them, there were the babies: a little cough, a growing fever, and dead. There was the tsar—a king's king, flashing with jewels, robes purple—a cruel master!

Mr. D'Arcy smiled, too, just so, and proceeded to give a carefully calibrated lecture in history, how the tsar entered the Great War enthusiastically, how most Russian factions followed him, how the separatist Bolsheviks held back, how the new war brought worse food shortages and more death, how the news was all gossip with no presses operating, how with the lack of food and information, anarchy and insurrection were rife.

"Now, I must mention Rasputin. Have you heard of him Robert? No? Then listen. Later you can read up and tell me what you think of him!" Rasputin, so Mr. D'Arcy said, was an opportunist, a satyr, a supposed monk, politely said to be "counseling" Empress Alexandra, who at his behest (so it was rumored) made secret deals with the kaiser of Germany, further alienating the people and now the nobility as well. Saint Petersburg itself was torn. The many factions gradually coalesced into two armed camps: the White Army, made up of the Bolsheviks, and the Red Army, made up of the Soviets. Alexander Kerensky and his revolutionary socialists were squeezed into power between these forces. For a young nobleman like Count Darlotsoff, there was no one left to trust. In desperation, winter 1916, he packed his townhouses and took his family to the dacha compound. Companies of soldiers roamed the countryside as brigands, in uniform or no.

Bobby listened intently and watched the map, from which the story seemed to rise.

"One day," said Mr. D'Arcy, "a band of forty came swaggering up the maple lane at Dacha Darlotsoff, straight to the grand doors! Hearing their shouts, the Young Count, though not feeling brave, stood up from breakfast, pulled off his napkin, yanked on his jacket, hefted his sword!" Alone, the Young Count stepped outside, barred the doors behind him, took a stand. Soon his uncles came running from their houses to support him, then his brothers-in-law, his five teenaged nephews, several young cousins, finally the three manservants who hadn't run off: nineteen youths and men, in all, standing against forty.

"The oldest was Uncle Pieter, my age now, eighty-one. The youngest, Cousin Victor (who had been named for Victor Hugo), your age, at a guess; he was twelve." The leader of the renegades spoke: "We come in peace." He was tall, with roughly cut leather pants, and for a uniform nothing but the vestiges of an officer's jacket, on its breast a badge from neighbor Simeonov's chest. The Young Count's heart pounded. But he was master of the estate and had established himself as a kindly one, generous and fair. He stood tall in his riding boots, said, "If you come in peace, then go in peace," a rather nice construction, as he thought, and all of the brigands and all of the dacha's men stood frozen till suddenly the great doors flew open and out raced the Youngest Count, a boy nicknamed Chimp, a baby of five years still in short pants and curls, shouting: "Turks! Huns! I kill you!" Waving his wooden sword and charging with it on an imaginary steed through the men of his family and into the phalanx of soldiers. And just when one would expect in normal times among normal men laughter and relief, a brigand in the third or fourth rank of men—that's how deep the brave Littlest Count had penetrated—picked the boy up, flung him in the air, caught him by the feet, and dashed his brains out on the stone stairs of the main dwelling. From the criminal's mates there were cries of disgust, but never mind—the Young Count struck their leader down with his sword, a perfect thrust through the neck, and the old uncles faced the next tier slashing, killing, but were overwhelmed by the advancing remains of the forty and were murdered one at a time, dying beheaded, bleating, disemboweled, gushing blood, as the Young Count and the brave young nephews backed up to the great doors. From above, sudden shots—the Young Countess and the Old Countess, as it turned out, firing the sophisticated hunting rifles of dacha Darlotsoff round after round into the band of criminals. And this saved the day: the ragtag soldiers had only three or four old muskets, slow to load. By the time the brigands turned and ran, twenty or more of them were dead on the stairs, piled on Chimp's tiny body, and on the bodies of the uncles, and the brothers-in-law, and on Feodor, favorite nephew, fourteen years of age, and on two boy cousins, nicknamed Marcel and Louis, and on the cook, the French tutor, and the stable boy, too, the loyal stable boy who'd come up from the village that morning.

Mr. D'Arcy took a long breath, stood erect, puffed his cheeks, blew out a series of sighs, looking over the length of the map as if he were staring out across the great expanse of Russia herself. Bobby flew the broken body of Chimp to Sweden first, then those of the three old uncles, one at a time, full ceremony each, then the others. He huddled the remaining family—mostly women and children—behind the Young Count, pictured the great wooden dacha doors closing safe behind them, imagined the shouts, the tears, the triumph of the women upstairs muted instantly by the tragedy they hadn't been able to forestall but only interrupt.

Mr. D'Arcy lowered his voice, continued his story. That evening, only two hours later, barely enough time to drag in the dead family members for lying-in, a score of brigand bodies still splayed out on the steps, the remains of the motley band returned with a disgruntled hoard of peasants from beyond the ponds. These hundred men hid behind the piled bodies, then stormed the great doors. The Young Count and his nephews and nieces and daughters, armed one and all with elegant and thoroughly modern hunting rifles but little skill among them, fired from the downstairs windows into the advance killing many, wounding many.

"Even my children fought, made murderers by those they killed!"

Upstairs at the dacha, the Young Count's pretty wife loaded rifles for the Old Countess, who was a masterful shot, picking off brigands like so many blackbirds in the stubble of rye. The brigands and their peasant conscripts were no better armed than earlier, died in growing heaps, but a handful managed to set the dacha doors on fire, filling the house with smoke. Then four of the beasts climbed the stones to the second story, surprising the Old Countess, who was still firing on their brothers. They overwhelmed her and tossed her bodily out a grand window. She broke on the ground below in sight of her son, died without a sound while the four brigands handed down their prize, the Young Countess, who scratched at their eyes, called them dogs. One could not shoot for fear of hitting her. One could not give chase, either, not with six young women and girls unprotected in the house.

Mr. D'Arcy fell into a deep silence while Bobby flew the dead to Sweden. First, the Old Countess in her plumpness, crack shot, then the rest.

The Young Count didn't know it at the time, of course, but this was the February Revolution in progress. The year was new, 1917. His darling wife carried off! His mother defenestrated! His horses gone. His barns afire. As for men, only the young German was still alive, that mere gardener's assistant, a coarse country boy the Young Count had never been fond of.

Bobby flew the tutor, the cook, and the stable boy off to Sweden, one by one. The Young Countess he held in his hand a minute—she'd only been carried off, perhaps to be rescued—so beautiful, the figurine he'd picked, the most beautiful of them all, flowing long red hair, red and silver gown. Mr. D'Arcy gazed at her, too, at length shook his head very slightly. "She mustn't have lived long at their hands," he said.

To Sweden with her.

Around St. Petersburg Bobby could see rivers of blood, smoke pouring from dachas, flames enveloping the finest houses in the countryside. Children carried off! Gentle milk cows slaughtered by starving roamers!

Mr. D'Arcy said, "Now—tell me, Robert." He was starting to pronounce Bobby's formal name just the way the part-time French teacher at West School did: *Ro-bear.* "If you are the Young Count, what do you do next? Remember—you have two living daughters and three nieces, aged sixteen down to seven, a lapsed nun for governess, a brave if stubborn young German gardener left. The only other adult is your sister-in-law, who has always been called Monique rather than her Russian name, which was Evgeniya. Now—tell me, tell me—what is your course of action?"

Bobby checked the figurines. What Mr. D'Arcy had said, his eyes closed, was exactly true: the Young Count was surrounded by eight, and only one a man. And Bobby didn't know what to do. His own heart began to beat in his own thin chest, all of him safe in this rich man's map room except his imagination. First thought that came to his careful head was of heroics: "The gardener and I go to rescue the Young Countess! The women hide? The women and girls hide in the tornado shelter!" This from *The Wizard of Oz.*

Mr. D'Arcy smiled at that suggestion briefly, said, "The German gardener is but seventeen, I should say, a hulk, quiet but impassive. And the house, remember, is smoking at the doors. These girls—all very lovely! Babies some of them, two of them your daughters! And Monique crying and moaning—she's lost her head—no help there. Do you see?"

Bobby thought desperately, gave a desperate answer: "We have to gather everyone and leave!"

And Mr. D'Arcy snapped back: "Just leave the dacha with all its furnishings, all your wealth, all your beloved objects, papers, portraits, pets?"

Bobby, trying to be in character, said, "But the *brigands* will be back!"

Mr. D'Arcy, not acting, not at all, almost in tears, said, "Leave the dacha and go . . . where? Where will they not be intercepted? Where should their flight take them?"

"The forest!"

"Exactly—the forest." Mr. D'Arcy closed his eyes, leaned back in his chair, rested a moment before plunging on. He told of the fires in the forest, the brigands lurking there, no escape route obvious.

Bobby smelled the smoke, saw all the blood, saw the corpses of the old uncles so lovingly arranged on all the couches of the grand drawing room, the nephews laid out on the floors beside their fathers. He said, "We'd better get going! Let's move!" He looked at the crackled old map, saw a stream named Ota just there where the dacha was marked in Mr. D'Arcy's own ink. He said, "To the stream? Is there a canoe?"

"Well thought, Robert. Except that, of course, the river Ota is quite frozen."

"A sled!" cried Bobby.

Yes, a sled. The Young Count and his daughter Petra (the only girl capable), along with the dour gardener, loaded one of the dacha's formal sleighs with food and firearms and family papers fast as they could, then escorted trembling Monique and the younger girls down to the ice, none too soon: a mob in the hundreds approached, bearing torches.

Bobby bit his nails, said, "We have to *hurry*!"

"Hurry, Robert, yes. The girls mounted the sleigh on their own. Monique, we had to push. And Dort and I acted as horses, took up the trace bars, pulled the sleigh out onto the Ota."

"Safe," Bobby said. "Safe!"

"Hardly," said Mr. D'Arcy blackly.

"NO HOMEWORK TONIGHT?" BOBBY'S father said at dinner.

Bobby, lost in thought, had to scramble to keep his cover, said, "Report."

"Report?" his mom said.

"On the, um, Russian Revolution."

"Oh, I know a thing or two about that," Bobby's father said.

"Romanovs. Rasputin. The tsar and tsarina and tsarlings eating too much caviar! It all leads them right down into World War I."

"Yes," Bobby said. "But the worst of it comes well after World War I begins!"

His father and mother both looked at him a long time, proud as pizza pie. Their faces said it all: Bobby finally taking an interest.

His dad said, "Let's get out the *Encyclopaedia Britannica* after supper!"

BOBBY RAN INTO THE woods, took the commando route, even crawled to the front door of Harbinger Hall—he was a long-lost nephew, a brave boy bringing news of the river Ota. At the great doors of Mr. D'Arcy's stone house, he didn't even have to knock: Hilyard was there. "Master Robert," he said.

"Hi," Bobby said.

"Mr. D'Arcy will be down from his bath in a moment. You are to wait in his study."

Yesterday, Bobby had had to ask Mr. D'Arcy to stop the game: bus time. And Bobby had worried about this in the night, feeling he might have offended the old man. He stood in the study not touching anything (Hilyard had said he had best not), only examining the grand bookshelf, trying without luck to pick out the secret door. Soon Mr. D'Arcy shuffled in, wearing a silk smoking jacket like the Young Count himself might, the jacket over pajama pants, lamb's-wool slippers.

"Good morning, Robert!" *Ro-bear.* "I see your smile is with you! You are ready for more of my dismal story, more of our game, I should say."

"Yip."

"But first, Hilyard has made me realize that there are some questions to ask of you. First: your family. Are you Robert Mullendore?"

"Uh, yip."

"And your mum, is she the Ann Mullendore who volunteers with the garden club?"

"Yip: Ann."

"So the redoubtable Hilyard did recognize you, I should say. The second question is about your studies: I'd made the rather glib assumption that this for you was a holiday week of some nature. Hilyard says no. So: why are you not in school?"

Seven lies went through Bobby's head, but the truth bobbed up in the light of Mr. D'Arcy's clear eyes upon him: "I am skipping."

"Skipping. I believe I know what that means. Dort says he saw you of a morning a month ago, creeping through the woods, then again perhaps twice, and then yesterday of course, leading up to his making your acquaintance."

So Bobby told the whole story of his desertion, his defection, his despair. Mr. D'Arcy didn't seem mad, more like amused, and listened carefully. "Well, never mind. Later we'll ask Hilyard to make a couple of phone calls on your behalf."

Bobby's heart sank. "Um, who's he gonna call?"

"On your behalf, my boy. No more to say. Not to worry, either. Hilyard has a very delicate touch. But you and I, we have a game to attend to."

In the map room Mr. D'Arcy flicked on the lights one by one, Bobby glum till he saw that the dead were still in Sweden, lots of dead. The living were arranged in their sleigh—a matchbox Bobby had rigged with paper clips for runners—rode upon the ice of the Ota. Mr. D'Arcy named all the figures in the sleigh: Monique, Petra, the other girls. The young German gardener last. Bobby picked this figurine up and looked at him long: peasant garb, greenish trousers, yellow shirt showing a tear, rake and hoe over its shoulder, a figure larger than any of the others, especially its huge little hands. Bobby said, "Can I ask you something?"

"You may, yes, ask anything, as you wish."

"Is Dort the same Dort?"

"And I may answer or not, as I wish!" Mr. D'Arcy said. He was more cheerful today, for certain. "For now let us just say that he is a young, silent, rather irritating gardener's assistant, and German to boot, with the one noble trait of loyalty. He is strong, he's nearly a horse himself, which the Young Count is by no means. The Ota has overflowed its own jumbled ice after a thaw, has frozen anew, slick and hard and black, I should say. Can you see it?"

Bobby could see it.

The sleigh sang along on the most modern polished-steel runners—the problem was in controlling its *speed*, the two man-horses slipping and sliding, holding the trace bars. The Young Count skidded in his riding boots, slithered at Dort's steadier side, had to keep shushing the girls behind them, who whimpered. They passed below the Petrokov Summer Palace, where flames silhouetted brigands passing furniture out the windows. A shout—they'd been seen!—and dozens of men came crashing down the great lawn through the crusted snow after the sleigh. But Dort was a horse and pulled the whole band along the ice at a sensational clip. The Young Count gave up trying to help, finally hoisted himself onto the broadboard, then into the sleigh and among the panicked girls, looked back to see a phalanx of scruffy, slipping soldiers and peasant men giving chase, losing ground. No comfort there: the milldam was ahead.

The Young Count hugged and kissed each girl and told each he loved her, kissed his daughters passionately as if he would never see them again, then took up arms. Petra loaded and handed him hunting rifles one by one. The Count picked off three soldiers and four peasants of a growing number, while all along Dort pulled and the sleigh skittered. At the dam the desperate family tumbled out, all but Monique, who was frozen with fear. The Young Count, the girls, Dort, thus forced to leave her, stomped in the crusty snow to the mill buildings, where they raced through the miller's abandoned house, down two flights of wooden stairs and back outside, out onto the ice below the dam, all of them falling and sprawling, the Young Count thinking to reach the far bank and the old sawmill, where they could take cover and fight. Just then over the dam came the sleigh, pushed by the brigands no doubt, Monique riding it down silently, thrown out on the impact, landing grotesquely twisted on the current-weakened ice, which broke too, dumping the sleigh and then the woman into the water, farewell.

The girls, the gardener, the Young Count, all held hands in a line, Dort first, then the Count, pulling all behind to cross a frozen mass of floes and logs and treacherous puddles on slickest ice. Petra held the one rifle they had salvaged. Of course, by now the soldier-brigands would have the weapons from the sleigh. Near the sawmill shore, near what might have been safety, the ice simply ended in a deep flow of river water from the millrace. And here came the soldiers, followed by the peasants. Twenty or more men and boys, firing the dacha's hunting rifles. Marta, the Count's younger daughter, shrieked and fell on the ice, dead. Petra, the older, fired back, hitting no one. The soldiers came forward, slipping in their tall boots on the ice in a crowd. Then suddenly the ice beneath *them* gave way. One head bobbing, then under the ice, many arms flailing, many men simply sinking under the weight of their stolen clothes and full pockets, two or three climbing out on Miller Gurevitch's garden banks where, as Mr. D'Arcy said, "We can only hope they froze."

All this left the family and gardener on a huge pan of ice that turned slowly as if it would reach the shore and save those still alive, but instead abruptly stopped, heaving itself up on something submerged, rising then on the slow current, and cleaving, dumping everyone. Petra and Dort managed to swim out, helped the Young Count to shore and safety, but all the others were lost. The survivor's garments grew stiff with ice. The Count was nearly out of his head with grief, ready to leap into the Ota and join the dead.

Dort had the inspiration to burn the sawmill building, easily ignited with the sawyer's tidily stored flint and steel, sparks in dry sawdust. Twenty minutes and the fire was famous, as Mr. D'Arcy put it. Half an hour and the survivors' clothes were dry.

Bobby studied the figures of the little girls. He flew Monique to Sweden first, laid her in line, squashed the matchbox sleigh with a slow fist. He thought hard in the silence, then flew the sleigh to Sweden, too. He could do that much. Then he flew Marta, shot. Then one little drowned girl at a time, till the five girls but Petra were in Sweden. Mr. D'Arcy watched solemnly. He said, "Saved from rape by death."

Silence in the map room, just the sound of a fan whirring somewhere in the walls. Abruptly, Mr. D'Arcy continued: The remaining threesome walked southwards into spring, avoiding towns, raiding abandoned farms for food, finding fresh scraps of clothing, always marching, growing wild, filthy, starved, thin as rats. The Young Count's plan was to cross the German lines—the kaiser more an ally than not, he thought—and perhaps as refugees or even as prisoners of war make their way to Germany, and later, God willing, *la France.*

At that, there was a very soft knocking, and the hidden door rolled silently open on its secret ball bearings. "You will take luncheon here?" said Hilyard.

"Yes, quite, why not?" said Mr. D'Arcy, an entirely different voice.

And the butler set up a card table, chairs, tablecloth. Soon he was back with a tureen of bright red soup, a small loaf of coarse bread, then strips of liver on fine plates. Next a salad of dark greens. Next a plate of cheeses. Finally chocolates. Bobby ate with best manners, Mr. D'Arcy delicately. No talk until Hilyard was back to collect the plates.

To him, Mr. D'Arcy said, "You've made some phone calls?"

The butler said, "Indeed, sir. I found everyone most agreeable once a certain level of astonishment wore off." And here crept the first smile Bobby had seen on that face.

An alarming smile spread on Mr. D'Arcy's face as well. He said, "And we will have Saturdays?"

"Saturdays, sir, quite so, though it took some persuasion." Those smiles. Both men looked at Bobby.

"What?" the boy said. He knew the calls were about him, all right.

Mr. D'Arcy said, "You mustn't shirk school, my boy. And from here forward, you shan't. I believe Mr. Hilyard has interceded on your behalf—you won't be punished, we believe, except by having to come here Saturdays through the school year for tutoring, to, um, rather make up, I should say, to make up for lost school." And that was that.

After lunch the little band—the Young Count, Petra, and Dort—made the German lines. Mr. D'Arcy leaned into his story in the golden lamplight, a hand on the map as Bobby moved the last three figures southward to the banks of a great painted river. Dort crossed first, shouting German so as to be welcomed. The soldiers he met shoved him and cuffed his ears but in the end allowed him to swim back to his friends. Dort, though, had read their intentions and thought the Young Count and he would be shot for the girl. So the little band hurried several leagues along the river until they found a crossing on rocks under the remains of a bridge. A Russian peasant came to them, begged for food. This was the river Dnepr, the peasant said. He took them to a ditched dredging barge he'd found, and the four of them launched that poor vessel and floated three weeks south, unchallenged. At Kiev they traded the dredging equipment to a docksman for bags of beans and grain, and the band floated on. Kiev was in German hands; Dort barked greetings to soldiers, sailors. And so the grieving band continued, all the way to Zaporozhye.

There, life seemed as it had always, high summer. The band found an estate the Young Count knew—that of a friend of his father's—untouched, its master gone, a very old man in charge, a blind great uncle. That old man welcomed them, shared the estate's abundant stores, comfortable beds, bathing rooms. This, Mr. D'Arcy said, was the worst period the Young Count had ever or would ever encounter in his life: the succor and the solace made him comfortable and in comfort every horror welled up: his wife, dead, his younger daughter, dead, his whole extended family, too, each a sorrow too much to bear. He'd sleep hard, wake happy, then remember—spend the waking day in tears. Dort, the same. Petra, however, was young and healed more quickly, spun on tiptoes among the flowers of the great, untended gardens, the sole ray of joy on the old estate. The Count did what he could to restore her to her studies, to be brave in her presence.

"You said 'we,'" said Bobby. "You keep saying 'we.'"

"Do I?" said Mr. D'Arcy. He thought a moment, trying to hear himself, said, "If so, I apologize. It is not I but a younger man I speak of, the Young Count Darlotsoff."

The old blind man of the manor came to the Young Count in front of the fire one midnight, walking in his sleep ("A true Tiresias," as Mr. D'Arcy said), and chanted: "Listen noble friend, listen to me: You will be well. You will find freedom via water. You will prosper in your new home. You will never forget, but you will come to accept. You will be wealthy again, in a new palace. You will never again marry. You will have no more children. Until one day a boy will come. You will tell him what you have suffered, and even in his innocence he will understand, and what you tell him will change him forever, and you will have an heir in him. You will live long, very, very long. You who have lost so much, will gain more back. And the boy you befriend will change the world in his turn." The Young Count found surcease in the old man's words, found the will to live on.

The Germans couldn't hold Kiev and in retreat took the manor, bunking there, preparing for what they did not realize would be their doom. The intrepid threesome was once again cast loose, headed once again southward. They reached the Crimea, spent what seemed a kind of mourning vacation in Sebastopol, then Yalta, a resort city where White Army thugs handed out random death. Dort found work on the docks, was accosted constantly, beaten twice for his silence, accused of being Red, or German, or criminal. The Young Count could get no work, was jeered and slapped for his aristocratic accent by anyone who felt the urge, but made rounds of the meanest back streets for scraps of food, for useful tins. Petra dressed as a smaller child, an urchin, used her fine manners to collect day-old bread, vegetables gone by, the odd soup bone. In fact, the band ate relatively well. They lived under a bridge briefly, then on the littered beach. Dort kept them in vodka, which was the coin of his realm.

One chilly afternoon as autumn approached, the Young Count discovered a day sailboat from one of the empty resorts, small open cockpit, hull perhaps five meters in length, sails partially rotted—it had been pulled into the reeds by vandals and forgotten. If one stayed out of sight of the piers (where White Army hooligans lined up young men and shot them just to watch the sea turn red), if one slipped into town at night, one might supply such a boat with food and water, might steal it unseen. Terror prevented immediate fulfillment of the plan, however; even a hobo's beach was more comfort than that little boat. Still, over the course of the subsequent weeks, they hid a fourth of their scavenged food under the boat's small foredeck among moldy life vests. On the penultimate night Dort took ill—vomiting, shitting, coughing.

"Surely I can say shitting, yes? You grin! American boy!"

The next morning, the Young Count fell ill, too. That evening, Petra. Dort came around healthy enough to look after her, then the Young Count came around, too. But brave Petra grew worse and worse, and there on the beach under the salvaged awning of a pleasure yacht she died.

Mr. D'Arcy cried silently for a long while. Bobby felt he could cry, too, but would not. He flew Petra to Sweden, felt that the others greeted her there—felt at least that she had company there, had family: her sisters, her mother, her grandparents. Who did the Young Count have? No one but Dort, the irritating gardener.

At length, Mr. D'Arcy continued:

The Young Count grew determined. Death at sea seemed a blessing. Even to be shot, heaven sent. The night after burying Petra in Black Sea sand, "so for the tides to find," he and Dort dragged the abandoned boat from the reeds, climbed in, and hand-paddled in a calm sea, no moon, paddled till they were pure exhaustion, then paddled more. Dawn and a breeze came up, good fortune, since they had not made the horizon, could still see shore. Then the breeze turned to wind and then to storm—more good fortune mixed with more bad: the boat was tossed and flung, but no other vessels were about, no one to spot them, and they made way. The Young Count had some aristocrat's sailing lessons behind him and kept the little boat before the cold north wind a full day, cruising ever south. In the night, Dort asleep, the Young Count held the tiller, groaned and wept, let his tears mingle with the heavy rain, the relentless spray. At daybreak, landfall.

"This was *Turkiye*, Robert, the country of Turkey, and freedom. And the Young Count did live on, as his Tiresias said he would."

In Berlin, some months later, posing as French, the Young Count took a new name. Protected by Dort's knowledge of the city, he worked briefly as a waiter till he could make it to Paris, well after the war. There, his money waited, so very much money that he found no obstacles to a voyage to New York, where he worked to became thoroughly American in a matter of months, hoping to shed his horror. But horror ever returned, returned unbidden at every sweet moment, even to this king of the banking world. And in time, the Young Count—not so young anymore—found his new-world palace, as had been predicted. And in a moment of weakness, of nostalgia, of irrational love and longing for the past, he sent for Dort, who willingly came and became his master gardener, as stupid and irritating as always, as loyal as always, the only one who knew Mr. D'Arcy's story, first to last.

BOBBY TORE UP DOGWOOD lane, pulling his sleigh full of doomed daughters, skittered on the ice that was Wahackme Road, raced onto his own road, all but skated along the tar and breathlessly home. Mr. D'Arcy wouldn't say a word more about the phone calls Hilyard had made, only invited him back for Saturdays, which invitation Bobby would honor nearly every Saturday of his coming youth and young manhood: lessons on the maps; lessons on a polished-brass microscope; lessons in a dozen languages; lessons in business, ethics, economics; lessons in math and mythology; lessons in what the old man called *charm*. Robert grew intellectually far past his peers but loved them and was loved by them and attended school in any case, daily attendance through college in Cambridge, Massachusetts, where with Mr. D'Arcy's help he was welcomed at Harvard with every blandishment the admissions team could muster. With the move to college, the Saturdays with the ancient man ended but never the game. Christmas break and summers, too, and many a road trip with friends to meet the master, sometimes particular girlfriends. Mr. D'Arcy approved only of a certain redhead called Marilyn, whom much later Bobby would marry. And though Mr. D'Arcy passed away on a winter's day, expiring quietly alone at his desk, the Young Count was always with Bobby, gave him his many powers, gave him Dort, too, and Hilyard, also the Connecticut estate and a fortune in stocks and bonds and real estate and numbered accounts across the great blue globe. Robert B. Mullendore would change the world, all right, becoming a figure in government, then diplomacy, finally international business, a paragon of ethical development, champion of peace.

HE WAS LATE, AND RAN, only slowing when he saw his parents—both of them, Dad home early from work, tall and concerned, Mom in her apron, head cocked somber—saw his folks standing at the end of the driveway waiting for him, Mrs. Applegate just behind them, arms crossed over her chest.

Kiva

MY FATHER, A GENETICIST nearly seventy, was raising me alone. My young mother, a formerly kind woman suffering from thoroughgoing mental illness, we'd left behind in the hasty move from Kabul, Afghanistan, some eight years before. Much younger than my father (whose name is Hammad Aravin Hammad, a sandwich of Arab and Sanskrit), she'd been returned to her extended family in their bombed and beleaguered border village of Khwost, and the marriage annulled. Which sounds cruel, but the woman we'd all known no longer existed. There'd been a political disaster, something I was too young to understand. Father was being helped by the Americans. He'd made terrible missteps under their guidance, and so he was owed.

Mother's illness and our move (to Punta de Fleche, New Mexico, a laboratory town invented along with the atomic bomb) had put Baba and me frequently in the way of counselors and therapists of all kinds, and the two of us had a really communicative relationship that we were at constant pains to keep fresh and loving around the hole in our lives. I really mean this and really mean everything I say; I'm not an ironic person, never speak in opposites. We were both a little obsessed by the idea of romance. If Baba dated, he respectfully told me of his plans, then told me logistical details only: where he and the woman had gone and what time, certain stretches of conversation, the plot of a given movie. If he had sex, I had no idea of it and would have found it highly gross to know in any case. If I dated, it was entirely because of his encouragement. I did not have sex, except for masturbation, which he liked to say without even slightly flinching was part of life, even provided me with the tamest possible men's magazines (breasts and bottoms and here and there some fuzz, no *inner workings*, to use his phrase), even while forbidding me porn on the web. On that basis in fact, knowing what boys are made of, he did not allow me my own Internet account but gave me nearly free rein with his own. You did not try to hide computer keystrokes of any kind from Baba; Baba was very nearly a computer himself. With a heavy accent, some might say, but I never noticed. His work at the lab was classified, and he never said the first word about it. At home we only spoke English, and I, having arrived in the USA at the impressionable age of eight, had become thoroughly American, with an American's sense of individuality that often troubled the old man.

"This new classmate," he said, sitting with me before dinner one night. Always we had candles. Always some music, a full CD picked by one or the other of us for appreciation, anything from Olmec tribal chants to Italian opera to Neil Young to, say, Alabama Shakes or Bat for Lashes or one time Li'l Wayne (okay, Father hated this: too violent, too disrespectful to women, sort of filthy, my mistake) to that day's selection, which was shakuhachi flute music from Japan, more silence than tones. Then talk, when the music was done, while he cooked: "Son, I think the reason she is dark is because somewhere back there she is partly Afghan."

I smiled at his joke. Claire Hesterly was Nordic blonde, lissome and fair, the band of her blue underpants visible when she bent to retrieve her New Testament: she was not Afghan. But I'd mentioned the girl's tan, and he wanted to hear more.

I said, "Oh, Father. She's wrecking the curve. She's in all the AP classes with me. She's matched me on four calculus quizzes running. She can manipulate an integer like no one I've ever seen. And she beat me in bio: 110 on the mids to my 108!"

"Anything over a hundred is a hundred, no?"

"And chem, the same. A run for my money. And I know I shouldn't put much stock in appearance, but she's exquisitely beautiful. She looks like someone in a shampoo commercial."

"And not stuck-up?" One of my expressions.

"Normal as wool carpet!" One of his.

"Kali Hammad, you must ask her out."

"Jeffrey Brick has already moved in. They're going out."

"Ah, the estimable Brick, in and out. She'll grow tired of him. He's a great athlete, and he has been kind to you, but he's no scholar."

"Well, then, Eddie Rennsalear is right behind Brick. And Eddie has not been kind to me."

"She loves science, from what you tell me. Ask her collecting."

"Oh, Baba! *Insects*?"

He gazed at me fondly, said, "Or ask her to the ancient Pueblo ruins."

"She's more like snowboarding at Taos."

"But, Kali, son, you don't know how to snowboard!"

"You are very swift, Papa."

We waited in companionable silence. Baba seemed to count his breaths: he was checking his mental lexicon. What had I meant by *swift*? He retrieved a bowl from the high cabinet, unwrapped his best knife, chopped parsley fine, drained couscous into the sink, unwrapped a small packet of meat, chopped eggplant, chopped tomatoes, chopped onions, didn't expect help: I was the cleanup crew.

At length he said, "I just read a new study. Question: how do the many male capuchin monkeys who are not alpha males pass down their genetic material?"

"They don't, Father. That's what makes the troupe strong."

He raised his considerable eyebrows, raised his chin, dropped a skillet on the stove, clicked a flame to life beneath it, poured a little oil in. "To the contrary," he said. "All and only alpha-male genes would limit the pool to the point of disaster in only a few generations. Was the hypothesis. Finding? In fact, the alpha male's genes in any given troupe were not predominant. They were not even majority. The sub-alpha males, alpha's direct competitors, had no distribution *at all.* Sub-alpha would be your friend Eddie Rennsalear, and that sad case Freddy Orco. So who, given that evidence, do you think was 'getting' the young women of the monkey troupe?" Baba paused for effect, just a beat too long, gazing at me amusedly. The oil in his pan began to sizzle. He lowered the fire.

"Who!" I said.

"The whole cadre of submissive males, that's who. They stayed entirely out of the alpha competition. Instead, they spent all their time with the females, engaged in female activities, grooming with them, helping with the young, looking for food. Huddling against weather, against the night. And very often while the alphas were battling for control of their harems, the *submissive males* were quietly mating, every day, all day, every night, all night, with any female they fancied."

I ate my hamburger, Baba's concession to my Americanized tastes. He always sautéed the ground beef in small squares with dried fire peppers and eggplant chunks, wedges of tomato, all of it served with tabouli, never French fries, because he could not stomach potatoes, chapati to be eaten on the side or used as a utensil. Hamburger buns made him snarl. I sipped my Coke. Coke he approved of for its caffeine, a kind of tea; he had once thought it was an Afghan product. I poured more ketchup. He approved of ketchup because somewhere in the deep past it had been Chinese, and he was very fond of the Chinese, who had birthed our religion, which was Buddhism.

Baba looked at me long with great affection, spread his fingers on the table, his nightly gesture before I did the clearing. It was nearly time for my homework hours, nearly time for his evening study. He said, "Invite Claire Hesterly to Bandelier National Monument. We will show her the ancient Pueblo ruins. Invite her sisters, too. Not Saturday night—that's for Brick and Eddie. Try Saturday morning. But first talk with her. Always talk with her. Talk with her Monday. Ask her how things are going with Brick. Listen very carefully to every word she says. Talk to her Tuesday. Ask about her sisters, their progress in school, sweet things they have said and done. Talk to her Wednesday. Ask about her dreams, both those in the night and those for the future. Pluck a stray thread off the arm of her sweater, compliment her eyes, any makeup she uses. No, please listen! On Thursday, talk about ancestral Pueblo ruins. Make your invitation— nothing to be nervous about. It's only cliff dwellings. And, most important: invite her sisters. And I will pack a purely beta picnic lunch for all of you and serve as chauffeur."

MEANWHILE BABA WAS BEING investigated by agencies unknown for reasons unspecified: he was a foreigner with a security clearance during a season of suspicion, an Afghani who worked at a secret lab, and overnight that had become enough. Three men in suits and tight haircuts, accompanied by his surprised section chair, had made a humiliating visit to his lab and taken away his computers and then (with his permission—they had no warrants), had taken away the numerous computers at our own dwelling, including the laptop that contained my homework and all my many school projects. Since in that way it involved me, Baba filled me in. He was convinced it all had something to do with Claire's father, one Morton Hesterly, who'd been a top-down appointment, dropped into the lab from above with high-level security clearances. Now I understood Father's keen interest in Claire. My father's new associate had arrived with his family in tow only six weeks before, was ostensibly a materials technician from somewhere in Maryland. But his hands were always clean, my father pointed out.

CLAIRE HAD ALL THE answers in calculus the next day, a beautiful thing. I had only to correct our teacher, Mr. Givens, once—he was forever dropping cubed roots in the tertiary wave sets. Claire gave me a look longer than necessary. Her hair was combed straight. She wore a smart red jacket, black jeans. Gathering my courage, I walked her to study hall, which was half indoors, half out. If you wanted to work or were on detention, you stayed inside; if your grade-point average was above a B, you could go outside. Claire's GPA was exemplary, but she elected to study. So I did, too, sat across from her at the large table and read my new library book: a photo compendium of women's hairstyles. I concentrated on the construction of the French braid, a fine skill for the beta male, but also spent time over the diagrams for the swing braid, the pretzel braid, the double-double and triple-double braids, the Russian interlocking braid, the Chinese bun braid, the warrior braid.

"Kali," she said, teasing me. "What kind of book is that?"

"I'm trying to learn a French braid. I always wanted to be able to make a French braid. In case I see my mother again. Don't you think it's the queen of braids?"

I showed her the page, its careful photo diagrams, the long-necked, exquisite model, who was in no way more attractive than my interlocutor.

"You can't learn to braid hair from a book," Claire said pleasantly. There was real kindness in her. Kindness, in fact, poured from her eyes, served as apology for her earlier teasing tone.

"Well, it's a start."

She went back to her book, and I to mine, but only briefly before she looked up. I could feel the warmth of her regard, breathed in it for several seconds before looking up as well.

Claire said, "Where is your mother?"

And I told her, the first time I had told anyone anything whatever about Mother Hammad's struggles.

Claire bit her lip and listened closely. "Not fair," she said when I was done.

THE NEXT DAY WAS her turn to share. She told me that she had had to move a dozen times since junior high school: horrible. She reeled off the names of a dozen towns, a dozen high-school mascots—Tigers, Sharks, Wreckers, Robins. And so forth, including American schools in various foreign capitals—Eagles and Warriors and Generals. She'd been able to keep a friendship or two going via Snapchat and Instagram, but mostly it was very difficult to be or to have a friend or maintain a steady romance. Her sisters were her best friends, sadly. Because both of them were quite "bent," as she put it. Antonia, one grade behind us, was actually famous for her weirdness, also for climbing the water tower during recess, also for calling Mrs. Chichester, the French teacher, "Mrs. Chimp-chester," repeatedly, without a blink from our simian instructor. There was a sister named Judith, too, still in junior high. "My phone-in therapist says they're damaged from all the moves. Also, my mother has been in a major depression since Judith was born. Also, my father is basically a Nazi."

"How did you come out so normal?"

"Oh, Kali. I didn't. I use studying to keep from noticing how crazy I am."

"But, Claire, Claire Hesterly, you're the sanest person I've ever met."

Instead of complimented, she looked crestfallen. She said, "My father says I'm unreliable."

I only looked at her—her lineaments much more complicated than I'd until that moment known, her beauty so mutable: first this face, then that, finally her own face, something beyond simple physicality, something that made her soul seem accessible to me. I noted a trace of makeup aglitter on her eyelids. I'd have to ask about that, about how one went about keeping glitter on the eyelids, for what could be more beta to know?

"Unreliable," I said, a quiet joke, since her father was so completely, obviously wrong. I thought of my father's advice and reached nonchalantly across the table to brush a crumb off the arm of her sweater, neatened her stack of books.

"Something in your teeth," she said kindly.

I took care of that problem with my tongue, unembarrassed. Then, after a very long time of quietly being together with her across the study hall table, I said, "Is Jeff Brick fun to date?"

And every complication left her eyes. Even her posture shifted: happiness. "He is *so* dreamy," she said. And then she went on, painful for me, a lot of stuff I knew about him, a few things I didn't: he was a kind of god, apparently. The team had won yet another game over the weekend, and Claire was effusive: "Did you see that pass? He's like a pro quarterback, Kali."

I had not seen the pass.

She said, "Forty-seven to seven!"

"Almost unfair!" I said, catching her tone.

"But I'll tell you a secret." She seemed to consider her impulsiveness, gave me a long look. "The boy can't *kiss*."

A kind of heat penetrated my chest. "Anyone can kiss," I said. Bravado, purely theoretical: I myself had never actually kissed anyone but Baba, and perhaps my mother, no doubt my mother. "You just put your lips together and etcetera."

"No, no," she said laughing. "Not at all."

"Not at all," I said, the heat from my chest reaching my face.

"And he's clumsy in other ways as well."

"Other ways?" I said ingenuously, then realized what she was saying. Something about *sex*.

Claire blushed very hard from her clavicles upward, skipped elegantly past our inadvertent subject: "Plus he's always got practice. And the team *studies* together! Can you imagine studying with *Freddy Orco*?"

I kept a neutral face, said, "Are you going to the game this Saturday?"

"It's all the way down in El Paso. Not a chance."

Beta heart pounding, I said, "I have an idea for something to do."

CLAIRE WAS SEVENTEEN, LIKE me. Her sister Antonia was the famously sullen redhead one grade behind us, just turned sixteen. The mystery sister, Judith, strawberry blonde, was thirteen. All the same height, and the same height as me. Enough looks to go around in that family! The girls came giggling out of their house—an oversize development federal just like ours—rushed for the car as if they were making a prison break. Their mother came out into the sunlight behind them, just as good looking as her daughters but sadder, the forever-trailing wife. Then the spy came out, Mr. Hesterly, and he was all smiles, too, like a steel girder in a good mood.

"Devil," Baba said under his own big smile, waving back from the driver's seat of our sensible minivan. And I understood suddenly that my old man was exacting a kind of preemptive revenge, and not only helping me, subtle man. Of course Mr. Hesterly thought his mission was secret from one and all. And doubtless he thought this innocuous playdate was a way to get closer to his target. If Father was right, perhaps the spy would tip his hand, or overplay it. I climbed out to wave to the oncoming females. Mrs. Hesterly gave me a long look. Oh, was her life sad. Her husband narrowed his eyes at her.

"How nice of you!" she cried.

"My pleasure," I cried back.

"Home by dinner!" Mr. Hesterly called.

Young Judith yelled, "Shotgun," and cut behind me, climbed in the front seat I'd vacated. I found myself buckling in between Claire and Antonia in the rearmost bench seat (the middle one having been removed by yours truly, and with some difficulty, for the scientific-equipment transfers my father was always making). Claire smelled of sweet soap, Antonia of the Walmart perfume counter, overwhelming olfactory competition, myself in the crossover zone. Baba found my eye in the mirror, nodded with pleasure for me, everyone's plan working perfectly. And we were off, an hour's drive to the National Monument. "I like that skirt," I said to Antonia, after my father's advice. Her thighs were freckled, hairless, thoroughly naked.

"Santa Fe," she shot back. "Grrl Power Boutique."

"It's mine," Claire said. "Actually. From like grade school."

"Actually, it's not yours at all, Cruella."

"And I like yours, Claire," I said. "I like the length." Past her knees.

"You can braid my hair first," Judith called back, bouncing in her seat.

So. Claire had been talking about me. The ensuing silence in the wayback was finally broken by her: "Are you ready for the bio test?"

AT BANDELIER WE CLIMBED out of the car, the only car in the large parking lot. The ranger station with its restrooms was closed, October being the beginning of off-season for the legions of summer RVs. We hiked along the wide trail into the mouth of Frijoles Canyon toward what informational signs told us was Tyuonyi, an Ancestral Pueblo Peoples' site, excavated in the early twentieth century, perhaps two hundred rooms arranged in a closed circle. Claire walked with Baba, talked with him seriously about her aspirations: she wanted to be a surgeon. "All that cutting!" said my father, disapproving. But then, he was never happy when humans played God.

Judith ran off ahead in her jumper—she looked like a very tall child, but built exactly like her sisters—high boobs, narrow hips, long legs. Antonia walked with me a few hundred paces, long enough for me to come up with words to say, but before I said them (something about how I liked the red and green of the ponderosa pines high against the blue of the sky), she suddenly bolted, ran off to catch her little sister. That Grrl Power skirt was no bigger than a paper towel. Her thighs, her hips, her shoulders were on another level of development from Judith's. Antonia was the beauty of the troupe, certainly. Her hair flowed about her shoulders; her speed was breathtaking. I slowed to walk with Claire and Baba.

Continuing their conversation with a mere nod at me, Claire intoned bookishly, "The population here is now thought to have been in the thousands. It all crashed at once."

"Disease?" my father said.

"Possibly drought," Claire said.

No, Claire was the beauty of the troupe, and she'd studied up on Bandelier.

"But no one really knows," I said: we were all good students.

We came to the central village, a great circle of a ruin, once a sort of apartment house, a communal warren of small rooms in a band around an elliptical courtyard containing three stone-lined pits in perfect circles.

Judith was already walking through the complex as through a maze, ignoring the signs: STAY ON PAVED PATH. "You'd have to walk through everyone's room to go to bed!" she observed.

Antonia was nowhere in sight.

"I believe they climbed in through holes in the roof," Father said. "And perhaps you need to climb out, young lady."

The circular pits were kivas, I knew, religious places.

As Judith obeyed my father's quiet authority, Claire read the self-guided tour booklet she'd found in the school library, paraphrasing for the rest of us: "This place was excavated around 1910. They just left all the original earthen mortar and mud plaster out in the rain to dissolve. The bricks have lasted—they were cut out of the local rock, which is volcanic. Um, later, the park service fixed everything up with cement. The kiva here was restored more recently. There would be an altar at one end and a hole in the floor at the other—an entrance to the underworld, the entrance that all souls, all animals and humans came through. The women kept them in repair. The men did all the worshipping." She snapped the booklet closed, said, "Apparently, sexism was part of nature to them! Anyway, as far as I'm concerned, kivas were just pits for heathen men to conjure up destructive forces. They actually give me the heebie-jeebies."

My father grinned, gave me a wink. "Males can be quite stupid," he said.

"I'm all for religious tolerance," Claire said.

I didn't quite get what was so funny about that but laughed heartily with the two of them. We continued past Tyuonyi, took a right on a path that brought us directly to the foot of the cliffs, where ground-level thatch-roofed dwellings had been reconstructed.

"Very dark inside," Father noted, never having been a fan of darkness.

The path climbed upward, and then higher yet, and we looked into cavity after cave after excavation, beautiful little rooms—"cavates," Claire's booklet called them—higher and higher above the canyon floor, great views of the ruined village below, petroglyphs in zigzags, prints of ancient hands.

"Cliff kiva," Claire said, pointing above us, still reading. "Large room, small anterooms."

I left Father and Claire on the path, climbed a new ladder built authentically as the Ancestral Pueblo Peoples had built ladders, looked stupidly into a warren of rooms, seeing nothing as my eyes adjusted to the darkness. A thin stripe of hot sunlight lit the smooth rock floor. The ceiling was black with ancient soot. I wriggled inside as into the maw of the leviathan Claire and I had just read about in classics. Suddenly I heard a splashing sound. Startled, I stared.

"Don't look," Antonia hissed. And that's when I made her out, a dim figure squatting with tiny skirt hiked up and white underpants down, clearly peeing into a hole in the floor, peeing into the underworld from whence all life came, nothing untoward to see but those long legs shining, underpants practically glowing.

"Sorry," I said, and backed away, feet first right out the entrance and back down the shaky ladder.

"Claire says that each kiva is thought to indicate a family group," said Baba, skeptical.

Antonia appeared at the top of the ladder with her skirt askew, climbed down: best not to look.

"There you are, *Toni*," Claire said.

As a troupe we followed the path, looked into further evocative rooms, trying to imagine what had once gone on here, what the air in the place must have smelled like.

Judith came running up from behind us, when I'd thought she was ahead.

"I lived here in a past life," she said, breathing passionately.

"You were an insect," Antonia said.

Baba laughed at that.

Antonia scowled, wheeled, trotted away from us.

I followed, trying to be discreet, hurried after I made it around a corner and Father and Claire couldn't see. Ahead, Antonia suddenly left the path and headed upward, climbing bare rock—easy handholds—even using the DANGER: NO CLIMBING sign for a step. Twenty feet up, she disappeared into the cliff face.

Then her bright face appeared, high above. "Check this out," she called.

I hurried, climbed up as she had, looking back to see if Father were in view, and Claire. They were not. I followed Antonia into a big cavate, beautifully shaped, much more light than the earlier example, perfect round windows, hearth, small secondary rooms, heartening view across the valley.

I said, "This must be the men's restroom."

"Go ahead," Antonia said sharply.

"Don't worry. I thought your peeing was funny. Just sort of, maybe, sacrilegious."

I hadn't ever seen her smile before. "Just *sort of, maybe* yourself," she said. "It's totally religious. I'm an *anointer.* You'll be anointed next if you don't watch out. This place is so fucking boring."

"I like it," I said.

"What we need is a big fat joint."

"You take *drugs*?" I said.

"WELL," BABA SAID, "ALL this climbing about is making me hungry. Let me go prepare our picnic. You teens go on down into the canyon—it continues on a mile more—and let's meet up back here in an hour or so. Twelve fifteen? Okay? Twelve thirty?"

"Oh, I'll help you," said Claire.

"Not necessary," said my dad. "Not necessary at all."

But Claire insisted. She was alpha property all the way, and in this crowd Dad Hammad was number one. The beta male was to spend his time with the beta females.

So Antonia and Judith and I set out on the diminishing trail through the extraordinary canyon, at first strolling three abreast, then Judith skipping far ahead, finally Antonia and I alone, shuffling under cliffs filled with yet more carved-out chambers, the ruins of ancient housing. In a slight meadow I spotted a mule deer buck, its antlers very like the plants it stood among, good camouflage. "Deer," I said, pointing.

"So what's all this shit about braiding hair?" Antonia said, trying to pick the animal out of the background.

"Just an interest," I said. "Hair. My mother."

"My ass, your fucking mother. Claire's never going to go out with you, dickwad."

"Well, no, I know . . . I mean, I didn't ask her to go out. I have no interest, is what I'm trying to say. In going out with Claire."

"Never, never. You hear me? She will never go out with you." She put a quick hand on my chest, said, "Let's slow down here."

I knew from anatomy class exactly where my adrenal gland was and felt a squeeze there, just under her hand, as if in my heart (which is the confusion countless generations have suffered). We silently watched Judith skip around the shaded corner ahead and disappear.

"A big fat joint," Antonia said. And tugged me to her and gave me my first kiss, and then my second, and then instructions: "Open your mouth a little, pretty-boy."

Her tongue was a revelation, carefully compact, finding mine, probing my molars. She kept her eyes open, still looking for that mule deer over my shoulder.

Quickly arose a virginal teen boy's most profound embarrassment: the happy erection of nights and private musings arriving in the presence of *company*, arriving out there in the light of day under the cliffs of glowering ancients, pushing at my trousers, practically knocking, as at a locked door. And then more so, Antonia's gripping hand, even as the kiss continued, even as her eyes continued to search for antlers. Embarrassment building toward disaster, I lost my reserve, pointed my tongue like hers, found her individual teeth, the ridged roof of her mouth, pressed her lips with mine. I had barely the nerve to put my hands on her back.

Judith's call in the nick of time was like a fire alarm, an extended shriek.

Antonia and I unclenched in a millisecond—but the shriek hadn't been about us. Judith wasn't even in sight. The youngest Hesterly shrieked again. Adrenaline squirt upon adrenaline squirt, we kissers loped to catch up, I increasingly less hobbled with every step, but Antonia very much in the lead. I put on the afterburners and we made the corner together. Judith was arms wide like a statue in the middle of the path, and just beyond her—and I mean just a harrowing couple of feet—a large diamondback rattlesnake curled with head raised, ready to strike.

"Back up slowly," I shouted.

But Antonia was more proactive. She picked up a large rock, barreled forward for the attack, her tiny skirt swishing about her businesslike fanny. She shoved Judith out of harm's way with one hand, flung the rock with the other, a dust-raising thud unfortunately just behind the animal, which lunged toward her, clearly perceiving no other way to go. In hiking boots and bare legs, she kicked the creature even as it struck her boot, kicked again, and again, until the awful, innocent thing—fully six feet long—sidewound its way out of her purview.

"Motherfucker," Antonia said, breathing hard.

Judith, having fallen in tall weeds that might have been hiding any kind of creature at all, shrieked again.

I may very possibly have shrieked as well.

AFTER SOME TREMULOUS DISCUSSION of the close call—Judith wanting to go back and find my father, Antonia not, I voting despite my better judgment with Antonia—the three of us continued on.

"It's an ancestor spirit," Judith kept saying. And, "The snake is my spirit animal."

"You know nothing about that shit," Antonia said. "It's nothing but a snake. There are snakes around here. Get over it."

Ahead there was a path, I knew, one that would take us to the cliff face and then up almost vertically through rocks and crags to a series of reproduction ladders that led to a remarkable, fully intact kiva dug inside a cavate halfway up the cliff face, the best and most complete of all the kivas on the site.

I told the girls about it.

"How big can this thing be?" Antonia said.

"Yeah," Judith said accusingly.

"It's not big," I told them. I'd been up there with Baba, and just the two of us fit inside. We'd taken the occasion to breathe together, as he would say, something on the order of meditation, not quite prayer. I'd found it unsettling: the kiva had been built for different lives altogether.

"Then, okay, if there's only room for two, you better go up with Ju-ju, and then come back and you and me can go up."

"I'm not waiting down here alone," Judith said.

"We can all go up," I said.

"Judith's afraid to be alone, and you're afraid to be alone with *me*," Antonia said.

"Let's put fear behind and climb," I said, consciously sounding like Baba.

Up at the kiva I descended first, making my way through the little opening in the roof (authentically re-created by the park service out of loosely plaited pine branches and cornstalks) and down the ladder, which was nothing more than a pegged pole. Plenty of light penetrated the thatch.

"No snakes," I called, sitting.

Judith came down then. She sat with her back to me.

"Okay, I will have a French braid," she said. She was very different from Antonia and from Claire, now that I looked at her. Her hair was lighter, finer. She smelled like baby powder. She held her shoulders high, always perfect posture. She was skinny, but she was no little kid.

"Okay," she said.

"Okay what?"

"You can braid my hair. A snake braid. Do you know it?"

"I don't. I don't think I know any braids, not really. And, anyway, we need a comb."

"Just use your hands," she said, shoulders square. "The snake will guide you."

I tried not to scoff but put my hands in her hair, pulled it back, tried to remember the book instructions, divided the shockingly soft locks into three parcels, pushed one aside (that long, delicate neck), got to work braiding. When I was done she felt the braid all over with both hands, turned and smiled for me. She said, "Claire says you're a loser, but I don't think so." And then she fell into me, threw her hands around my neck, tucked her head on my chest, pulled herself up into my lap where she curled up like a puppy and *bit* me on my left pectoral muscle with her strong teeth, like biting my heart. The effect on me was profound, not exactly sexual, a first experience of caring, I would say now, a rush of feeling, a commotion.

Suddenly the kiva entrance darkened, and Antonia's face was above us. "Perverts," she said calmly.

"Ta-ha," Judith said.

"It's time to get back," Antonia said. "I'm fucking starving."

JUDITH AND ANTONIA AND I made it back to the circle village considerably more than one hour after we'd left, but there on a blanket was one of Baba's wonderful meals, dozens of small plates of dishes, exotic and familiar. There also was Baba, sitting peaceably, rapt in serious discussion with Claire, whom, I felt, I'd just seriously betrayed in advance. Antonia turned up her nose at the victuals, gave her big sister a hostile look, wandered off unfed, kicking rocks.

"We saw a rattlesnake," Judith said. "It almost got me!"

"Antonia chased it off," I said.

Baba looked alarmed.

"Snakes are a valuable part of the ecosystem," Claire said. And she turned to me, a distinct change in her voice—something more possessive—said, "Let's you and I go up there after lunch."

"He'll do your hair," Judith said.

Claire's look lingered. I recalled my mother saying I was a very beautiful boy, something I hated. And the girls at school called me cute or pretty, or even worse, sweet, or lovely, always feminizing the beta! Claire herself had once said my eyes were so dark it looked like I was wearing makeup. But she would never call anyone a loser—that was Judith's word. And of course Claire would go out with me—and soon. Antonia just wanted to mess her up as she messed up everything, including puking on the school bus once, some kind of green alcohol.

Judith picked up her charcoal-baked bread with wonderment, played at using it to pinch up bites of cucumber yogurt. I avoided Baba's eye. I avoided Claire's. There was nothing innocent about her sister's fancy braid.

"Antonia never eats," Claire said, holding her napkin with aplomb. I felt the adrenal squeeze once again, my mouth go dry: all sorts of physiology, all unbidden. My stomach dropped. I was no longer hungry. I had in addition a strong case of what one of my human ecology books called epididymal edema, something I'd never before experienced, exquisite pain in my balls, which if they weren't blue might as well have been.

"Your father and I counted two hundred forty rooms," Claire said.

"And that of course was simply the ground floor of the original," said Baba.

"There are more dwellings all the way down along the cliffs," I said.

"What a paradise this must have been," said Claire hotly. "Your Baba and I have been trying to map out the agriculture."

Judith played with her braid, seemed to see visions in the food, which she shuffled into arrangements before shuttling it to her mouth. Claire made a kind of sandwich. My father ate one item at a time making a perfect circuit of the dishes clockwise. I worked counterclockwise, though he didn't seem to notice. Anyway, we ate the lovely meal. Afterward Dad pulled his ornate box of dominoes from the basket and showed them to Judith, who was delighted, captured. The old man set up a children's version of the game, one I remembered well: only two could play.

Antonia had disappeared altogether. "She'll be in the car," Claire said. "She's always in the car."

BIG SISTER HESTERLY AND I walked side by side down the wide path into the throat of Frijoles Canyon. I pointed to the petroglyphs her sisters and I had spotted earlier, pointed out the deer still in its place, now with two females, showed her the spot the snake had stopped Judith.

"I'm so sad about your mother," Claire said out of nowhere. "So very sad. Your dad told me more about her. I didn't know she'd chopped her hair. Do you remember that? Was that the first indication?"

Yes it was. "I feel ugly," I said, not really meaning to.

"No," she said. "You are honestly the most, most *beautiful* boy I've ever seen. And such nice skin."

"Not that looks mean much," I said.

"They mean nothing," Claire said, someone who could afford the sentiment.

We walked in silence to the path that led to the ladders up the cliff and to the intact kiva, climbed silently, she first, a revelation of musculature above me.

In the kiva we sat side by side. I endeavored to take her hand.

"I'm a very loyal person," she said. "I can't betray the Brick."

"I know."

"You were nice to walk with my sisters. They are both nuts, you know."

"I like them."

"I have a new bra," she said.

Punch to the chest. And this time it really was my heart. I mean, it's not all physiology.

Claire pulled her shirt up to show me. The bra did look new. It was blue and very plain, and her living breasts were cosseted there. She pulled the shirt back down. We were very close together.

"Antonia kissed me," I said.

"As I said: nuts."

"And Judith bit my chest." I pulled my own shirt up, showed her the tooth marks.

"I shouldn't have let you alone with them."

I pulled my shirt back down. "As I said."

"You like them." She moved subtly closer to me. The light dimmed, perhaps a cloud above, or the sun leaving the canyon. Her kiss was of a different order than Antonia's, more stately, less impulsive, cautious almost, a little dry, no great hunger: she wasn't going to bite me. "There," she said.

"More," I said.

"My family will move away soon," she said. "We always move away."

"I'll find you," I said.

"You may hate us by then," she said.

"Listen, Claire, we know all about your father and his investigation."

Long silence. "He'd say he's only doing his job." She kissed me again. "He's heinous," she said. "Even he admits it: your father's done nothing wrong."

We kept kissing, me somehow without the urge to take it further despite my new sense of the possibilities, despite the blueness of her bra, despite the increasingly unbearable pressure inside my scrotum.

"Brick just jams his fingers in me," Claire murmured.

"He should respect you," I said.

"He respects me. It's just that he never lingers anywhere," she said.

I lingered at her lips—no idea what else to do.

"He's never kissed me this long, not once."

"You're a loyal young woman," I said.

"You should put your hand on my back," she said.

I did. We kissed some more.

After a while, she said, "Don't you know how to open a bra?"

"No idea."

"That's what I like about you, Kali." She reached behind her, quick gesture, and a certain tautness under her sweater was released. She had to actually put my hand on her breast, but it was my own idea after a great long while to open her shirt, my idea to kiss at her brown small nipple, to linger there, to suckle. She kneeled between my legs to allow me access and somehow in the process brought the pressure of her thighs to bear upon my pain.

"That's all I want," she said.

"Proper kisses," I said.

"I'm on the pill," she said.

My attention to her nipple deepened. She shifted her legs, shifted them again, then more so. Unbidden, very suddenly, honestly out of nowhere, I experienced my first orgasm in the presence of another human, positively geothermal in its propulsive power, a soaking mess in my trousers, great sighs and gulps of the dead kiva air, near total embarrassment except for the sudden groan of fellow feeling on Claire's part, my face suddenly in her hands, an even deeper kiss, acceptance personified.

"You're so, so, so cute," she said.

The kiva went a shade darker, and then another, Claire and I kissing, her hands on me, and mine on her.

JUDITH AND BABA HAD found a frog in Frijoles Creek, a robust little brook that still greened the Ancestral Pueblo Peoples' Eden. Claire and I took an interest, leaned over them to look, trying hard not to exude sexuality, my long shirttails strategically untucked. But Father cast an all-seeing eye on his beta boy. And then Judith cast her own eye at her sister, complicated tribal stuff.

After a while, Father and Claire packed the picnic back into the basket and cooler, and the four of us strolled single file out of the ancient village and back to the car. Antonia's legs stuck out the open side door of the van, making us laugh—Claire had predicted where we'd find her. Quickly we swallowed the mirth: one of the legs was swollen and veined red and purply black, dotted oddly with fat beads of sweat, and Antonia was unconscious. Baba checked her pulse: irregular, as was her breathing.

"The snake!" Judith wailed, and fell into tears.

In the scuffed toe of Antonia's right hiking boot, Father found the embedded fangs of the serpent. The sneaky animal had found a way to delay its wrath: Antonia's kicking at stones had gradually worked the fangs through the leather and to her skin. Baba eased the boot off, put a finger to a pair of simple scratches. "She won't die," he said. "But we must hurry if we are to prevent tissue damage." In the trunk of the car he had a doctor's first-aid kit, made up for the Southwest and therefore complete with antivenin, a tiny hypodermic shot he administered expertly under Antonia's swollen knee. We pulled her further into the car across the carpeted floor, covered her. I couldn't help noticing her exposed panties: dirty pink, not white at all. Claire sat on the floorboards to be beside her, a cool hand to her sister's brow. Racing, I stuffed the picnic in the back, slammed all the doors, and we were off.

"Her boot saved her," Father said, less calm. "But we've lost a lot of time."

He drove evenly out of the canyon, yet very fast, up the long inclined road to the level of the surrounding desert, where finally his cell phone worked. We met the medevac helicopter at a crossroads—unparalleled drama, at least in my life—two businesslike military EMTs loading Antonia in while giving her another shot, wrapping her in a space blanket, covering her face with an oxygen mask. Claire went along for the short flight to Albuquerque, all the passengers the helicopter could handle.

Judith wept and wept on the slow drive down and out of the monument—she had suddenly found herself alone with virtual strangers—sobbed and demanded I sit in the back seat with her, molded herself to me, fell asleep.

AT THE HOSPITAL WE discovered that Antonia was fine, the main problem not having been the slight exposure to rattler venom but its combination with severe dehydration and the fact (discovered in the process of treatment) that she was several months pregnant. "Gravid," as the ER physician put it to my dad. Apparently, she had announced in her waking delirium that I had tried to "stick" her.

"Not at all," I said.

"Impossible," Claire said.

"I was with them the whole time," Judith said, catching Claire's defensive tone.

Antonia was asleep in her hospital bed, an I.V. tube taped to her arm.

The doctor said all the same to Mr. Hesterly when he finally arrived from White Sands that evening, and translated the word *gravid* into normal English for his benefit, mentioned the accusation of sticking, added that Judith had been with us the whole time.

"Pregnant!" Mr. Hesterly roared.

His eye fell upon me.

I said it again: "Not I."

But Mr. Hesterly leapt upon me, knocked me to the tiles, pummeled my face with efficient fists. The doctor trotted off to get Security. Claire and Judith and Baba got Mr. Hesterly off me but couldn't really restrain him—he kicked at me through their legs, spat at me over their heads, threw punches through their arms, a study in sustained fury. Security arrived in the person of a young man in a tight uniform who went down as easily as I had, covered his face and curled up on the floor beside me. The real police came next, bop-bop with their nightsticks, and that was the end of that, Mr. Hesterly jerked out of the room in handcuffs, still cursing me, cursing my father, cursing Antonia.

No shortage of nurses to see to my bruises.

FATHER'S COMPUTERS WERE RETURNED a few days later, no explanation, files intact. Rumor had it that Mr. Hesterly was released from the Punta de Fleche County Jail within minutes of his incarceration, rushed away in a black car. The very next week Claire and Antonia and Judith moved with their parents to Palo Alto, California. Claire contacted me every day—emails, text messages, Facebook, paper letters, phone calls, hot Snapchats, Instagram, Skype—enormously pleased that I wrote and phoned and messaged her back, virtual kisses constant. Jeff Brick moved on to Josephina Fox, gorgeous niece of the former Mexican *presidente*, never a harsh word between us. Nothing more was said about Antonia's pregnancy, and there was never a baby. Baba allowed me to meet Claire and her sisters during spring break for a nearly ski-less ski trip to Taos, during which I saw Antonia but once, Judith only twice, and was taught to make love by Claire, condominium nights.

I've enrolled as premed at Johns Hopkins, Claire the same at UCLA. We're just kids, we both realize, and though I must say I was more than willing to put a label on our relationship, she says that's not the thing to do. So perhaps I'll resume my beta ways, make new friends among the women of my program, while Claire takes charge of hers, alpha being alpha, and gender no barrier to the hierarchy she seeks to dominate, not anymore. She and I have a loose plan for Thanksgiving, and that's as far ahead as I'm allowed to discuss.

My mother died just after my Taos trip, hacked at her hair once more, hacked at her breast, my uncle informs us, and finally flew to heaven. Baba says, "Oh, we knew it was coming." But of course that's no comfort, and wrong: I always thought I'd see her again.

The Fall

THEY'D DRIVEN WHERE UNCLE Bud had shown them on his tattered maps—west on a long unmarked logging road deep into the woods, through two unattended paper-company gates, then north on a faint jeep trail, once much used, no longer. They were to look for a particular boulder. And the pickup truck did fine, as her uncle had said it would, even with no four-wheel drive, Timothy confidently pulling the shift lever and kicking at the heavy clutch, bounding them upward through the deep ruts and grassy sections and *singing*—Timothy singing!—except Jean knew him just well enough after two years to know that the singing meant he was anxious.

Jean was tense, too. "Where do you think we'll pitch camp?" she said. And, "I really do hope I can manage that pack—you said thirty-five pounds but it's forty-six now and I'm quite trepidatious about my back, sweetie. It's hurting now, just from packing."

Timothy glanced over coldly, said, "She's trepidatious."

"That's all you're going to say?"

"You're strong enough to carry *me*, for Christ's sake." And he bumped over a great log submerged in the mud of the old road, very slowly, one mile an hour, said a soulful "fuck."

Which made her laugh. She clamped down on her lower lip with her perfect teeth—he always said she had perfect teeth, but with a kind of disdain, seeming to hate even what he liked about her. He also said she talked too much, which of course led to fights. But she did chatter at times. Something she ought to be able to prevent on a vacation week in the warm August woods and by force of will did: she didn't say another word.

Pretty soon—before noon, just as planned—they were at the unmistakable rock Uncle Bud had described, mossy and dark under old trees that Timothy said were hemlocks. He parked the truck and turned off the motor leaving silence. They had wanted remote, and this was remote, all right, Jean's idea, actually, she who'd snorted when Timothy suggested two weeks with his folks and his brothers on Cape Cod—*again*—after what had happened last August, dismal visit. And then Christmas, my God, was he demented? Two weeks in that paradise of stifled resentments and overbaked competition. But he'd gone for this. He had. Jean had to hand it to herself. She'd known him two years and had come to handle him passably well.

They had arrived so she talked: "I'm just saying forty-six pounds seems like a lot of pack for me." Jean was petite—especially small compared to Timothy (who didn't like to be called Tim and certainly not Timmy). One hundred five pounds, five foot two, eyes of blue, twenty-five years old, not the greatest beauty in the world, in her own estimation. Timothy was her giant bear, gruff, rational, reserved, a stark contrast to her more excitable (and, in her opinion, more exciting) nature. He said nothing, just pulled her pack and his easily from the back of the truck, her uncle's truck, old wrecks, uncle and car, both of them. Uncle Bud in his cups last night had confided to her amusingly that he thought Timothy a stiff and a cold fish, though he was glad to meet him: now he could warn her off him. Wasn't the boy a tad bit too much like her father, speaking of stiffs? Speaking of emotional *deserts*? Uncle

Bud's laugh was so infectious, even with his being so nasty. Wouldn't she do well to wait to get married? "Thirty is even too young, but at least, I beg of you, wait till then," he'd said. "I'll be your best man. I'll give you away! Find someone who's not so *angry*." They laughed and laughed until Timothy came into the big rustic room from one of many constipated visits to Uncle Bud's nice outhouse, and even then they could not stop laughing. Timothy, for his part, did not crack a smile and did not ask what was funny. She'd never thought of her father as *angry* before, and so that had given her something to think about in the night.

At the parking spot in the deep woods, Timothy put his hands on Jean's shoulders, pulled her up out of her reverie, as he so loved to do, said, "We'll drink up that gallon of water in your pack there and that weighs eight pounds alone." He'd said this before ten times. He said, "We'll eat down the food." Ten times. He said, "And every day it'll weigh less. You'll be fine."

"Well, I'm worried about your pack, too."

He didn't answer but hefted her pack and held it to her back, let her find the straps. He wriggled into his own without help, a staggering seventy-four pounds, way too heavy. But he found his balance as she had found hers and they hiked into the woods on the faint trail that would take them up Talon Ridge to Independence the back way, Uncle Bud's way. For the first twenty minutes her thoughts were all ajumble and slightly furious—Timothy had talked her into too much *weight*. And too much weight for himself, too, always showing off. And no sign at all that he felt this was an especially romantic trip. But it was. Their relationship was the whole idea. And that you didn't always have to be off with your brother someplace, or some replacement brother, doing manly things, making fun of everything on the planet, including Jean, for sport.

Was that what her beautiful uncle meant by angry?

Jean and Timothy, hikers now, passed through thickest woods, mossy earth, an untouched old forest that loomed over a recent clear-cut so that there was a view out at times, to the hills south, and to Mt. Abraham (she thought she recognized, but said nothing, not to invite derision in case she was wrong), all in a balmy updraft gusting at times to wind. Her pack felt light, actually. Her pack felt fine, to tell the truth. No problem walking. Timothy pushed her to greater heights, and that was a good thing. They climbed, mostly: switchbacks, lichens, boulders right and left, warbler song, chickadees, wood peewees—what a place Uncle Bud knew about! Timothy hadn't said two words.

"How's your pack?" Jean called forward.

"Heavy," Timothy said. He could say just the one word *heavy* in such an ironic way that it meant everything about the little argument they'd had last night and the bigger one this morning, and about all her complaining, and yet how good she suddenly felt, even climbing up the big rocks here. Looming in the woods above them was a gargantuan boulder, yellow where all the rock around them was gray, a glacial erratic, Jean knew from a half-forgotten geology class, a mammoth presence, dragged by the ancient glacier all the way from Vermont, likely, cracked magnificently along the way, fallen into two pieces you wanted to push back together. "That is a glacial erratic," Jean called forward. Timothy said nothing, hiked on, though she knew he had heard her by the brief and infinitesimal tightening of his neck.

Well, altogether she had preferred art history in any case: Bonnard, Kandinsky, Cézanne, Max Planck, Otto someone, Courbet, Delacroix, Manet: why were they all men? Someone had complained and Professor Della Sesso had agreed, stopped his own class, rewritten his own syllabus in front of them, come back the next week with slides from Käthe Kolwitz, Vanessa Bell, Suzanne Valadon, Mary Cassatt, Romaine Brooks, Natalia Goncharova. He'd stopped the class! Of course it was all planned, to make his point, a great point about the place of women not so much in art but in art history. He was a beautiful man. Jean missed her college days. Her publishing job was basically secretarial, second assistant to the curator of the image bank at Time Warner. At least it was about art.

They stopped a little higher, sat on a kind of wide shelf of cool, dry granite, pulled the top layer out of Jean's pack, ate a lunch of chicken roll-ups she'd made this morning, two carrots each (Timothy had peeled them unnecessarily, making fun of Uncle Bud's garden—its very existence when there were grocery stores), and then two big pieces of the carrot cake she'd made for Uncle Bud—carrots were the theme—a quart of water between them (which would be altogether nearly three pounds less for her to carry).

"Here's to Drunkel Bud," Timothy said.

Then he was silent, merely ate. He was often silent. He was twenty-five, too. Jean knew he was thinking and not to interrupt. He'd listen if she said something—but if she did talk, then he wouldn't say whatever was coming, whatever bit of conversation he was brewing up—this was the silence before the talk, and she loved to hear him talk, loved him, in fact, from the bottom of her shoes, despite what Uncle Bud had said, late (Timothy already reading in bed), poor, unshaven Uncle Bud slurring his whispered words, eyes liquid, but so full of warmest caring and gentle humor: "You'll marry him and stay with him like your mother stays with your fucked-up father, even not loving him, thirty years to realize it's so, yes, Jean-Jean, it's so for her as for you, and she still can't shake him, just lies down for him, bed of nails. Nothing can stop you, I know. No, no, I know it's true, Jean-Jean. No, no, I'm right, no use to argue: it's misery you're courting, since that's all you've known."

Jameson Irish whiskey speaking.

There in the forest, waiting for Timothy to speak, Jean finished her sandwich and repeated to herself what she had whispered back to Uncle Bud (who had finally let her talk, listened unbelieving): she loved

Timothy and felt just wonderful about him. And it was true—she could hardly remember what they'd argued about last night when she'd come to bed, what they'd argued about this morning (or ever, for that matter), and wanted to be his wife.

Suddenly Timothy spoke: "It's hard to imagine," he said. "Hard to think of ourselves like, fifty years old, like Uncle Bud, huh, isn't it? That such a thing could happen? I mean, what if it's just a kind of joke they play on younger people, just to make 'em feel bad—right?—like, they know goddamn well that we're going to be always just like this, more or less like this—I mean, there are young people, which is one unchanging species, and then there are old people, which is another—and the old-people species have as a kind of group joke that they pretend it's all one-in-the-same species—that we young ones are on a long trip that leads to their sorry-ass state."

Jean laughed for him and he smiled and that melted Jean, that very handsome smile. She looked in his eyes and said, "But, Herr Doktor, I distinctly remember being younger. I'm not sure you've included all the evidence here." Two years and they had this whole kind of private vaudeville act together, where she played graduate student and he played crazy brilliant professor. She really, really wanted to go to grad school, art history, to follow her favorite prof to his new position in Paris—he'd emailed her twice inviting her to apply—but that would have to wait.

"Well, right—but we're the kind that go from zero to about twenty-six and just hover there, always almost twenty-six, like someone in a book—always the same age every time you read it. We're the somewhere-under-twenty-six-always species."

"What about a book where the characters grow old and die? I can name a few.

"Written by the Olds! Self-serving tripe! What on earth garbage have you been reading?" Even being funny he sounded harsh, like the joke was on her.

"I don't read trash," she said, trying to keep the tone of high comedy, failing.

He wasn't listening anyway, just shuffled through the side pocket of his pack, eventually tugged out his tiny jar of insane pot. Methodically he rolled a parsimonious and perfectly cylindrical joint, then lit it, one of their twelve waterproof matches, and they had two tiny hard-sucked puffs each.

Coughing a little, trying to suppress it, trying to rescue the moment, Jean said, "So we're the species that gets only so old. So I'll get to catch up to you, yes?" She was three months younger than Timothy.

He didn't rejoin.

The feeling of the pot overtook her immediately. She knew he'd have little more to say for a while. No one was around them in the woods, so Jean (in love) put her ear on Timothy's chest to listen to his heart, and he leaned back against the rock and mulled his important thoughts while she undid his blue jeans just partly, just enough to get her hand in and hold his dumb, dependable willy, which rose tenderly to greet her grip. This, she liked. And he liked it, too, and tucked a hand back of her blue jeans and kind of hefted her on top of him for a long kiss, and on the moss there on the side of the faint trail they gradually got their pants down and wriggled to get his jacket on the rock beneath them without taking their hiking boots off, even, and had a very brief grind 'em (as he liked to call it—she didn't mind so much anymore) and then some kissing, which showed that he was in a good mood, too, a very lot of kissing, as when they first met and would make love for hours in her old sublet, a great apartment in the Village now long gone, pretty white walls with art, and she couldn't orgasm at all, he made her so nervous, and if she brought it up (she believed in communication) just said that orgasm was not a verb. Here in the woods and more firmly in herself she surprised herself coming quickly, if not too hard (coming was his word), *orgasming* to his overeager fingers while they kissed. Something about the forest made it easy and different, also that he bothered.

"You are a glacial erratic," he said.

"That is an insult, Doktor," she said, quite pleased that he'd been listening earlier, just saving it up. He'd know what a glacial erratic was, knew a lot about the world and the woods. They cleaned themselves up some with a paper towel that she dutifully stored in a baggie and pulled their pants up and hefted their packs. She could feel that hers was lighter.

Timothy kept talking, named each bird and tree as they continued the hike—he knew so much. Ash tree, birch polypore (a familiar, bulging fungus on a dead paper birch), this warbler and that one, all the little plants everywhere. Jean liked it all but cared more about nineteenth-century women painters—that was her thing, she'd decided, and still dreamed of Paris—no reason that, married, she and Timothy couldn't live in Paris. Goldman Sachs must have a job in Paris for their wonderboy. Two years, that's all it would take.

She felt great, if a little soggy in the underpants. "You are a glacial neurotic," she said.

Timothy rewarded her with a hearty laugh. This was one of those jokes they'd keep going for the weekend and that for years to come would tag this hike in their memories. She laughed, feeling light, suddenly; the pack was as nothing on her back. They could stop fairly early—no rush—perfect weather, get a really great camp arranged, set up that little stove, make spaghetti with the red sauce Timothy carried in a jar for a special first-night dinner only. She'd had stomachaches over the camping part for two weeks but felt free of every anxiety now. They had great equipment and great food and Uncle Bud's advice, which was famously good advice, if not perfectly sober. ("Your mother told me last phone call that your father has never once said he loved her.

Never once.") Well, Timothy's family was worse: aggressive teetotalers and potheads.

They broke out of the trees suddenly in a dry-pond meadow (Timothy called it) and were in sight of the bald blade of the famous ridge that hunkered just beneath the famous mountain peak, and the view of it all was just—it was just *spettacolare.* She said that word with exaggerated accents and giggled (the marijuana), and Tim giggled with her and they walked side by side, holding hands. The trail tightened then, so Jean dropped behind him, and they marched on duck boards thoughtfully placed through a mossy bog. *"Thuja occidentalis,"* Timothy called back, and these words were as beautiful to Jean as the trees they described, big white cedars curving up from hummocks and snags. The bog resolved into a pond—a beaver flowage, as Timothy called it—no beavers in sight, and at the deeper end they stopped on another flat rock and soaked up sun and, very hot from the hiking, stripped down and had a swim. Then they kissed and petted nicely, cold fishy gooseflesh skins pressed together. She climbed up on the next rock naked and he leaned against it and it was hot in the sun—he licked her legs, not altogether seriously. He licked her legs, then he licked her (she didn't like to say it, the word he always used), and she had a deeper orgasm this time and said so, using his word, which made him grin and go cocky. And then he climbed up and fucked her hard on the rock, an uncomfortable performance. Her neck was bent back. He was too rough sometimes, but she could let that go. He stopped thinking of her, stopped thinking altogether, called it boning. You traded one thing for another. (Wayne, her last boyfriend, was tender and very slow, but he couldn't kiss.) And it wasn't ever long in any case. She would have to remember to take her pill each day of the hike and wondered if she'd get a rash from the sleeping bag, as at Girl Scouts, and thought of Mimi Stevens, her counselor, the witch, and of the particular way the logs of Cabin Twelve came together. And Timothy grunted and groaned and then laughed a little and that was that and she rose back up through several layers to him and kissed him a while, but he wasn't into it. "Better get moving," he said.

"I love you," Jean said soulfully.

He spanked her bottom, said, "You love me."

They had a quick swim and she rinsed him off her and out of her and they dressed side by side. Her socks felt wet and her T-shirt, too, and her underpants, everything a little damp from the earlier sweat and now the swim, but it was a hot afternoon and beautiful in Maine and there was plenty of time to get to the camping place Uncle Bud had told them about. She should be glad. She knew what it was—the pot. Also the orgasming, which sometimes let you down. And now she felt a little swollen and uncomfortable down there, walking. Twice in three miles of hiking! Well, that was love. And there were worse ways to be sore.

She followed Tim up the very steep path, which was nothing but a field of rocks. His butt was cute, what there was of it anyway, that was one thing. "You're just plain erratic," she called lightly to no response.

They came to the beginning of the open granite ridge—what a view. The stoned feeling from earlier had settled into a headache. The sun hurt her eyes. Something in her belly ached.

"One hour," Tim said, tugging on his pack straps to adjust them.

"That's all?"

"That's what Drunkel Bud said. One hour from the cairn." He pointed up the hard stone slope to their left.

She hadn't noticed the massive cairn. And he was competing with her, that condescending tone: he'd seen the cairn, she hadn't. He'd only win if he could annoy her, though. And she didn't feel all that bugged. Her pack felt like nothing, nothing at all. She thought about how to cook the dinner, how good that would be, their neat little gas-bottle stove, precious folding pans: boil water, cook spaghetti. It would never taste so good! And here they were, already at the verge of the famous Talon Ridge, which was superdramatic, something a nineteenth-century male artist would put in a painting, finding the curve of it complex, a kind of bridge to the mountain, a mile terribly exposed (imagine a storm blowing over it!), none of the soft fields and cloud vistas of women, more subtle, the tensions interior, or such was a lecture she recalled.

To both sides, the granite sloped sharply twenty or thirty feet to sudden drops. To the left, a kind of bog, not far down, a lot of dead spruce trees, beautiful skeletons, but to the right, a sheer drop of hundreds of feet. Ahead the talon sliced that direction, just enough that you could see some of the long face of the fall. The impression was that you were walking the apex of a cathedral, the Abbey Church of Saint Denis, perhaps, a place she'd written about once in a paper—got an A, too.

"Here we go," Timothy said, and led the way.

Jean followed sprightly—with Timothy, you always felt you had to hurry.

The bog side was brightly lit, the cliff side dark in its own shadow. She tried not to look down. She actually panted—this was what *breathtaking* meant. The trail had been carved out of the plain rock. "WPA," Uncle Bud had said, fondly.

"Welfare," Timothy had snorted. Why did he have to call him Drunkel? Why especially that name, which she had repeatedly told Timothy annoyed her. It's what her father called Bud, who was not a drunk, not really, just bereft, a very kind and calm and gentle soul, her mother's only brother, a sweet, poignant man who'd built his own eccentric, amazing house and lost his wife to cancer before they could live in it, thus the retreat to his cabin. Why shouldn't he drink?

Timothy got walking faster, the way he did when excited by a competition—they were almost to tonight's campsite, and he'd be first. Just along this roof of granite, then back into the woods. It was as if the incredible view to all sides—even down—simply weren't there, the only direction forward. The camping spot was on a bigger pond than the first one back there, and just under the mountain proper, Independence

Peak. Uncle Bud said it was the nicest camping in all of Maine. She and Timothy would have an easy morning there tomorrow, swimming, sunbathing, bird-watching, no doubt making love, then onward—up the mountain, then a few days on the Appalachian Trail, then the Fire Warden's Trail down from Bigelow Mountain, finally back to Uncle Bud's truck, a grand loop: seven days. Ahead, the trail became even narrower, just a shelf carved into the rock and strewn with loose stones.

Tim hurried faster. "Hey," Jean called. She wanted a kiss from him right now on this precarious place. She said *hey*, and he didn't hear. A kiss just to slow him down. He was almost jogging, and tonight if she nagged him about it he'd frankly love the attention and crow and mock her. She slowed. Walked at her own pace. Breathed at her own pace. Enjoyed the view up to the mountain, the view down into the gorge beside them. She had come to the end of the bog and now the mountain was a wall to her left, the abyss to the right all the deeper, the talon coming to a point ahead, Tim's bright pack bobbing as he ran.

"Hey," Jean called again.

But he was too far ahead.

And then he slipped. She saw him slip. His flying foot hit a nothing of a rock, which slid under him, and he dropped to one knee. He reached for a handhold on the path, missed, went down on his shoulder, couldn't quite catch himself, continued to slide in gravel toward the fall. It was all so slow. He put the other hand out, grabbed a large stone that was sliding, too, tried to turn, awkward under the weight of his pack. He couldn't get around to sitting, so he dropped down on all fours, visibly putting on the brakes. But all the rocks large and small around him were moving now, a slow, gentle slide with Timothy part of it. He dug the toes of his boots in, gripped the solid granite of the ridge with his fingernails.

But he just kept sliding. Jean trotted, then raced, to get to him—there was a length of rope on the side of her pack and she reached back for it as she ran. But Timothy and the rockslide picked up speed as she did. He didn't shout, didn't cry out, didn't say a thing, just looked back at her, a profound look, grabbing at the rocks around him, starting everything he touched to movement. And with everything around him he slid to the edge of the drop. Rocks flew off the cliff into the sky below his feet. His boots hung over, then his knees. He bent at the hips, legs dangling, still slowly sliding. Jean threw the rope perfectly. But the overweight pack pressed Timothy down, restricted his reach. He missed the rope end, missed it again, arms flailing. Then with a sharp cry he went over the edge. The rumble of rocks continued briefly, then everything stopped and there was silence.

THE ARGUMENT THAT MORNING had been about her iPhone. She'd promised she wouldn't constantly be looking for a signal, wouldn't be Snapchatting friends little stupid photos, it would be for emergency only. He had won—you entered the wild on wild terms—and she had left the phone behind in their sweet little room at Uncle Bud's. So her first thought got her nowhere. Her second thought was to scoot on her butt down the incline to the cliff edge, get a look, dangle the rope. But that would be stupid and impossible: she'd go over, too. Her heart pounded in her throat, her ears.

"Timothy!" Jean called, to echoing silence. "Timothy Beal!" Nothing.

Best to stay calm. She stripped out of her pack, left it at the exact spot he'd stumbled to mark the place. So many loose rocks—new ones had simply replaced those that had slid and then fallen with Timothy. Free from the weight of the pack she sprinted back down the ridge the way they'd come, a sense almost of leaving her body, of perfect ease on the loose gravel, fearless warrior. At the forest end of the curving ridge she skidded to a stop in gravel, fell to her knees turning, that anxious to look back. Her pack was nothing but a blue shape perched on the ridge. The edge of the cliff wall, what you could see of it, was dark. The odd tree grew up from rough rootholds. You might land on a ledge. A tree might break your fall. You might be okay. The bottom, not visible. Rocks, no doubt, more trees. Oh my God, oh my God, oh my God. Run for the truck? Drive out for help?

Or go to Timothy? She trotted back up the harrowing talon and to her pack, more cautious now. Oh my God, oh my God. All was quiet. Squawk of a raven below. Breezes warm and flowing upward. Jean returned to her body as if falling into it, her sweaty body, that edge of headache, the cramp in her womb from making love. She kept having the urge to turn and ask Timothy what to do.

Be calm, she told herself. Make a plan.

She checked pockets for her phone, but no. They'd been maybe four hours to this point—all uphill and with two long stops. She could run it in an hour, maybe, get in Uncle Bud's sweet old truck, two hours on the faint jeep road, then two more on rutted logging roads to where? To that gas station? So five hours. In that time she could maybe also get to Timothy, give first aid, set a broken leg—she'd taken a course at summer camp ten years past—staunch any bleeding, give comfort if nothing else, take his advice from there. He knew about so many things. She hefted her pack, slipped into the straps, kicked some stones into a pile to mark the spot, pathetic. So she took the pack back off, built a proper cairn of ten large stones to mark the spot for any possible rescuers, a helicopter even, only then shrugged back into her pack and ran, buckling the hip strap even as she flew, the decision coming as she ran: truck. The trail got easier off the ridge, the deep shade of trees somehow comforting. She ran fast, then faster, clear to the beaver flowage before she remembered that Timothy had the keys.

WHERE THE OLD TRAIL pegged upward to Talon Ridge, Jean broke into the woods and headed down over tangled deadfall and among the boulders of eras gone by. Quickly as she made her way the cliff below the ridge established itself, sheer and cold in hard shade, but with so much fallen rock at the bottom that it wouldn't be that high a fall, she thought, not really. After a full and difficult hour, breathing hard, climbing rocks, skirting crevices, the cliff wall soaring higher, the scree field tilted steeper, rocks tumbling under her feet, Jean rested. She had no idea how far she'd traveled. She couldn't have missed him, not with that crimson backpack, pure attention. She tacked lower—found a faint path maybe made by deer, moved more quickly, examined every ledge and crack in the cliff above her, stopping to listen for cries. Below her a stream tumbled—good: she'd be able to wash Timothy's wounds even if their water ran out. That joke he'd made about carrying him? She couldn't carry him. She could stabilize him, do whatever was necessary, make him comfortable, put the tent up around him, cover him in their sleeping bags and all their clothes, be to the truck by nightfall with the keys, best plan. The cliff was so high. She prepared herself in case he was hurt badly. Tourniquets could be dangerous, she recalled. Splints could be made with sticks. Underwear, T-shirts, flannel, hers, his, it could all be used for bandages.

She came to a fault that ran the width of the narrowing canyon and created a sharp drop, nothing compared to the cliff, but twelve solid feet at first guess, and sheer. She could jump down, perhaps, but how could she climb back this way to get the truck, and help? Maybe use the rope, tie it to that tree. But then she wouldn't have rope for later, and who knew? Wasn't there some knot you could tie and then free with a twitch once you were down? Timothy would know it. If he could only have caught the rope when she threw it *so well*. The stream had to make the drop, too, and the roar of the little waterfall invaded her thoughts, made them urgent. She breathed, took off her pack, dropped it down there just so, exactly right, where she could land on it to break her fall. The pack took a foot or more off the height of the break, too. Still, it was a long way down, fifteen feet, at second guess. The rope was down there, tied on the pack. Oh! She could have tied the rope to the tree, climbed down using it, then simply *cut* it with her Swiss Army knife, just left the remainder behind, keeping plenty. All this in Timothy's voice, carping, as she lay down in the dirt and loose rock and scooted herself over the edge of the drop-off till she was hanging by her fingertips, barely gripping a fragrant spruce root. She hung a long minute, without the arm strength to pull herself back up in any case, finally got the nerve, and dropped. She hit the pack hard with her feet and fell backward into loose rock.

But she was fine. She was really totally fine. Her butt wasn't even bruised. That she was sore was from before. The cut on her hand was nothing. He'd fallen feet first, too, and so there was at least some chance he was only slightly hurt, a twisted ankle, dislocated knee.

The canyon fell deeper, darker, the stream louder and closer, more narrow, the scree looser, her footing more insecure. Jean forced herself to walk—what else was there to do? She picked her steps carefully, watched her feet intently, stepped on his hand.

Timothy was sitting up straight, that famous posture, his shoulders pulled back by the straps of his pack, head back, too, legs buried in the rocks that had accompanied him, hips twisted more than perpendicular to his shoulders. Jean didn't have any moment at all of thinking he was alive, no need to check his breath or heartbeat. He was dead.

HIGH UP THE CANYON wall she saw the last sunlight climbing, orange. It would be night very soon. The stream roared and echoed in the canyon. Timothy smelled like *defecation*. Also spaghetti sauce—their jar for dinner must have broken inside his pack. But the spruce smell and the oxygenated stream smell was strong, too, and a breeze moderated the stench. It wasn't like she was going to eat. She sat a long while in perfect calm, perfect acceptance, which was not like her and which she tranquilly thought must be shock. In a way it was easier that he was not in need of first aid. She didn't cry anymore but simply sat and thought, long elegant lines of thought with no bearing on the emergency: she remembered meeting Tim at her brother's best friend's wedding. Horrendous blue tuxedoes, all of them. She and this handsome groomsman made love steadily, it seemed, for the next three weeks, till he had to go back to New York and his internship at Goldman Sachs, which turned into a job when his MBA was done. Very remunerative, as he liked to say. Things she was ambivalent about: investment bankers (Professor Della Sesso had often talked about such people, called them *bloodsuckers* in a beautiful accent, and *ricattatori*, roll that first *r*); suburbia (Timothy's dream was Greenwich, Connecticut, ask Uncle Bud his opinion of *that* place); any one of Timothy's friends, including her own brother, who was a certified pig.

And her brother, come to think of it, was exactly like their father, as was Timothy, when you thought about it, from banking to suburbia to his chilly reserve. Why was she with him? "You are beautiful," Uncle Bud had whispered. "You are capable. Does he make you feel either? What can I do to convince you?"

She didn't touch the corpse. The sunlight climbed out of the canyon, was gone. The stream grew louder, comforting in a way, but hiding who knew what scary noises. A lone bird sang briefly, good night. And then it was dark, and darker. And chilly, then cold. Jean dug in her pack, found her flashlight, pulled her sleeping bag out awkwardly, unfurled it from its stuff bag. Such a good sleeping bag, old gift from Uncle Bud, bright blue. She got herself in there, moved more rocks, leaned back as if to sleep. But despite all, she was hungry.

The bulk of the food was in Timothy's pack, as was the little gas stove. In her pack were useless things like couscous and expensive freeze-dried chicken divan in foil packets. Oh, but gorp—there was a one-quart baggie of gorp—and this she ate in little absent increments till it was gone. And she drank water from her metal bottle. And felt she could sleep some, get through the night somehow. If Timothy weren't such a show-off and always in such a heat to *win* they'd be camping right now. Or if they'd left the first pond just one second earlier or later? They'd be camping. Thoughts of the campsite, which she'd been picturing for two months, brought her to Uncle Bud, that idiot, sending them into danger and Timothy to . . . this.

Then again, the whole backpacking trip was her idea, her own, and she'd fought for it over going to Timothy's horrendous family reunion on the Cape, and that bunch, oh, that bunch would blame her squarely, squarely. Every happy thought she'd ever had of marrying Timothy these two years had foundered on the image of that screwed-up family. She sat and thought the same moody thoughts as always about him, added these to Uncle Bud's observations of last night, only last night.

All moot now.

The stream down there was loud, luckily loud. She was spared the gurglings and belches of the dead, sounds she knew well from working at the veterinary hospital every summer through high school, back when she was going with that kid, Bruce, who was no Timothy, but sweet and talkative and a listener—funny you could ever miss Bruce, but she missed him now. Timothy did not twitch, did not jump, all that was over.

JEAN WOKE WITH A start, kicked her feet out and sent rocks tumbling, sat up, reached for Timothy's hand, found it—so cold, and worse, stiff. She let it go with a shudder—it was not in his possession any longer, it was not his, or him, but a disgusting object.

Oh my God, oh my God. She wanted to feel his spirit was with her, but she was profoundly alone, hard stars above, no known constellation, just the hard line of the killer cliff and across the narrow gorge the jagged line of the tops of fir trees. She listened to the stream a long time with deliberate concentration.

How could Timothy be so *clumsy.*

How could he be so *stupid.*

SHE WOKE TO THE sound of the stream. High above, a group of stars was familiar, but unnamed. Funny, but she could relax. She'd been so unfair! He wasn't to blame—the trail was unsafe. He was hurrying for *her*—he knew how much she wanted to be at the campsite, be set up in their tent, be eating, cooking. He was so *good.* Such a good person. She would marry him despite all. Best if Mountain Rescue found them together here. She'd never leave his side. She'd sit here through the days it took to starve, and in a few weeks Uncle Bud would look up from his Jameson's and remember where his old truck was and call the family, who'd call the police, who'd call Mountain Rescue, who'd come out looking and certainly find the truck (probably they'd already be well aware of the truck and wondering about it)—find the truck and follow the trail clear to the campsite on the beaver pond—no sign of Timothy and Jean. Perhaps the scrap of a cairn she'd built would alert them. She should have written a note—how stupid—several hikers a day must pass; someone could be going for help right now. But no. Things were exactly as they were.

Perhaps after days of futile searching, the youngest member of the ranger team, the most insecure of them, would notice the cairn, the plight of rocks, and they'd all be led to the tragedy—broken Timothy and his girl, starved at his side, his bride in death. Oh, she loved him! And she reached to touch his hair, which felt lovely, soft and fine as always, accepted his condition, which would be hers soon enough.

But not soon enough. She should write a note in the morning and cut her wrists to be his bride. She'd be his bride by his side in death the endless night.

SHE WOKE TO DAYLIGHT next, birdsong. The stream, too. She blinked and stretched and was surprised they'd slept under the stars and sat up and remembered. She wriggled out of her bag, made her way out of Timothy's sight, peed behind a boulder, clambered back, had a long look at him. His face was no longer his. His fingernails were all broken from trying to stop his slide. She worked to get his pack off him, struggled with the resistant arms. The smell was no longer so bad, or she'd adjusted. His upper body was simply loose on his hips. Oh, Timothy! She worked around the spill of red sauce, found the loaf of raisin bread he'd allowed, wiped it off, crackers in a small box, block of cheese, block of chocolate, found his compass, retrieved the little stove just in case, their little tent, his hunting knife, the keys to Uncle Bud's truck (in Timothy's moist front pants pocket), stuffed all this in her own pack, stuffed her sleeping bag in its sack, tied it carelessly to the pack frame, pulled the pack on, balanced step by step and rock to rock and got out of there, quickly backtracking upstream and all the way to the drop-off by the waterfall.

She tied their rope to her pack so she could pull her belongings up if she made it, attempted a hopeless free climb with the rope in her mouth, fell four times, not even close. So she tied the free end of the rope to an oblong rock, tried to toss it over the one practical branch of the high spruce up there—impossible. She stacked rocks to make a climbing platform—exhausting. After an hour she had a solid block of stone only a few feet high. To get her all the way up the drop in that fashion would take days and days and all her strength.

She gave up, made her way back to Timothy. She'd had what he would call a paranoid thought. Digging in his shirt pocket, she found his tiny blue jar of pot. Fast, she emptied the powdery potent stuff to the wind, threw the jar into the stream. His rolling papers, into the stream. She felt in a rush of horror that she was abandoning him so sat a while beside him.

Unbidden thoughts: there were other boys. She'd even recently been going back and forth with a certain college flame on Facebook, but that was nothing. She'd be a tragic heroine, very attractive in that way. She'd be wary of love, magnetic in that way. She stood, pulled on her pack, made her way carefully through the rocks he'd brought down with him, rehearsing the story she'd tell and basking in the sympathy and wonder she'd receive. Sinful, disgusting thoughts. She shut them off. She tried to pray for Timothy but hadn't prayed or been to church since she was ten. Her last confession (to Father Mark, a saint) was about stealing Barbie accessories at a slumber party. Timothy! So impatient and disdainful. Just as Uncle Bud had said: the dude was just like her dad. There were other *kinds* of men. Start with Uncle Bud. Subtract the tragedy of him, and the drinking. That beautiful house he'd built! The far cabin where he was holed up now, bottle in his lap. Timothy called it a shack. Timothy thought him soft. Think of all the men she hadn't met!

Sinful thoughts, disgusting.

And now flashes of yesterday's sex assaulted her, and Timothy's fall, too, the way his fingernails dug in, sex and fall somehow equally unpleasant, even horrible, braiding into one thought. She stepped faster, picking her footfalls, a good old athlete, scrambled down the scree, got to the stream, drank from it, the hell with giardia and all microbes forever, drank deeply, washed her face, struggled to stand under the new weight of her pack and the growing feeling that this was all her fault, secondary feeling that it was all Bud's, and worse, that Bud knew it would happen.

Had she slept even two hours last night?

She headed downstream. There was no trace of a path. But a stream always went somewhere. By the time the sun got into the canyon an hour had passed. She'd find help. The stream would cross a road. She'd find help and they'd recover Timothy and she would be something of a tragic heroine and perhaps even Professore Frederico Della Sesso would see this new thing in her eyes, the deep sadness and horror in her eyes and take her crush seriously as he had decidedly not, take her in his arms there in the oaken doorway of his dust-mote and sunbeam and bookshelf office somewhere in Paris. Bad thoughts. He had called her Jean d'Arc, their little joke. She closed him out, pushed on. By noon she was out of the canyon and the forest had opened somewhat. The walking got easier for a mile or so, gently downhill alongside the stream. But then the stream widened, became a bog. She slogged her way halfway around to where it was more of a pond, stood on a lone knoll, looked out over the water, and was at last overcome. She tugged her pack off, threw it down violently, threw herself on the ground after it, wailed and wept, clutched the mossy duff. Then came a vision as if from above of herself in this position, the dirt of the forest sticking to her tearstained cheeks, herself spread out on the ground in grief and remorse and horror. The rangers would listen attentively to her, when she finally found them. They'd be older guys and have bluest eyes, three sweet men, beautiful eyes.

She cried more, at her own shallowness, felt a wave of love for Timothy, felt in the same wave that she came back to her true self ("You are not yourself," Timothy would say when she was upset with him). But what if the true self she'd always known was false? Jean stood, crossed her arms over her chest, grasped her own ribs in confusion. And started walking. She'd go back to him. Only as an afterthought did she return for her pack, only absently shrug it on, aware uncaring that it was open and that things were falling out of it. She walked very slowly, deep thoughts of Timothy, his humor for example—a certain joke ("All your intelligence is in your brains, Jeanie"), his tricky smile. She was starved. She stopped at a sunny rock, pulled out crackers and their block of cheddar cheese (these had been on his back!), ate feverishly, found their bag of baby carrots, gobbled them all, a pound of them (his dead back!), sucked at her water bottle, found their large chocolate bar, ate half of it.

There'd be raisin bread for later. Uncle Bud had offered it, and though Timothy said no—too heavy—she'd accepted the small gift. She lay back on the rock in tears.

WHEN SHE WOKE, HER mission was pure again: get help. She retraced her steps around the bog to where she'd thrown the pack down, picked up her sleeping bag, her wading sneakers, four blue pairs of panties still neatly folded, the keys to Uncle Bud's truck. What had she been thinking?

She carried on, climbing to higher ground, made her way around the bog till she saw the beaver dam and climbed down to rejoin the stream, which was three times wider than in the gorge. She fairly jogged, singing loud then louder, whatever song came to mind, "My Favorite Things," for one, screamed it out as she ran among trees in the old forest, leapt boulders, pushed aside underbrush, downhill and always down alongside the stream, singing as hard as she could to stop her thoughts of Dr. Della Sesso, which had grown pernicious. Frederico. His gaze had always lingered on her eyes. Now he'd find her so *dolorosa*, so *tragica*. "Origin of the World." He was Italian but lived in Paris. She'd been there herself, a month in junior year, hadn't been able to commit to a year or even a semester: Wayne. Who couldn't kiss.

There was a ranger station in Carrabasset. You could get a ride there, and the kindly men would explain that this was no longer a rescue but a recovery, no rush. The other rangers would all gather around, they'd pat her face, they'd kiss her eyes, and Frederico would come to fetch her, fetch her back to France. She snapped herself awake: Carry on, Jean, carry on.

The stream fell through a steep glade, quite straight for hundreds of yards, but just before it turned and flowed out of sight, promising nothing but more hard bushwhacking, Jean could just discern a hard horizontal, painted red: a bridge. She made her way to the road—narrow, nicely graded gravel—and simply lay down, her will collapsing, flopped herself down pack and all, lay there frozen by her thoughts, exhausted, killed.

In an hour, two, hard to say, a father and young son from nearby Quebec on their way to the store in Kingfield for camping supplies (she'd learn later), stopped their Subaru and leapt out to her aid. She heard their guttural French Canadian accents—so different from the French of Paris—heard them clearly as they leaned over her asking each other what had happened here, touching the pulse point of her neck to be sure she was alive.

She opened her eyes to see the boy, who might have been eight, saw his sweet concern, cherubic, like something on a chapel ceiling, blue brushstrokes all around his head, the wings of angels.

"I never loved him," she said.

"Alors," said the father.

"I never loved him one bit."

"You are shivering," the father said. The shivering seemed to make him cross.

"I only want to sleep," Jean told him.

"Elle veut dormir," said the son gently.

"We will take you into town," the father said, gruffer. They helped her sit up, helped her out of her pack. The boy put it in their car, then father and son helped her to her feet, so unsteady, helped her into the back seat. She curled up and lay across the nice leather, let them cover her with her own green sleeping bag, which the boy had untied and unrolled.

Murder Cottage

I WAS DOWN THERE so much for tide-pool research, camping in summer, that dumpy motel in winter, that I started to think of getting an apartment of some kind, one of those cool places over an old drugstore or in an abandoned mill—stilled machinery, homeless cats. But, really, in those rural Maine burgs there aren't any rentals, or only terrible ones, trailers and broken houses, the drugstores all gone to big box, the old mills now malls or past saving. I thought of house-sitting some richie's shore house, but turns out that's not easily done either, several leads that all foundered on my teaching, that I'd have to be back in Bean Town for the fall, when all the caretaker duties really begin: winterizing, leaf management, constant reassurance.

But then in the Bluebird Diner I picked up the *Pennysaver* and, idly paging, spotted an ad for a house. Ninety-nine thousand, which seemed to me a desperate number. The photo accompanying the ad was grainy, of course, but showed a rustic-looking and tiny building alone on a rock, grayed cedar shingles, the ocean in the background. Clearly, something was wrong with the place.

The real estate agent, one Bonnie LeDoux, very cheerful, confirmed my intuition immediately, right on the phone: "It's an outstanding value," she said. "But there's a bit of history to it. Ready? The couple who owned it, they were murdered. Newlyweds. Shot in their beds. In the house. And that's made it hard to sell. The Bangor Savings Bank owns it. Six years on the market."

"Murdered?"

"Shot in their beds. They caught the guy immediately, so that's not a worry. It's just . . . well, I don't know. People are superstitious."

"I'm a scientist," I said.

"The most superstitious of all. I mean, if superstitious means believing things that aren't true!"

"I'll let that go."

She had an open, hearty, honest laugh, laid it on me.

At the house twenty minutes later, I was amazed. Especially with the view off across rocks to the ocean. Two acres of rocks, in fact, with patches of dirt where things could grow and did—lavender and beach plums, sedges and alder—also a rock beach. We looked at the house itself last. Bonnie was a robust gal, tall and pink cheeked, jeweled jeans well filled, that good humor in every joint, kept punching my shoulder with her knuckles, strong. "They weren't found for a week," she said. "You should have smelled it."

"You smelled it?"

"Yup. Along with real estate and driveway plowing and blueberry picking, I'm a first responder. You need more than one job down here."

"You're an EMT?"

"Forest ranger." She pulled a badge out of her canvas purse, punched my shoulder with it, hard, showed me the gun in there, too, put it all back.

I said, "So forest rangers are cops?"

She shrugged to say, Not exactly. "But often first on the scene."

Inside, no terrible smells. Part of the wallboard in the bedroom had been sawed rudely and removed.

She said, "That's the cleaners did that."

"Thorough."

"Listen, Mr. Autumn, my sense is that the bank is pretty motivated here. Try a figure on me."

"It's Autun."

"Ah-Toon."

"Ten grand."

"No, seriously."

"Twenty-five?"

"You'll only get one shot with them. What do they care? But they need their expenses covered."

"Thirty-five."

"You've really got it? Cash? Can get it?"

"Yes, really."

She said, "It was a love triangle."

The bank and Bonnie and a couple of local lawyers and I closed four weeks later, and the little sweet crime scene was mine.

"You know what happened in that place . . . " one of the bankers said the second my signature was dry.

FIRST THING, I HAD the wall repaired where the cleaners had had to remove the gore-soaked Sheetrock. Otherwise, there was no particular sense of death there. Bonnie knew a carpenter who'd known her ex-husband, was the impression I got going into it, but while he ate the little lunch I made him, we talked and I learned that he himself, in fact, was Bonnie's ex. I said she seemed like a good person, just a pleasantry.

He said, "Don't fuck her whatever you do."

"Oh, I have no . . ."

"Don't get me wrong. She can do whatever she wants. I'm just saying, she'll break you, that's what I'm saying. My God, the legs on that woman."

He did a masterful job on the Sheetrock, even taped and primed it for me, several return trips, and all for seventy-five bucks.

THEN IT WAS BACK to Boston to teach, fall semester, hard to go back to the big city. But finally it was December. I'd been thinking fondly about my little cottage for months, the peace of it, the rocks, the ocean, the price: I'd gotten the place for probably a tenth its true value. I didn't spread the word, however, never told the story—I worried that if the murder thing got widely known, potential girlfriends (my ex, Charlene, had left me for a job across the country and then, after a few years long distance, for a colleague who played guitar, sad) might not want to come along on the weekend dates I envisioned. But there'd been no weekends for me—I was chair of the department during that stretch, sixteen-hour days. My chairmanship ended with the semester, however, and then my sabbatical began. I sublet my apartment to a fussy grad student who would take perfect care of Charlene's ancient cat—no moving that distinguished animal—and loaded the old Civic with everything I'd need, not much. My idea was to do three things: read books, practice my amateur painting, not die of loneliness. The study of tidal rockweed reestablishment after winter storms, despite my sabbatical proposal, would be number four, if at all.

I had no phone reception of any kind on the rocks there—*my* rocks!—a tumbled promontory bounded on all sides by Nature Conservancy land, paradise. And of course no Internet. I could have added a dish to the side of the house and got some coverage, but the point was not to have coverage. And losing all of that all of a sudden was like withdrawing from crack, or whatever the kids are playing with these days. I paced the house, noticed every little noise, got my paints out, set up my easel, stared out to the ocean through the picture window an about-to-be murderer had stared through the other way, his heart pounding, at a guess.

Third day there, Christmas Eve, and Bonnie LeDoux pulled up in her mini pickup truck, surprise. "Welcome Wagon," she called when I stuck my head out.

Inside, she admired the new Sheetrock. "That guy does great work," she said.

"Your ex?"

"Aw, he wasn't supposed to say. I just want to keep it professional, you know? Your real estate agent? No life of her own? Only *your* life matters?"

"He also said I shouldn't fuck you."

She went pink in a rapid flush that ran right down into her décolletage. "Oh, that rat!"

I kept my eyes firmly on her handsome face, said, "I liked him."

"Everyone likes him. I like him. I love him. He just says stuff like that. Undermining stuff. I hope you didn't listen to him. Ugh, that came out all wrong. Listen. Here's your welcome basket. Made it up myself. Just now. A little *rrr*eposado tequila, some elderflower liqueur, also limes. Also cucumbers, I hope not too suggestive! Except of summer. Cucumber margaritas."

My loneliness fled. I said, "I have salt."

"We can sit out in our lawn chairs on the rocks in our insulated coveralls and contemplate eternity."

"I don't have insulated coveralls."

"I brought some for you."

"I don't have lawn chairs, either."

Before long we were lounging in her lawn chairs out on the far point of my rocks, the freezing offshore breeze pushing our hoods firmly onto the backs of our heads, drawstrings batting our faces, huge seasonal waves charging up against the rocks, high tide, whitecaps retreating, king eiders and common goldeneyes and black guillemots paddling peaceably amid the mayhem. Those coveralls were insanely warm. And the drinks were rays of sunshine. Bonnie, too, in and out of my peripheral vision like a lost memory, intoxicating.

"It's *your* salt," she said every time I sighed, two drinks, three, four, not terribly strong, but who can tell with rrreposado? Bonnie just kept leaning out of her lawn chair, adding one ingredient at a time to her giant backwoods Thermos, shaking 'em up good, pouring me fresh jelly jars full.

We watched the ocean, the birds, the high-cruising clouds.

"Where do they go?" I said at length, philosophy overtaking me, the sun hitting the low scrub behind us.

Bonnie knew just what I meant. She thought a while and said, "They go everywhere. Molecules far and wide. Matter can't be destroyed. You die and you're all broken into irreducible bits and then transformed into the next thing."

"Your husband said something very complimentary about your legs . . ."

"I used to squeeze the breath out of that little squirt, that's all. Like trying to get blood out of a cornhusk. Or at least a little juice."

"And you're a forest ranger?"

"It's seasonal, doll. You'd be surprised how much I know about deer populations, though."

"Driveway plowing?"

"Who do you think plowed yours, city boy?"

I hadn't even thought of it. I'd just driven right in, neat berms of snow both sides. We laughed and laughed over that. She took my hand and held on, a crushing grip across the abyss, lovely.

"Happy housewarming," she said.

■ ■ ■

INSIDE LATER, AFTER A couple of hours of increasingly libidinous and rumbustious lovemaking, I cooked us up some food. I'd stopped at Drummond Pier for my traditional huge lobster, and it was enough, even for two large and famished people, also a bag of smallish potatoes, also green beans, also a pound of sweet butter from the honor fridge at the farm up the road. We talked about sex, the way new lovers do, licking butter from our fingers, little compliments, daring phrases, slugs of margarita, insatiable.

She said, "I liked when you carried me around."

I said, "I think my hips are dislocated."

"I could squeeze harder, believe me. That was like, I don't know, a five."

"We're really great together, Bonnie LeDoux."

"That was me, Ah-Toon. I'm really great. You, you've got a ways to go."

We listened to the waves a long time. Finally, I said, "Just something about it."

And Bonnie said, "I know. Doing it right in the room where they got shot."

"Just something about the actual stakes we're all facing. That whole walls have to be replaced."

"Like, eight bullets each. Dude had to reload in the middle."

"Or maybe he had one of those double magazines."

"No, he reloaded. Took his sweet time, too. Lined the shells up on the kitchen counter there. Sixteen altogether."

"And just coldly shot his former love!"

"And her boyfriend. Then drove to the state police barracks and turned himself in. Forty to life." Bonnie sucked a lobster leg clean, stuck a potato in her mouth whole, then green beans, those capable long hands at work, so alive! She chewed contemplatively, her beautiful mouth, looked at me long, then away. She said, "I've never been in love before."

"Well. That's what murder will do for you."

"All those splattered thoughts."

"I'd hate to be one of the cleaners."

"They're busier than you think. Motels, lobster boats, campsites."

"Your cheeks are so red from the wind."

She softened, just something I hadn't seen in her, the feminine side. She said, "The legs on this girl."

"You want me to say I love you, too."

She laughed, just ha-ha. Then, "Only if you mean it."

"Okay, I do."

She said, "We called it the murder cottage. Back at the office, I mean. I should have told you that."

"We can get a sign made for over the door: MURDER COTTAGE."

"Murder Cottage. I like that. Beats, like, Rocky Roost."

"Or Bonnie View."

"I like that you say we."

"We, then."

"Come let me crush you like a bug."

"But you've got a gun in your purse."

"Ah, guns are like lipstick, these days, an accessory."

"That's no way to talk in Murder Cottage."

"Your voice is so low."

"I do love you. I don't mean to sound surprised. I just really do. Whatever it means this early in the game, I do." I did.

She thought a long minute, said, "It means this." She gestured to the two of us, the cottage, our coveralls on the floor, the new drywall, not a sign of Christmas anywhere, that thing that was happening elsewhere and without us.

"It means this," I agreed.

"Plus all the emails all fall."

"Those were good emails."

"It's all in the subtext. Even early in the game, you creep."

We cleaned up a little, ran the lobster shells down to the ocean, threw them in, then made the short journey back to the cottage and bed, made love to the sound of the crashing waves, the increasing wind, sixteen shots from a phantom handgun, then thirty-two, then sixty-four, then exponential everything unto millions, our link to eternity, the smell of lobster and butter and ocean and sky and every human effluent, and kisses and second tries and new ideas and confidences and snuggling and dozy intervals then at it again: life.

Princesa

A FAMOUS ACTRESS WAS supposed to arrive. Everyone Robert and Phillipe met found a way to mention her: Tessa! She was shooting a film across the island with the great director Pedro Almodóvar, whom Phillipe claimed to admire, no one Robert had ever heard of. The hotel driver who picked them up at little Ibiza Airport talked about her the whole way, mostly in Spanish superlatives, beside himself with the pleasure of her, that such a luminary would grace the Royal Mediterranean Hotel, kissing his fingers to the air: Tessa Embrodar!

Phillipe caught the bug immediately. He'd heard of the actress one way or another. Shame on Robert for not knowing Tessa! Was the attitude. The actress had been in a dozen European films, none Robert had ever heard of. But she was in that Harrison Ford movie, too, Phillipe kept saying. They'd seen it on a double date when Robert had first met Julia, who'd adored it! What was it *called*? Robert had no interest, Harrison Ford or no, and certainly no wish to be thinking about Julia, not on this trip. The name Tessa Embrodar meant nothing to him whatsoever, even repeated a number of times by guests and hotel employees alike in various faulty accents around the buildings and grounds as Robert and Phillipe toured the place and were introduced to simply everyone (none of that all-American anonymity here): Tessa Embrodar is coming! Robert was superior with Phillipe about it—some obscure actress in some second-rate Harrison Ford thriller, not even one of the big ones, give him a break. They made a gay-straight joke of it between them, he repeating the actress's name in mock awe, Phillipe shaking his head in not-quite-mock disgust at Robert's geeky philistinism.

Phillipe's aunt was an executive travel consultant for the likes of Mercedes-Benz and Berkshire Hathaway and the Saudi royal family and had secured for her favorite nephew this golden sojourn. Double occupancy and Phillipe with no boyfriend at the moment, unheard of, thus bereaved-and-boring Robert. Robert had had to look up Ibiza. It was one of the Balearic Islands, in the Mediterranean off of Valencia, Spain. And now that he was here he had to admit it was spectacular. Plus, they were paying less than ten percent of the standard price because a castle suite had come empty at the last minute. Suddenly they were jet-setters.

Robert continued to complain—that was the game—but he was very satisfied with the Royal Mediterranean, extremely pleased, in fact, especially with everyone else paying something on the order of fifty thousand American bucks—a castle and vineyards and olive groves once owned by the Contessa of somewhere or other, attentive maids and obsequious bellboys and unobtrusive waiters and insistent concierges everywhere all but brushing your teeth for you, multiple spas and restaurants and swimming pools and tennis courts and beaches and boating and archery and surf lessons all included. How many massages could you take, how many high colonics refuse? Robert and the late Julia had spent their honeymoon all those twenty years ago at a Motel Six on Lake Erie near Buffalo, where she was from. Phillipe (he'd been Phillip until after college), well, he'd gone to the big city, dabbled in acting, secured sugar daddies one after the next. Or at least that's how he told it—famous rich Republican closet cases who supposedly lavished him with gifts—though he wasn't exactly rolling in cash.

Ah: magnificently manicured gardens and walled walkways meandering down to the Mediterranean as viewed from their three private patios or from the great windows in their separate and equal bedrooms (massive round beds with canopies, glorious baths); the old castle and village visible from their "drawing room," which was a beamed expanse of foyer complete with astonishingly vast and real medieval tapestries, huge windows, the vineyards and hills and horses and scrubbed cattle out there in ancient pastures, the stone fortress wall probably seven feet thick on that side, vines growing right into the room, not just antique but *ancient* furniture carefully buffed and polished, olive wood crackling in the fireplace tended by their various valets, their clothes folded and ironed and hung every time they turned their backs, their shoes left in military precision and polish in the stone stairwell, their dirty laundry attended to daily, cuckoos calling outside all afternoon, nightingales all evening, scent of flowers opening at dawn and eventide from bowers everywhere, cocktails after breakfast if you weren't careful to say no, which Phillipe wasn't always, in fact wasn't ever, rare bottles of wine at every meal.

THE ACTRESS NO DOUBT gained the more attention by being the only person her age who would grace the place, certainly the only single woman. There were small children and a handful of teens, most of them traveling as au pairs to the very few young heterosexual couples. The rest of the clientele was well into retirement years, all wattles and jewelry and tall coifs and powders. After that a handful of gay men in long-term pairs, but Phillipe seemed undeterred: in his world love and commitment didn't preclude sexual adventuring, and he meant to make himself available.

You were seated arbitrarily at dinner each night with other couples, which is what Phillipe and Robert were apparently perceived to be. The first night it was almost unbearable, three ancient husbands with their three ancient wives all dressed formally, a long discussion of international interest rates, much of it in German, Robert in torn cargo shorts, Philippe in Italian leather trousers and waistcoat.

The next day after tennis together and then with various partners (a certain gaiety descending), and after a long swim in the warm blue Mediterranean—groomed hotel beach, islands out there—Robert and Phillipe climbed in the horse-drawn hotel "conveyance" and visited the expensive village. The great church ran a high-end thrift shop, and there, to Robert's protests, Philippe outfitted the two of them for castle life: tailored shirts, pegged trousers, suede loafers. The second night they felt almost refined, joined the talk about global warming, heartily blamed America as the others were doing, brought China and India and eastern Europe in for some inspection, or Robert did, anyway—he was a laboratory manager at Rochester Institute of Technology and knew from climate change. The respect he was accorded as a scientist was like nothing he'd ever felt at home, where his career had not gone exactly as he might have hoped. But people made assumptions when you were able to afford castle life. He fell into a resurrected, youthful confidence, waxed expert to eager ears.

One of their fellow diners seemed to fall in love with Phillipe over dessert, gripped his arm, gazed at him almost teary eyed, old codger who let it be known he owned a string of polo ponies, also a shipping line, said the hotel reminded him of his home—he wanted to show Phillipe the horse farm he kept in the countryside, kept speaking of gifts.

"Go with him," Robert whispered. "You could use a pony."

"You would trade me for a Rolex," Phillipe spat.

"I'd trade you for a cigarette, and I don't even smoke."

But the old stud fell asleep during the cheese course, was rolled away in a custom wheelchair.

THE HOTEL OWNED BOATS, and the evening champagne cruise turned out to be a hoot, as Phillipe wrote his aunt, though in fact it was a trial, he having to dance with one noble nitwit after the next. Even Robert danced with Phillipe. It wasn't like there were available women.

Day three and the two of them got involved in a lawn-bowling tournament, then bravely split up. Robert headed to the volleyball courts, played a genteel match. Phillipe joined a hike through the hills (singing and foreign banter and great elaborate stops for wine and cheese, he'd later report, maybe a touch eerie and far too rocky, heady nonetheless).

That evening they found themselves seated with Vedat and Maria, a voluble pair from Yalta, a place neither Robert nor Phillipe had heard of. "But is on Black Sea!" Vedat remonstrated. "Is site of peace accords after Vorld Var Two!"

"Tessa Embrodar," Maria suddenly gasped.

"We've heard she's coming!" Phillipe said passionately.

"No, no! By the saints, she arrives!" the lady said.

Her husband exclaimed something in their Ukrainian dialect, translated for his new friends: "Permission!"

"Perfuction," his wife corrected.

Robert didn't want to crane but managed to catch a glimpse—of a corpulent older man and his equally voluminous wife in elegant suit and gowns, chins high, making their way out to the terrace in a cortege of hotel staff, a college-looking girl following in tall blue jeans and cropped flannel shirt, oblivious dark-eyed survey of the room as if all the excitement had nothing to do with her, her hands managing her mane of bright chestnut hair as best they could in the tumult of ocean breezes in bright sun. The whole dining room seemed to have noticed the arrival, and conversations that had died long since came back to life as if some subtle, happy gas had been introduced to the hotel ventilation system. Robert distinctly did not recognize her: just a girl, admittedly striking.

"Let us claim table on terrace," Vedat said. He rushed out there embarrassingly, but in seconds a wave of hotel employees was transferring their bottles of cava and blown-glass flutes to a table not too far from the famous one.

Up close, the young woman's face was, in fact, familiar, and now Robert *did* remember her, the graceful bearing, the pouting mouth, the sudden shy grin as she caught his eye, the indifference as she dropped it, the really magnificent sweep of her shimmering chestnut hair, the fine cheekbones, the deep color of her skin, the tilt of her pelvis as she stood waiting for her chair to be wiped of dew, the tidy, small breasts pushed up mechanically by a not-invisible blue bra to make at least a little cleavage, the pretty, half-buttoned pink-plaid flannel shirt, her huge eyes scanning the room for anything more interesting than her companions and even her skyrocket career, unforgettable girl from the unremembered movie with Harrison Ford, startling in reality. She'd been riding a horse. Through the desert. In the film. She found Robert's eye again, held it merrily, no idea of her powers, dropped him when her aunt said something that required a petulant answer.

Best to stop staring, of course.

"I belieff Robert is in luff," Maria said thickly, leaning on his shoulder.

"No, it is I," said Vedat, leaning to kiss Phillipe's cheek.

VEDAT AND MARIA'S MANY rooms were at the far end of the castle in the height of one of the towers, sumptuously furnished, and with a den and deep couches to which the odd couples repaired for a nightcap and some surfing on the Internet to get a look at Tessa Embrodar in action. They watched film clips in several languages not

English, the girl from about age sixteen to the present, which was still pretty young, not even midtwenties. On the terrace she'd been an actual person, manageably beautiful; but even on the laptop screen she was more a world treasure, exquisite in every proportion. The camera loved her, as the saying went. The camera was agog. Vedat found a romantic scene between her and a narrow Italian man with a chiseled face, a lot of kissing, those upturned breasts.

"He turns all red," Maria said heartily.

Yes, Robert's neck was burning.

But Phillipe and Vedat were already onto the next clip—the girl riding a horse effortlessly across a barren landscape, that gorgeous banner of hair streaming behind her, her hips as she posted, full gallop, no stunt person standing in, what a rider!

It was the Harrison Ford movie.

Maria clicked it back again and again, the girl riding the overly enormous horse across the barren American plain.

"Vee have DVD of *Princesa*," Vedat said. "Vee borrow from front desk. They havink every Tessa film."

"We'll make a study," Phillipe said.

Anyway, the two of them left to go set up the bedroom television, Vedat carrying his magnum of cognac.

Immediately Maria put her hands on Robert, felt both biceps, patted his hair. She was older than he'd thought, with jowls and sad eyes, smelled floral, powdery. She clicked the computer again, and again Tessa rode off across the vast plain. "That girl, she luffs you," Maria said, "She luffs my Robert!"

"Just something about her," Robert said, gazing into the computer screen.

They watched the clip one more time, Maria rubbing Robert's hands lovingly. He wasn't sure later what look must have been on his face as he turned away from the screen, but Maria said, "Oh, oh. I'm sorry, Robert. Poor Robert." She put her hands to his cheeks, gazed into his soul, clucking.

Forgotten emotion! Or perhaps emotion unknown. He shook it off, helped Maria up off the couch (not an easy process), and shortly they joined the others in a cushioned nook that must have been a weapons cache at one time, anyway, there were shelves carved into the stone and the remains of iron brackets, a medieval crest in crumbling mosaic. Also wide couches and a flat-screen television so clear and gigantic that it was like a window. Vedat and Phillipe were waiting, Phillipe with the remote control tight in hand, his mouth looking unusually moist. Well, so what: he and Vedat had been kissing.

Tessa's face was the first shot in the film, a long close-up, a princess thinking dark thoughts and planning something, a luxuriously lengthy shot the likes of which you'd never see in an American film (as Phillipe pointed out): just trust the camera and the girl's spectacular presence, no need for anything else, holy shit.

IN THE MORNING THE actress appeared at breakfast alone. She might have been anyone's brilliant grad school kid, T-shirt and capri pants, flip-flops, another highly visible bra, this one fire red. Not three tables away, she ate a huge pile of croissants with jam and butter, as Phillipe pointed out.

"I don't need a report on every fucking bite," Robert said, his back to the girl. He wished he had worn pants and not his bathing suit, an old pair of surf jams he'd had for over twenty years, when you thought about it, from when he and Julia were first dating, bright pattern faded. Phillipe was badly hungover, not so much Robert, who wasn't a drinker. They could only imagine, they said, what Vedat and Maria were going through after the way they'd chugged their Armagnac, two in the morning. The four of them had minutely dissected the

Harrison Ford movie, which wasn't very good, not really, even despite Tessa's performance, dazzling. Very late they'd watched her most recent Spanish film, which was so very subtle, psychological, transgressive, eccentric—funny, too—the girl really had it all.

"She's putting salami on a croissant," Phillipe said. "That's her fifth one." She'd been naked for half the scenes, or nearly naked, no discretion in the filming. Her aunt and uncle ought to have protected her, Phillipe had said, and repeated at every fulsome peek of flesh. He was oddly moralistic for a slut, as poor Julia had often pointed out. Maria and Vedat thought the nudity was fine—it was the story that was egregious, that a man would disown his own daughter in that fashion, shocking, and that even so she could behave that way in the end, even in medieval times. They translated from the Spanish as the movie went along, probably poorly, as no script could possibly be that halting and melodramatic. Robert had remained silent but thought it was the most beautiful film he'd ever seen, with the longest cuts imaginable, like looking at photographs, Maria with her hand on his arm, Tessa's protean beauty five minutes at a stretch, Phillipe finally changing seats to escape Vedat's little kisses.

"She's getting up," Phillipe said.

And then she was standing at their table. Tessa Embrodar, the very girl. That face from the movies looming over the breadbasket, but in color and with a small pimple on its forehead. "Hi," she said, acknowledging Phillipe and Robert equally. She beamed—any smile from her was a beam. Her hair was pulled back carelessly. She still had the lines of the sumptuous hotel sheets cut deeply into the side of her face.

"Oh," Phillipe said. "Oh!"

"Good morning," Robert said coolly. He felt a little mad at Tessa for the way she'd acted toward her family. But that was in the movie. He felt a little betrayed by the things she'd done naked with the Blue Knight of Grenada, too. But here she was, just a regular girl, and a little shy.

"Do you swim this day?" she said, indicating Robert's suit, his horrible bathing suit.

"I love to swim," he said.

She formulated the foreign sentence without inflection such that it sounded more like a command than a question: "You want to swim to the island."

"You mean the Royal Mediterranean Island Swim Challenge?"

The Blue Knight of Grenada had torn her clothes clear off her. She didn't get his sarcasm, said, "Yes, of course. They doing it every Wednesday, yes, today. I need this partner for the rules. You swim. It is most safe. The hotel boat follow. It is the popular hotel swim. One kilometer. Like nothing, nada." She pulled up her shirt and tugged down the waist of her capris to show that she wore her bikini underneath, long smooth belly.

"I swim," said Robert.

AND SO IN AN hour Robert in his jams was diving into the Mediterranean Sea beside Tessa Embrodar. There were three other sets of swim partners and an odd man out, a middle-aged German fellow who had no buddy and didn't care what the lifeguard said. Nor did the lifeguard care much about the rules, just a shrug: what was one more drowned German?

Tessa's aunt and uncle were aboard the hotel's pontoon boat under the canopy in lounge chairs, perfectly content to be chatting with Vedat and Maria, who had decided to come along. Soon Maria was topless, her breasts already deeply tanned, enormous round brown balloons slightly deflated. Phillipe, terrified of boats, had gone to town with the pony man for lunch.

The swimmers started in a knot, various levels of ability. The lifeguard paid no attention to them at all, got into a passionate talk with the boatman. Tessa, at least, took the buddy system seriously; with quick, strong strokes, she swam close beside Robert while the others fell behind: a gay couple in perfect physical form doing breaststroke to keep their hair dry, laughing and chatting together, also one of the young hetero couples, happy for the time away from their kids, choppy swimmers. The water was warm, the current speeding them along. A kilometer wasn't far to go. Robert had been a champion in college. Tessa must have had coaching, too—excellent form. Halfway across, the two of them broke out of their speedy crawl and into a tandem breaststroke as if by plan. The water sheeted off her shoulders, her face. Her aunt had braided her hair for her in front of everyone. The lifeguard shouted—they were getting too far ahead of the boat. So they stopped, treaded water in the dulcet sea.

"You swim as a dolphin," she said puffing happily.

"Leaping and spouting," Robert replied, same.

But she didn't get it.

He tried again: "Leaping and spouting like a dolphin," he said.

"You are beautiful to look at," she said.

"And you are too," he said too hotly.

She'd meant swimming. And, anyway, to be beautiful to her was as normal as putting on shoes. She stroked away from him—no more thought of the lifeguard, the boat—and burst quickly into a very fast backstroke. He caught her up within twenty strokes, and they swam on their backs like that through the gentle swells side by side and fast. Quickly again they were far, far ahead of the others, though when they stopped once more they saw that the odd man out, the German rule breaker, was catching up, thrashing the water, his balding head burned bright red. The hotel boat stayed with him, since he had no partner. Ahead the island was coming into focus: great rocky cliffs topped by sparse trees and a bit of meadow.

"We is the best swimmers," Tessa said.

"No, you. You're the best. If you took off, you'd leave me behind."

"Never would I!" But she did, she took off, full mermaid.

No, the kilometer wasn't long, but arriving at the island seemed a fine achievement. You swam around behind it and out of sight of the boat, found the hotel dock, which looked out on the open Mediterranean. Tessa beat Robert there by a full minute. But he beat the German by several more, and the German beat the boat. The rest of the swimmers were only halfway across the channel, twenty minutes or more behind. Robert sat on the perfect steel dock with the German, the actress dripping between them. Her suit was less than scanty, tiny crocheted sails. Her skin was brown as her hair. Her shoulders were wide, her arms muscled. She was a kid used to trainers and gyms and dance class and riding, capable of anything.

"You schwim gudt, lonk leks," the German said to her.

She modeled her legs for them, turned them this way and that, modeled them quite a long while, inviting both men to ogle, in fact ogling them herself, and why not, these great works of nature. Robert looked out to the channel. Tessa was used to attention, all right. She punched his arm to regain his gaze. He had to remember forcefully that this young woman was not the murderous Princesa of the beautiful movie but only herself, a young lady.

Robert said, "Tell us about the project you're filming."

"I am sworn to silence," she said, that beaming smile.

"Just tellink: who ist direktor?" said the German.

"Top secret," said Tessa, wagging her finger, putting the phrase in audible quotation marks.

Ah, yes. *Top Secret.* That was the name of the Harrison Ford film.

THE BOATMAN AND THE lifeguard laid out a decadent picnic, enough food for a camel caravan. Tessa was a watermelon fan, it seemed; she pushed her whole face into a tremendous quadrant, let the juice drip down her chin and into the top of her bathing suit, heedless. When she was well painted she walked to the end of the dock and fell languorously into the sea, swam a long time alone.

She and Robert were the only ones not drinking wine.

The German, happily, had joined the young parents in a bottle of champagne and they'd walked up onto the shore out of earshot with a second bottle and crystal hotel glasses, lots of raucous laughter among them. Even the skipper of the boat pulled at a flask of something. He was ancient, unbowed. The lifeguard turned into a valet and darted among everyone, replenishing drinks and snacks, wiping up spills, even dabbing at Tessa's uncle's chin. Robert walked to the end of the dock, sat and watched the actress swim.

Vedat and Maria were drinking cognac again, barking out jokes in their broken and incongruous Scots English and in several other languages. Tessa's aunt and uncle were dressed elegantly for the heat, all silks and linens, clearly loving the company, laughing decorously. They hadn't stepped off the boat, hadn't so much as stirred from their lounge chairs, clearly found the whole island-swimming affair perfectly charming, a spectator sport. The gay couple laughed with them a while then wandered ashore and disappeared along a faint path holding hands. Soon they were out of sight.

"Blow jobs," Maria said cheerfully to laughter, even the boatman.

Well, Robert thought, those weren't the only words of English that had made it fully around the world. He pretended he didn't hear. The proximity of the actress had made him delicate.

They couldn't return till the tide came back in—that was the program: swim with the tide both ways.

The girl was still out in the water, tireless, guileless, doing flips and spins and spouting water, delighted with herself and her freedom: no cameras, no script.

The boat had a head and Robert used it. Maria grabbed his hand as he passed. "There's a path that way, too," she said suggestively. "It goes all the way around." And when she pointed you could see it—a rough path across the rocky shore. "Take her," she said.

Tessa's aunt gave Robert a long look but added nothing.

"If Tessa would like," he said.

"An adventure, this she like," said her uncle, then put his fingers in his mouth, whistled impressively. And here came Tessa, swimming full speed up to the stern ladder on the boat, which she climbed easily, bursting out of the water, flinging her head back, arc of shining droplets. Any small part of her would be famous, Robert thought. Any single square centimeter would be a star!

Her aunt said something, almost a song, in Spanish.

Tessa replied, a long, even more musical sentence. Then to Robert: "I'm not to walk alone."

"I'll accompany," he said.

Maria nodded happily, shooed them both with her hands.

Vedat said, "Stay, talk. We make celebration."

"A walk," Tessa said emphatically.

The aunt wrapped Tessa's lower half protectively in a thick hotel towel then rubbed the rest of her vigorously and unashamedly with sunblock (even the kid's breasts, blunt fingers under her bikini top), and so Maria wrapped Robert and rubbed him, made a child of him, too, and in the end he and Tessa couldn't get away fast enough. The two of them kicked into their hotel-issue flip-flops and climbed off the boat, fairly trotted away down the dock and marched resolutely up into the island. They passed the youngish couple and the German immediately, declined to sample their champagne, laughed at all the grinning and goofing: happy drunks.

The German looked painfully burned, roasted pink. "Hi-ho!" he shouted, oblivious.

THE PATH WAS VERY dry and rocky, but Tessa's land pace was like her swimming pace, and soon she and Robert were sweating and puffing, making a long hill that took them around a corner and out of sight of the boat, though anyone looking through a telescope from the hotel could have spotted them. Ahead the gay couple was naked and frankly lying on one another petting, no move to hide themselves.

"We sit," said Tessa, unraveling herself from the huge towel. She laid it on the ground, then boldly unraveled Robert and laid his towel alongside hers. They sat close and immediately she took off her top, not even worthy of a comment, just a person getting ready to sunbathe.

"You have children," she asked, no question mark. She placed the bikini top neatly on her flip-flops.

"No, sadly."

"Your boyfriend, he is beautiful."

"Just my friend," he said.

The girl didn't get the carefully modulated irony that anyone back home would have picked up easily. She said, "His eyes are so."

"I was married," he said. "My wife passed away. Several years ago now."

"She passed away where?"

"She died."

"No!"

"Yes, she did."

"Tell me her name."

"Julia."

Tears came to Tessa's eyes, deep tears, true feeling. She cried silently for Julia. Then she was done. The sea was deepest blue at this hour, the sun blazing over them, a breeze swirling, fragrance of rough pines.

"Life goes on," Robert said.

"Phillipe adore you," Tessa said.

"Friends," said Robert.

"Like you and me," Tessa said seriously.

"Maybe not just like that," Robert said, then wished he hadn't. She smoothed her skin. Her breasts were naked and tanned and it didn't matter that millions of people had gazed upon them.

She said, "You are sweet to me." She lay back in the bright sun, wriggled to get comfortable.

Robert thought through several complicated sentences about movies, about geopolitics, about the distribution of wealth, couldn't find anything to actually say. At length he came up with: "You are very sweet, too. Not at all the Princesa."

"Oh, terrible she!" She took his hand as if in fright, squeezed his fingers.

"But beautifully acted."

"I am so happy you came swim. I was so, so sad. No one around but all the old ladies, but now I shall not have been a bore. Now I will have something to remember!"

"No, I think it's I who will remember," he said, gaining an elbow to look at her. Her eyes were closed in the sun and she was so long and brown and he drank her in, her perfect peaceful face capable of such cruelty onscreen, the dips over her clavicles, the almost square angles of her shoulders, streaks of her aunt's sunscreen on her chest, her small breasts brown in the sun, nipples brown and tight and famous and frankly sexual.

He hadn't much poetry in him: "You are the most delicate sweet equation."

"And what is that?"

"A math problem."

"Mathematics! No. I am more of a problem than that! Mathematics can be solve!"

He tried again, the thought he'd had earlier: "Every part of you could be famous alone—your hands." She squeezed his fingers at that. "Your ankles." She kicked. "Your belly." She sucked it in. Such that her tiny bikini bottom gaped between hip bones and pubis, perfect sine wave beneath a taut horizon. Oh, to slip a single finger down in among those shadows! She opened her eyes, saw him on his elbow staring, rose on her own elbow, putting them face-to-face.

"All the little parts of you," he said. "They all add up."

"There we have the mathematics again," she said. "Men and their obsession with the parts."

"You're the sweetest young *whole* person. And I'm just an old lab rat."

She leaned closer, inspecting his face, that radiant, camera-beloved intelligence in her eyes, the kindness. She said, "You are no older than Harrison Ford."

"I'm younger than he! I'm younger by far!"

"But something reminds me."

"You were in that movie with him."

She put on a very convincing American accent: "I played his daughter, Elizabeth Bowen. Willful, a little wild, dead in the end." Then back to her own: "Not too many lines, so I get away with it."

"Anyway, you were magical in it, riding that horse."

"I'm a lover of horses," she said. "Also the hot sun. Harrison Ford, not so much."

She was so close. Impulsively he kissed her cheek, her temple, her ear, quick succession. She didn't protest, didn't move away, so he didn't have to act as if it were a joke but kissed her neck, her chin, kissed at the side of her mouth. She seemed both willing and unwilling at once. He kissed her forehead (coconut, lemon, that sweet tiny pimple), kissed her chin (watermelon, saltwater, salami), kissed her coarse eyebrows, her surprised little nose, kissed her eyes one at a time as she closed them again, kissed her open but unresponsive mouth, kissed that watermelon chin, kissed those clavicles, kissed her breasts, her belly, might have tripped all the way over the line, but she squirmed away at the precise moment.

Looking out across the sea she said, “It’s sad you have no wife. And sad you have no child. He’d be a dolphin like you. A beautiful swimmer and a dolphin. If only you were young for me.”

“If I were younger, you wouldn’t look at me twice,” Robert said.

“I am not looking at you now,” she said.

“You are very beautiful, dear girl.”

She said something in what might have been Latin, then translated: “The beautiful is the radiance of the true.”

The breeze picked up nicely. The gay couple had turned face-to-face, talking, too far away to hear anything or see what they were up to. Tessa’s breasts, honestly. They’d been in the movie and here they were in life. He tried not to see them separate from the woman, tried to see the radiance of the true. Semblance of restraint, he nibbled at her sun-hot shoulder. She didn’t seem displeased, didn’t seem anything, so he put a hand on her belly, kissed her neck. This made her sigh. Passion or irritation, he couldn’t tell. He was terribly aroused. He felt the vast brevity of time, wished he could quote some Latin back to her, but he was only a computer geek and a widower from Rochester. He kissed her arm. She gazed up at the sky. He leaned and kissed her chin again, kissed her mouth. No response at all, like kissing a sleeping beauty. He thought of Phillipe, a fleeting thought of Julia, then the insistent image of the cruel Princesa. He leaned further, kissed the slight cloth of her bikini bottoms.

Tessa opened her eyes, gazed at him at length. “You all pink,” she said.

He did feel hot. And under her gaze he grew hotter, all the blood in his body rushing into his face, also into his bathing suit, so it seemed. She seemed to be reading his face, deciphering the lines of his face, solving the problem of him. This was serious work, not to be interrupted.

She said, “I am only twenty-four, Robert.”

“I know.”

"So. Why you doing this?"

"Because. I don't know. Because, as I said, you are very beautiful."

"Others are very beautiful, too. But you do not kiss them."

"Others are not *true.*"

She put on that perfect American accent: "Is this what's done in Rochester, New York?"

"No. No, no. Nothing like this. You don't like it?"

"I like it a little." She smiled slowly, pure radiance.

He wriggled down and kissed her long thighs, which she did not let fall open, nor yet clamp closed.

"Perhaps if you had a daughter you would not," she said.

He kissed her knees. "I just like kissing you. And I like you. I can't seem to help myself. I like you quite a little." He started in kissing her calves.

"Only a little," she said, a question.

"I mean a lot," he said.

"You make no sense," she said.

He kissed the tops of her feet, kissed her toes, kissed his way back up, kissed her thighs again.

"You going all perfectly red," she said. "Your neck. So burned."

She rolled away from him, pushed his face away from her, sat up.

He sat up, too.

She placed her fingers barely on his chest, withdrew them, examined the white spots left behind. She said, "Burning up, you. Burning to death. Shall we go up into the pretty trees?"

"I want to give you something to remember," he said, breathless.

"Oh, from you I have plenty to remember already," she said. She stood quickly, gathered her things, started barefoot toward the trees over the rough rocks and fossils, coarse gravels all loose and sharp. Her legs were so long! She minced and stumbled, waved and flung her long arms for balance, precious. Robert scrambled to his feet, grabbed his hotel towel, slipped into his flip-flops losing time, but because of the footwear caught up to her quickly, reached for her quickly—he had more kisses to bestow, that's all—reached and slipped on a loose stone and only snagged the string of her bikini, not what he meant. The very casual knot untied itself easily and the tiny bit of cloth slung sideways as she spun, her mouth flying open.

"Señor," she said, adjusting the bikini in no hurry, adjusting it in such a way that she was utterly exposed (what a shot this would make in a movie!), then repositioned the cloth, tied the strings as carelessly as ever, looser than ever, hurried away from him, fleet and agile. He did feel himself going pink—he was pink with excitement, with misjudgment, with loneliness. He rushed after her, his flip-flops ungainly on the rocks, she exclaiming over jabs to her feet as she escaped him.

Just at the edge of the wood—a deep, piney, fragrant, cool, inviting wood—the actress stopped to wait for him. She hugged herself seriously, safe in the moss and shade, a vision.

Drinking her in, rushing forward, far too excited, Robert tripped on a stick and pitched bodily into a pile of craggy rocks, caught himself too late, hit his face, his shoulder. Tessa threw her hands to her mouth, gasped. Robert struggled to his feet, touched the blood welling on his forehead. The actress seemed terrified, shook with surprise, burst into tears.

"Oh darling," Robert said. "Princesa!"

But she wasn't crying, she was laughing, couldn't seem to help it, laughed into her long hands girlishly, nothing malicious about it, only delight.

He tried a self-deprecating grin, brushed at his scraped knees with scraped hands, meant to simply carry on, but his nose began to bleed, one drop, two, and then a gush. He pressed the corner of his towel into his face, reached up to her for a hand, stumbled again, dropped to his knees. "Princesa," he called again.

Tessa backed away lost in giggles, stumbled away, wrapped herself tightly in her towel as her aunt had wrapped her, slipped into her top, tied the strings expertly behind her, eyes alight with fascination at Robert's predicament (he was struggling to stand), adjusted the cups upon her breasts precisely, ran a hand inside her bikini bottom to straighten it through the crotch where he'd misaligned it, gave a sudden shriek of laughter as once again he stumbled and dropped to his knees.

Far at the other side of the rocks, he realized, the gay couple was watching them—they must have heard her strange shriek. One of them rose to get a better look.

Robert pressed the towel to his face, realized how bloody it was, maybe funny, why not? He grinned despite himself, got to his feet, managed a few awkward steps. Tessa took off running down the upper path, sure on her feet. Robert staggered after her. She passed the gay couple with a burst of fresh giggles for their benefit.

Robert made the path and ran after her. "Princesa," he called.

Tessa ran all the faster, gasping with mirth.

The gay men watched bloody Robert speed past, their mouths open in perfectly double wonderment.

THE INJURIES WEREN'T SERIOUS, but Maria acted the emergency medical technician, anyway. She berated the lifeguard and boatman, who shook themselves from their Tessa trances and searched together for the first-aid kit Maria had demanded. The actress stood with her aunt and uncle, still gulping breaths and crying with hilarity, couldn't even get words out to explain.

Maria tutted and patted at Robert's scraped palms. "Children, she is," she said. And, "Is not serious, nothing serious." She had him tilt his head back and pinched his nose firmly. When she let go, it had stopped bleeding.

Tessa's uncle lectured her, and Robert could almost guess what he said: one didn't embark on a walk and come back with bloodied men! The aunt took Tessa's hands and gave Robert opprobrious glances, muttered to the girl. The uncle talked over the aunt, urgent advice, and from what little Robert understood they seemed to be saying that Tessa's director would be unhappy with her—girl under contract and involved with such misadventure! Or, anyway, the director's name kept being repeated: Almodóvar this, Almodóvar that. Tut!

The lifeguard slouched over with the boat's first-aid kit, a huge white briefcase of a thing with a red cross on it. He laid it on the dock but couldn't open it, bashed it a few times with his big fist, nothing.

The German man stumbled up from the beach. "I am physician," he said. *"Doctore."* He looked closely at Robert's chin and nose, turned him this way and that. "Best tink ist schwim in the sea," he said.

The gay couple arrived, trotting. "He was chasing her!" one of them cried.

"No, no," Robert said.

Tessa broke into a new gale of snorts and giggles.

The gay couple was not to be deterred. The thin one said, "He chased her right by us!"

And now the doctor went to attend to *her*, Tessa! She might, in fact, be hysterical, said his posture. Perhaps she'd been attacked, said his bustle. The male couple followed the German. Then Vedat, then the boat's captain, even the lifeguard, all in a tight circle around Tessa, who couldn't talk for laughing, fresh gales.

"He was kissing on her!" the thicker gay man said.

"She ran to get away!" said his partner.

"No, no," Robert repeated. But he was excluded from the knot around the girl, who only laughed.

The doctor checked Tessa's pupils, even as she tried to fend him off.

Maria gave Robert a long look. She backed away from him, his only ally, and joined the group around Tessa.

"Princesa," Robert cried.

"He calls me Princesa," said Tessa deadpan, tears of joy in her eyes, and now everyone laughed, even as the doctor took her pulse.

Robert could still feel the skin of her belly on his lips, the humid knit of her bikini on his tongue. He saw her riding that horse. He climbed down off the dock to the beach alone, rinsed the blood off his face and hands, the salt water stinging fiercely.

"All gudt!" the doctor pronounced.

Tessa kissed both of the man's florid cheeks. "I swim," she said merrily, hands to his face. "You come!"

Great laughter from everyone, great relief: she was okay after all.

And Tessa ran to the end of the dock and dove. The doctor quickly stripped out of his shirt and handed it to the lifeguard, trundled and dove behind her. Robert left his bloodied towel on the rocks, waded into the sea, dove in after them, his wounds stinging with the salt. It didn't take him long to catch up—Tessa wasn't swimming with her earlier vigor, and the German was a plodder full of champagne. Alongside, Robert slipped into his most powerful lifeguard sidestroke. Tessa seemed aware of him, doing a strong breaststroke, wouldn't catch his eye, matched her speed to the doctor's, clearly holding back for him, a man who swam like a windmill fallen on its side. Behind them, Robert saw the gay couple enter the water, begin their swim, those busybodies. The young parents climbed back into the hotel boat: unlike the doctor, they knew when to quit. Tessa Embrodar turned suddenly onto her back in the water, made a few strong strokes, then pulled up. The doctor stopped, too, and Robert, too, the little knot of them treading water.

"All gudt?" said the doctor to the actress.

"You swim like a dolphin," Tessa told him passionately, ignoring Robert.

The doctor didn't understand the words, Robert saw, but Tessa's look had been plain enough: she'd been bored by everyone on the little swimming adventure, but now thanks to the doctor she'd have something to remember. The German pinkened further and sputtered happily, feathered his way very close to the actress, grinned manly when she splashed at him, sighed when she touched his face (as if Robert weren't there at all), and without so much as a look at her former swim buddy, the two of them took off stroking and kicking, turning their heads to breathe in tandem. Robert watched them pull away as he treaded water, heard the party boat coming up behind, his hands and face and knees on fire. He kicked anyway, kicked and stroked, gave it his best, easy to catch them up, easy to pass them by.

Broadax, Inc.

MY OLD CHAMP AND pal Frederick Duk Nuhkmongamong simply appeared at my office—first sign of trouble, no phone call. Marie allowed him past the reception desk because I guess he was so beautiful in that suit, so clearly belonged in the corporate suites, or maybe she recognized him from the photos framed in my otherwise empty bookshelves—I never asked. When I looked up from the telephone there he was, determined as always and self-possessed, but something else, too: diminished.

I stared at him bluntly, kept snarling at one Ann Spray from Digital Carnage, or whatever it's called, some half-assed proposal I was tearing limb from limb, showing off a little. But my friend did not crack his usual smile or make the usual word-mouthing fun of my business style.

I hung up, thought a minute, jotted a note, only then looked to my friend. I said, "Ducky," fond as I could make it there in my role as shark.

He said, "Broadax."

We were the fellows who'd been roommates at Stanford—was it really twenty years? I said, "One-nine they want, out in *Bethel*."

He said, "One-nine in *Bethel*? Ha. They heard deep pockets."

"Why so grim?" They'd find license plates in my gut when they finally croaked me, whole propellers from ships, sure, but there'd be this lump as well, poisonous, lead-smelter slag: *guilt.* I felt a cramp. I felt myself sweating.

He looked away from me, first time since he walked in the door, looked back, and out with it: "Jilly and I have split."

"Oh, no, Ducky, come on, you gotta be kidding."

"It's a bad marriage, Ted, nothing to get sad about."

"Don't make small of it, Duk. This is terrible news! This is rotten news. I could cry! I am crying! It's . . . nuts." And it was nuts indeed, if he was initiating it: Jilly was brilliant and incisive and rich, too, a predator herself, but devoted to causes, hungry for life, a player of chess, no board required. A perfect wife as seen by the man who had nothing. I dried my eyes—I really had started to tears. "Nuhkmongamong, you idiot, I care about you! Have a seat—please, let's talk."

Duk collapsed into one of my grilling chairs, hands on my desk, leaned at me across the expanse of teak. I saw he'd been crying, too, that in fact he was all cried out: there was that dewy kind of redness at his eyes, his black, deep eyes. His tie was orange that day with the thinnest red diagonal stripes—no concession to sadness there—narrow knot pulled up so tight that his Hong Kong collar was a suicidal garrote cutting his thin neck.

"How to proceed?" he said businesslike, even rolling his French-blue sleeves.

"You're asking me?"

"You've been through it!"

My own divorce was six years old already, so I guess I was the expert by default. "Ducky, brother, this is a different case. Every marriage is different. You want my advice? You go home and you two work it out, is my advice."

"If I could!" Ducky spouted, and lo, he was not cried out after all:

here came a gusher of the hot and salty. His hands flew to his face, a guy, honestly, who might never have cried in his life.

"Talk when you're ready," I said. I could just reach his elbow, the veins of his forearms standing up blue. He was so thin. I leaned and reached and tapped his cuff affectionately. He said nothing. I pictured Jilly, pictured her perfectly, and smelled her, too—clandestine perfume, secret sweat. An unkind and suddenly consuming thought came through my brain: Jilly Webster-Nuhkmongamong was available, a brain and a boss, as I have said, but generous and beautiful, too, very tall with a kind of bow to her shoulders from making herself shorter for most of her life, and shorter yet for Ducky, who was five-five in thick soles. I didn't look down on her, though perhaps she was not quite so tall as I. She was a sylph in earth tones, always in earth tones: dark browns, rusty reds, black sometimes, soft grays, all to offset her paleness, her unhidden freckles. She looked at my mouth when she talked to me, looked in my eyes when I replied. Her hair she dyed auburn, the roots coming in dark, and her hands were always in it: tying it back, untying it again unconsciously, tying it back and out of her face, untying it again, a glorious mess.

But I put all that out of my head. That was shark stuff, the stuff that made Broadax, Inc., tick, granted, but to be repressed among friends. Beautiful Ducky, let's get back to Ducky, the Thai stick, we used to call him in college, 120 pounds of imperfectly repressed fury, about as Thai as you or me (but then maybe you are Thai—my apologies), the only vestiges of the old culture after three generations American being his food sense, eleven kinds of basil growing in handsome glazed pots that covered his deck-with-view over at Microsoft, a kind of vague Buddhism of outlook. Instead of stories of Jesus with loaves and fishes—the kind of stories in my head—he had Gotama under the tree about to be enlightened, stories mostly serving the same purpose: reminders to kill the shark, or rein it in.

In college Ducky and I and our pals talked about this stuff deeply through drunken late nights, big bags of pot strewn on the coffee tables of several communal dwellings, lines of white stuff, rolled up twenties (no hundreds in sight, not yet), talked solemnly, thoroughly, with mutual respect for the faiths of our fathers and mothers, back when we thought how different we two pod peas were.

Frederick Duk Nuhkmongamong met Jillian O'Reilly Webster during an officers' retreat at Microsoft before that company was macro and before the whole industry leapt to giant money and, of course, before the whole industry got so limp. Jilly, with all her other talents, was awfully well to do: M-soft stock options played timely, retirement at twenty-nine years of age. And her sticky-app start-up, like a rocket, pure genius, snapped up by Yahoo! for plenty of tens of millions. Ducky had been less timely with his own options, but he was no pauper (prenup agreements: their money separate except for what the Duk told me they called their "grocery account," joint checking, seven-figure groceries, I guess—maybe they shopped at Whole Foods): twin Jags in the drive, house like a castle, what lacked for happiness in that marriage?

"Tell me," I said, patting that long, elegant hand.

My own divorce was no matter for tears: Myra wanted to get back to set design, wanted to do it in New York, where set design would mean genuine theater work. And that was pretty much it. We liked each other fine, had a nice, long lunch after the final court date, boomeranged home and made love two hours—we'd never lost our lust for each other, a kind of proof of the divorce: it wasn't about your everyday death-of-sex issues but about a lack of love between us. I don't remember being sad, though I must have been.

I'd had two fairly wonderful (but in the end faulty) romantic connections since, no tears in parting, no one at the moment of Ducky's visit, though quite recently a couple of pleasing dates, and a particular and particularly painful make-out session, about which more shortly.

I was forty-one and certainly successful, if not so gorgeous as a certain Thai American roommate I once had. I was enjoying playing the field, deep center, as I pictured it, Dodgers Stadium, the big-time, seldom a hit my way, but still I was tense, my mitt oiled and ready, waiting to keep that one big home run of a love ball from going over my head.

But that was not the thing to tell Ducky. Ducky belonged with Jilly. Heart in my throat, I said, "What precipitated this? I mean, it's sudden, isn't it? Can you say?"

"Something I did."

I breathed, relieved, and waited—this was painful for our boy, and I had never seen his brow knit so tight. It was not I who was at fault, that was just my narcissism talking. Jilly hadn't confessed. That one brief encounter, like nothing. Ten minutes urgent osculation on a friend's balcony drunk, dinner-party aftermath, already a year past. Okay, maybe more like a half hour: one kiss. And you'll blame me, blame my inner shark, but it was not only mine, Jilly's got one too, some fish, a killer whale, black and white and spouting, all mammal, plenty of teeth, eerie song one hears for miles. Oh-ho, wow, toot, bleat, some kiss.

Duk stopped his crying, looked at me square: "Something serious."

I said, "Okay," keeping my face open, nonjudgmental. He'd an affair, so what? Jilly was no angel: to that I could attest.

He said, "Do you remember Monkey Six Internals?"

"That chip outfit? The 'biological chip' debacle?"

"I was in on the ground floor."

"Ugh."

"Lost all."

"And you didn't tell me?"

Ducky: "Ashamed."

"And, what, you didn't tell Jilly?"

"Worse."

"You told her?"

"No, no. Okay, dude. Here it is. I'll tell you what. Here we go, Broadax. I invested, got cocky, quit M-soft, as you recall, watched my money falcons ride the thermals, bro, put the works in Monkey Six, every cent I could leverage, from their APO to the crash last month: one hundred thirty-two dollars a share Thursday the fifteenth, fifty-nine cents Monday late."

"Monkey Six was a shell game."

"Well, dude, we all know that now."

"No, we talked about it then, Duk. We talked about it at length. When did you stop listening to me?"

"I'm listening to you now."

I stood, went to the window, the world out there, just a moment to breathe, then sat close beside my old friend, no thick desk between us, put a hand on his back, like a plank with ribs, his heart beating in there, ragged breaths.

I said, "So. You're saying Jilly is going to leave you over Monkey Six. But I'm here to tell you: no way."

Long silence, then: "Way, dude. I was overextended and needed big money very fast and couldn't ask her so I just went into her account and took it: one million, first sweep, so easy, then the rest, total eleven million."

"You can't just *withdraw* that kind of money!"

"Full scam, Broadax. Suffice it to say, I pulled it off, her brokerage account to our joint account, simply—listen to this—imitating her voice on the phone"—this last in a perfect Jilly voice— "and, um, using her signature, number of other simple tricks, joking with Mitch Markham, you know, the loyal broker. Of course he did whatever she asked, commented on her sore throat. And the cash was mine. But it was good money after bad and, within three weeks, gone."

"Gone!" I cried.

"Unforgivable," my man moaned.

"Stupid, too," I said. "Monkey Six!"

"Stupid is not the word. Criminal. Is the word." He was my brother and his despair was mine. I patted that back, surprised as he collapsed the rest of the way onto my desk, even more so as he wept hard, five minutes like that, time to absorb all my man had laid out for me and time enough to structure a rescue. I got it all straight, got it all planned in my head, easy to find the heart to help a genius of Duk Nuhkmongamong's caliber.

Gently, almost a whisper, I said, "Ducky, I can fix this. Here it is. We put you to work here. Obviously, this is not charity. We need you here at Broadax as much as ever, or more. I can preempt our international meat patrol with a call right now. You, sir, are now chief executive for Programs. Adjust the title to suit over time. Partner four years. Signing bonus: eleven million all-American dollars. Which will represent an advance on your yearly bonuses for three years hence, if recent payout is any indication. And we will disburse now. Today. You leave here with a cashier's check. You show that to Jilly over dinner—in fact, you give her the check, that's what you do. And tell her exactly what went wrong—how *scared* you were. She'll know the feeling! You tell her you start here next week, and in the meantime, maybe the two of you snatch a little trip—jump over to Maui? Use my place?"

The beauty of it hit him, you could feel it: "Fuck, Broadax." And that was plenty for thanks.

I recircumnavigated my desk, took the commodore's chair, flagged a quick note TOP URGENT to Human Resources, cc: contracts, cc: Marie. "There. It's done."

Nothing to do then but wait. The Duk pulled out his phone, and I pulled out mine—two captains of industry getting back to work. But I found I couldn't: fondness for my friend. After a ponder I said, "Do you remember when we hiked into the caldera at Yellowstone? All those hot pots and miniature geysers and miles of wild lands, not a soul to disturb our communion?"

He finished typing whatever message into his phone, then, still distracted: "College guys."

"I was terrified, remember? I was terrified of the bears. Complete surprise how afraid. We saw that mother and cubs. I mean, we saw them after lunch. Very nice. But then we're camping that night and I'm freaking out, Duk, I'm in my tent and I'm quaking and panicked and you, you heard me whimpering in the dark. And what did you do when you heard me? No words, only action. You collected your sleeping bag and backed out of your fancy-pants REI solo tent and eased on over to my silly Eureka pup tent and you wriggled in there and you held me. Not a joke, no teasing. You just held me all night, and let me quake. Some kind of panic attack, never before or since. And you were there, you were there all night."

Duk nodded, "I still have the key chain, bro. I still use the key chain." He dug in his pocket, and there the thing was, too big to be practical, the little gift I'd had made for him in lieu of ever mentioning that night again, this heavy bronze grizzly bear, true ruby eyes, key ring through its nose, even nicer than I recalled.

Marie buzzed and I buzzed her back and she brought in the instruments. Duk signed them, page after page, and then I wrote my old friend his advance-on-bonus right there, handed it over. He looked at the check a long time—small change here at Broadax—finally folded it, tucked it in his pocket. And gave a little bow, the likes of which I'd only seen him perform once, in the direction of his wizened father at his wedding to Jilly. God, the gesture meant everything: my investment was sound. I dug through my top drawer (new desk, everything neatly arranged by Marie, thus impossible to find item one), tossed him the keys to the beachside condo, Maui. King bed. Old cognac. Housekeeper/cook (Leda Loa is her name, $36,500 annualized, prebenefits, and worth every penny). Volcano views, top surf. Another marriage saved.

BUT YOU CAN'T LEAVE love to chance, or to guys like Ducky, so Saturday from home I called the condo, got my own voice, *beep*, said, "Mr. and Mrs. Schlebster-Dukmongamong, greetings, Broadax here," very cheerful, confident of the best, and sure enough the Duk picked up, jovial, full of good jokes.

"Yes, yes, Boss Broadax! We are here! Life is good! Leda Loa says aloha. You are a lovely man, she says! Jilly says *mahalo*, Broadax. Your cook can sure cook! We haven't left the place yet!" And so on, many a warm phrase. The guy was back on his game, and I was glad to hear it. In the background, Jilly giggling, shouting something out, and Ducky shushing her comically. "Kind of caught me in the middle of something, here, Boss Broadax!"

"I'll let you go! Or come! Or whatever you're up to! And see you Wednesday. They're putting your office together right now! Opposite corner from mine, the power precinct. Tell Ms. Loa I will see her down there in two weeks time, guests in tow. Those clowns from American Express. Gonna be a deal, Ducky, and you'll be selling-point one."

All pleasantries, right to the click.

And then a Saturday stroll amongst 'em. The pleasures of the single man: no one to inform, no one to call, just an aimless Saturday alone, glowing with my coup: Ducky was the best systems man in the known universe, a security guru as well, and everyone knew it industrywide, knew he'd been employed by M-soft preemptively—they didn't use him well, but no one else could have him. His hobby there had been busting into every program they had running the place and offering up groundbreaking cures, you know: fifteen minutes on a Friday after lunch and he'd be into the bowels of Systems, say, or flashing smiley faces on Big Bill's most private screens. At Broadax, Inc., we'd been trying nine years to hire him, with offers far more garish than the new one. I was fairly skipping.

Down to Santa Monica, maybe a latte, maybe a bite of octopus with the folks at Hinterland, take a little walk down to the beach after . . . springtime, hell, you might see someone you know. And it might be a woman. And of course I did: Jilly. Something was rotten in Hawaii.

THE LIES IN FRIENDSHIPS are generally small: *Can't make your party, sorry, I'm so sick. Can't take your dog, sorry, my houseman is allergic. Didn't kiss your wife a long half hour on the master-bedroom deck at Lorraine Lemoile's.* Well, come to think of it, they can get pretty big, but tell me, are they really lies having gone untold? Yes? No? Not even to one another did Jilly and I ever mention the kissing, not in one conversation after, of which we had ten thousand.

Jilly, Jilly. She rushed up to me on the hot Santa Monica beach walk, all adither, cried, "Ducky's gone!" Said, "Have you seen Ducky?" Said, "He's been acting so *oddly*!"

There was nothing in her face of a woman who'd lost millions. After a hug, after some gentle reassurances from me that I'd just spoken to him, after yet another lie ("He's taking a little thinking time in Hawaii alone"), I said, "Have you checked your brokerage accounts lately? Talked to Mitch Markham? Been to the bank?"

Jilly is good looking—did I say that? It's her self-possession, so like Duk's, the centered being behind those smoky green eyes. She's about to laugh at all times, and is about to laugh now, looking into me practically twinkling to see what is the joke. At thirty-five she could be ten years younger sometimes, ten years older other times, her beauty protean. She's got the maturity. She's got the legs. She kicked me sharply in the shin, ha-ha.

My reply was this sad and sober face: no jokes here.

And on a beachside bench I finally convinced her to dial up the twenty-four-hour account access Markham is so proud of. She poked in a dozen numbers, barked a dozen commands. Her mother's maiden name was O'Reilly—I hadn't known this. The freckles are Irish, the precision English, the passion rising from the fires in between. Real beauty, it doesn't fade in the face of bad news: her face dropped, yes, her mouth drooped, sure, her posture sagged hard—of course—a naked hand flew to her forehead in shock. But the thousand passersby to a man and to a woman turned their heads to see her anyway: she looked an actress, movie star, box-office gold. The role here was tragic. She moaned back in her throat, moaned with each piece of the electronic news: lots of small numbers where the big ones had been. Mitch Markham she found on the golf course, private cell. We shared the earpiece, heads together.

Markham was all pro: "That's right, doll. Right. We left the seven accounts active, yes, as discussed. And as per your call the other day, we've drawn 'em each down to minimums, account transfer; yes, honey, as you requested, and don't forget I fought you: fascinating move, I still say so, going real estate and munies in this crazy market? I just wanted to know what you've heard! All the figures are on my desk. All the paperwork available in your portal. Is there a problem?"

Very cool, our Jilly: "Mitch, thank you. And yes, there is a problem. I will call you Monday to explain."

Eleven million bucks, her personal money, broken into seven chunks and fired over to their joint grocery account. We hurried up the palisades stairs to the ATM at the bank on the corner of Santa Monica up there and found the rest of the news: no grocery money, fifteen dollars only.

Next call, of course, was to Hawaii.

Leda Loa rather sings when she talks, lovely deep voice, and it was she who picked up: "I drove him to the airport. His wife, she got off in town."

"Where was he going?"

"Malaysia, so he said."

"Malaysia."

"Via British Air. I have seen the tickets. Two weeks you and American Express clowns, yes?"

"Two weeks me and the clowns, Leda, yes."

She giggled. But not I: that check I'd written Ducky for eleven mil had joined another eleven mil and headed west.

ON A MORTGAGE THAT size, they foreclose pretty well immediately. As a fellow chondrichthyan, of course, I understand their thinking: all those rows of teeth have to bite something quick. Broadax, Inc., can absorb eleven million with only some raised eyebrows; Jilly Webster, private citizen, cannot. And the eleven million was just for starters. The Duk had ingeniously hidden three months of nonpayment, all their bills. Phones were dead. Power off. Furniture repossessed. Tow truck, two trips, hoisted the Jags. A stout fellow from the supermarket, even, looming on her doorstep demanding a check. It would be some time before she could harness her company's funds to rescue her personal self.

No, we didn't call the cops; Duk's desperate moves could await an explanation. And no, we didn't make prodigious or even simple efforts to find him. Jilly didn't, for example, call his family. Why worry them? At Broadax, Inc., I simply told Doug Blauveldt to resume the executive search: our man had changed his mind. My personal check to cover the blown advance would follow, ouch.

Jilly's theory was that Duk would come back when his crisis resolved, that he was only acting out a lifetime of suppression, the forcible containment of emotion, and she and I told each other this theory repeatedly in different forms, elegant each and every one. Still, she lost her house. Yes, that fast: Duk had apparently come to terms with their lender. So, a matter of expedience, she moved into my guesthouse. And there she bore down, operating her business from the kitchenette, a few phones and computers from my offices, set to work reclaiming all the things she'd lost.

My guesthouse, just down the hill in that lovely canyon. It had been a neighbor couple's home till I bought it, an offer sufficient to make them shout like lottery winners, dancing and hugs. Not that I'd foreseen this moment: from my kitchen windows I could see when Jilly was by the pool, watched her pace topless, talking on her phone.

Sharks do fall in love. It isn't all just gnashing and splashing and arms coming off clean. Jillian and I shared the loss of Ducky, for one thing, an actual missing person. We also mourned Ducky the nice guy: dead. I brought her a breakfast tray every morning—prepared by my private chef, so not exactly a community-service merit badge, but still—left it on the steps. I brought her a tray when I got home evenings—snacks, a magazine or two, cocktails in a shaker, just left it quietly on a little table down by the guesthouse pool. She'd come out to greet me only in the second week, thereafter daily, often cried on my shoulder. I held her, that's all I could do. I listened.

Fifth loss, discovered incrementally: her business had been sabotaged up and down the line, big to small and back again: the Duk, subtly hacking. There wasn't going to be a recovery. There wasn't going to be a release of cash. Well, no reason Ducky's job couldn't become hers, an adjustment here and there to play to her skill set, which was prodigious. She'd have to wait on her signing bonus, but why couldn't it be eleven mil? And nice to have the other corner office occupied, extensive remodeling already paid.

MY INVESTIGATOR, JACK WAX, found that Mr. Nuhkmongamong had indeed embarked on a British Air flight to Taipei. Not another clue further. Jilly figured he was in Bangkok—he'd many a relative still living there. My own vote was London—just a hunch. I knew it to be the city Ducky loved most, a place he could actually speak the language, which he could not in Bangkok, ancestors or no. Weekends, Jilly took to sunbathing naked, let our greeting hugs linger friendly. No further kissing, however. She'd let me know when, or if, and I was content to wait. Plus, we were colleagues now, something further to negotiate. The search for Duk continued.

Meanwhile, Broadax, Inc., throve. Jillian Webster, no longer Nuhkmongamong, was one tectonic plate and I was the other, she riding high, I sliding under, mountain ranges lifting, unstable structures falling, victims trapped in elevators. She was worth the zeroes of her signing bonus immediately, surpassed all our expectations, these soaring ideas, these practical implementations. Business was rocking, business was rolling. Our stock soared while around us the industry flailed. The world passed our desks, and we ripped off big bloody bites whenever we felt the urge. Four lawsuits settled in our favor, one after the next. A glowing segment on *Sixty Minutes*, listen to this: "Best Boss on Earth." Trade barriers dropping in Asia, in Europe, in South America, the right amounts of cash to the right presidential campaigns, all of it paving a golden path, the ongoing uptick.

Life was good.

Then Ted Brunk called up from Accounting, asked for a face-to-face, unheard of, but the right call: $150 million was missing from the overseas fund. And then Kiki Minimizawa from Customer Relations: in a single month we had lost some eighty percent of our long-term accounts to a young British company that seemed to have copied our business plan exactly and then bid into our base using information you could only call proprietary. I got on the phone for most of a horrendous afternoon. I heard this rumor and that rumor about Broadax, Inc., all lies that had to be quashed. My fellow chairs and CEOs would not speak to me. Except Harvey Barnard back east at humble New England Graphics, that honest gentleman, who explained how he'd been wooed away and told me all he'd heard about our product failures! We had had no product failures of any kind ever!

"Rumors," I said.

Harvey pointed me to articles in the *Wall Street Journal*, the *New York Times*, *Crain's Businessweek*, and the *Financial Times*, all forthcoming that day.

"I'd hardly call them rumors," Harvey said sympathetically. "We've had the information a couple of weeks, just like you. One of your competitors, I'm afraid. And we felt to protect our softer flank, we must go with that competitor. Which is offering quite a value, I might add, straight across the profile. My sympathy, Broadax." Said as one speaks to a shark from the diving cage—safe enough but still scary. I quizzed him hard and at length he caved: our new competition was Nuhkmongamong Ltd., of London, England.

THAT EVENING, OF COURSE, I was agitated. I brought the usual tray of drinks down to the guesthouse. Jillian was wearing her laptop and a frown of frustration, staring into its screen, just the leading edge of the news I already knew. I sat at her side, wearing my own frown and a sporty new square-leg Speedo, bright blue.

Slowly I said what I had planned to not say: "I fear Duk is getting ahead of us." And went on to outline the subversion of our patents, the seduction of our client base, the careful placement of disinformation in the highest quadrants. All of it quite likely the result of a supremely clever touch with the keypad and spreadsheet.

Jilly let her eyes roam to my mouth, smoothed all that hair out of her face

I said, "Let's speak directly. Did you tell Ducky about our balcony night?"

She said, "I'm so happy you bring it up."

I put my hand on her shoulder, turned her as if for a kiss. "I mean, did you tell him?"

And she leaned into me closer, like, *this close*. She said, "I told him because he knew." And then we kissed, only our second but deeper somehow, the depth of new respect, I suppose, of heightened friendship, attraction untamed, not to mention shared disaster. She said, "Apparently Lorraine Lemoile observed us from an upstairs window—that was some kiss, Broadax." This one was, too, and we carried on, I lifting her to her feet, backing her to the sun bed, kissing, kissing. "And Lorraine felt *embarrassed*. That's what Duk told me—embarrassed for him." We lay down, quickly tangled, sweetness that would save us. As the thunderheads gathered, as the hot rain began to fall, as the wind picked up around us, as she worked my Speedo down with her toes, she said, "And that's all I know. I've withheld this information too long, Broadax, and I'm sorry."

And then what can I say? We were making love, corner offices no more, just two bodies in collision, positively planetary. I thought of the view from my kitchen, thought of my chef up there, hot show. We'd have to build a bower, provision of privacy, the oddest thoughts in flagrante delicto. "You and I didn't discuss maternity leave," Jillian said after, one of those jokes that burrows in and lines a safe chamber with downy pluckings. Giggles subsiding, we stood up, dunked in the pool, climbed out, found our towels, our drinks, the silence of contemplation: the price of this love.

I really wanted to know: "Duk's reaction?"

"Duk wept."

Lorraine Lemoile, cat-eyed sharkette, always with eyes for Ducky. Sunset glinted off the pool. Some kiss, Jilly had said. She watched my eyes. I said, "But surely that is not what precipitated this . . . vendetta."

Her eyes again found my mouth. "No. It was something worse. Something else I've withheld. I don't know why. Let me show you." She rose like a vision, slid into the guesthouse naked, reappeared shortly, clad in one of my old House of Kwo robes, a thick letter in her tomboy's hands. "That's my handwriting," she said. "And this is a draft of an emotional letter to my sister, Kate, one of those letters you do not send.

And if you do not send it, Broadax, it might very well be in your sock drawer a month or two, or even nine weeks, and your husband might then find it and read it."

First line: *Dear Kate: I am in love with Ted Broadax.*

I DON'T HAVE TO say much about the Broadax collapse. It's been the subject these last three weeks of every op-ed column and all the TV pundit palaver a man can stomach and even *The View.* Competition from Europe is the official line—the president of the United States said it herself, part of her brilliant address to Congress. Competition from Ducky, she should have mentioned. First our products and services, then our client base, then large numbers of our best people defecting, even Brunk, then Blauveldt, moving to London. Last our patents—all quite legally if unwisely sold to him, all traceable deals (these hard drives hold everything—every email, every transaction—whether you've really written the emails or made the transactions or no). It's a brilliant, malevolent, fully electronic fiction. A fiction I can't counter, because every traceable link, every clue, every witness, says it is *fact.* Even my secretary, devoted Marie, seems to remember certain phone calls I never made. Marie is moving to London, by the way. She always wanted to head up a subcorporation, apparently, and she loves Carnaby Street.

My personal financial collapse is another story.

The first sign was the Mayflower moving van at my guesthouse—all my belongings there removed under the eyes of the biggest sheriff I've ever seen. And then the lovely young couple I'd apparently sold the place to, moving in.

Jack Wax? Moved to London.

Next, Duk got my house. My legal team? Suddenly a conflict of interest. "A new client" was all Buzz Dorfmann would say.

My retort: "London?"

"I'm not the least bit sorry, Broadax."

My personal checking account: frozen. My credit cards: maxed then canceled. My cars, all four: leases terminated. My life insurance: never existed. Every last little souvenir I owned: sold, checks from eBay users around the world all countersigned by me, all deposited by me, all spent, apparently, all gone, all the objects dutifully mailed by my houseman just before his own Heathrow flight. Seventy-three bucks in quarters, dimes, and nickels from the jar in my empty garage got Jilly and me a night at the Hi-Ho Motor Lodge under the freeway. This gave us an address to receive a wire of five thousand dollars from Jilly's sister, the loyal and lovable Kate, all done old school via pay phones, Pony Express.

Kate's gift of cash, unintercepted, brought us to our final frontier. Ducky had won. I put in a call to Leda Loa. Coming as planned. I owned my Maui condo, our last bastion, free and clear. But Leda Loa didn't answer. A call to her home, and her sweet old mother just barked at me: Leda Loa had moved to London.

The hell with her. We'd cook for ourselves. But in Maui my condo was occupied. A gentlemanly fellow who worked in advertising. All the transfer papers were in perfect order, title and deed, my signature unassailable. I'd sold the place. Made a good profit, too.

"Do you want this?" the ad exec said, opening his big closed hand. "They said it was yours."

A heavy grizzly bear key chain, true ruby eyes, key ring through the nose.

"No," I said. "Keep it. It goes with the house."

SO JILLY AND I camp on a hidden beach on the vast family land of a loyal old Polynesian pal, island to remain unnamed, man who's never once used a computer, let's put it that way. Shelter of driftwood and castoff plastic sheeting, my darling and I just two more of the familiar homeless beachies hereabouts: sunsets, starlight, long walks daily, long nights, storm and calm, peace and quiet. We've got nothing but our talk, but our talk ranges widely. My beloved reads to me, sweet bedtime tones, some really excellent books from the lost-and-found at the public beach not a morning's walk away. That's where I got my flip-flops, too, and where we've found all manner of useful things, from snorkels to hair ties to shampoo. We bob in the surf, we live in the moment, we run in grass skirts, homemade hats big as umbrellas. We couldn't avoid a little industry, help the local kids tie-dye T-shirts to sell to tourists, cash only, enough for sundries and the occasional bottle of good gin. The picking crew over at Dole donates surreptitious pineapples, coconuts fall on the roads, the spear guy on the rocks by the jetty offers fish we don't even recognize, practically free. The old lady on the hill has her garden and if we help, we eat greens and beans and tomatoes and poi. Fire on the beach with our kind, everyone adding a little something to the kettle: stone soup. We're breezy in love, famous for it here, a bun in the oven, whole lives ahead, permanent family leave. No more Broadax. No more Webster. New names secret, location untraceable, not a kilobyte in sight, sharks unto minnows, part of the scenery.

Good-bye to you Duk, good-bye.

The Tragedie of King Lear

DURING THE INTERMISSION OF *The Music Man* at the Rocky Pond Summer Theatre, Miller Malloy stayed in his seat. He'd never been to the place without his late, beloved wife Lou, who was the theater buff he'd never been, an actor, in fact—at least she'd been one in her college years. He'd never been to any show alone before, but there it was, loneliness in a beautiful old theater built in a venerable New Hampshire dairy barn back in the 1920s, a very familiar musical, a surprisingly robust and talented cast, many reasons to smile, many to weep. He examined all the biographies in the playbill. Some of these folks had been around the block more than once. The female star, playing Marian the Librarian, had played the title character in the TV series *Supergirl*, it said, but Miller had never seen the show, no idea how impressed to be. At the back of the little booklet was a notice in jovial font, no doubt an advertising slot that hadn't been filled:

ATTEND! FUND-RAISE! DONATE!
VOLUNTEER! ROCKY POND!

During the second act he couldn't concentrate for the possibility of volunteering. He saw himself staffing phone banks, cleaning the toilets backstage, taking tickets at the door, attending cast parties. Then he saw all that again and added a position on the theater's board of directors, eventually gave himself the chairmanship, bringing his extensive corporate experience to bear, making the company hum, the retired savior. By the time the last stirring note of "Till There Was You" was sung (that Supergirl was dynamite!), he practically owned the place. And that was before the smashing finale and reprise of "Seventy-Six Trombones," which made his heart pound luxuriantly.

Next morning, the last Saturday of his solo vacation, late August, he found his excitement hadn't abated. And so he went to the Rocky Pond Summer Theater box office when it opened and bought another ticket. Then he asked after the company manager. Who, it turned out, was the one selling the tickets—a chubby, cheerful young woman in overalls and kerchief, indefinite tattoo on her hand. Or not that young, fifties—Miller couldn't tell anymore.

"Oh, we'd love it if you'd volunteer!" she said. And pulled him by his own, inkless hand. "I am Marcia." Backstage, nothing whatsoever was going on, yet even abandoned it was a lively place: dressing rooms, props he recognized from the night before, costumes on racks, graffiti more and less amusing, a large blackboard filled out in a grid, neat lines of permanent paint—the title of every Rocky Pond production from 1923 forward, room for only nine more.

Marcia said, "I need someone to get ice for the cast party tomorrow. And, really, if I gave you money, someone to do all the shopping? We need cold cuts kind of thing, cheese, crackers, soft drinks, not too much wine, if you please, even less beer, maybe a big bag or two of chips. Napkins, all that stuff. Paper plates, what have you. Your first job, should you decide to take it on!"

"Happy to take it on. And I'll donate everything besides. No need to give me any cash."

She brightened, softened, already seemed to love him: "Now we're talking. It's the end of the season, not just the end of the run, so it's a big bash. About forty actors and musicians and crew and their friends and donors and family, including kids? No idea how to add that up. A hundred? In the back of the theater here. Everything to be set up by one o'clock. Matinee starts at two, ends at four thirty, five. The big rehearsal room in the back? It's where they used to milk the cows? Do I seem pushy?"

"Push away! I'll help serve, too, if you like."

"Oh, I'd like. Oh, my dear man! I'd like it divinely. You'll be alone, in fact. Though I'll try to lend a hand. Our indentured servants, I mean interns, have had to go back to college. You're a godsend! Literally! And proof of Her existence!" She gave him a grin and a hug and a pat, and bustled back to the front of the house.

Miller wandered out onto the stage, looked up at the spotlights, all the colored filters, the expanse of empty seats, felt a surge of new life in his breast, just as his therapist had warned he'd feel, wonderful.

But, Lou.

HE DIDN'T THINK HE'D gone overboard, though he could hear a voice saying so: "Off the deep end." The two of them had been well to do, however, and by now he was very well to do, even if retired, and after the performance Saturday night these talented kids and friends and fans and family deserved the best, and plenty of it. In the rehearsal space, which was huge and ancient—low beams chopped from chestnut, stalls built of native oak, a cement floor at the back where the whole structure opened up to a soaring milking parlor, pulleys and ropes and steel rails still in place, hayloft back over the milking stalls, actual bales of hay up there, also old theater props, all sorts of crazy furniture and backdrops, fascinating—he set up a party of his own devising.

He filled the old industrial fridge with four cases of assorted beers and ales and twenty bottles of assorted high-end white wines, juice for the children (also soda pop, wouldn't kill them), and the signature potato salad he'd made that morning, and the five dozen deviled eggs, ditto, also the gigantic cold-cut platter and the vast cheeseboard and the three big vegetable platters and assorted cold salads he'd driven down to Hanover for—you didn't want grocery store cold cuts and coleslaw when you could have DiGiacomo's, price triple at least, not to worry given the crusty old-world perfection of DiGiacomo's baguettes and the wicked Tuscan and Umbrian cheeses, golly. Plus, old man DiGiacomo had helped him calculate how much to buy.

The ice cream and the ice cream cake he placed in the enormous freezer beside the fridge—old dairy room equipment—also the five hundred pounds of ice he'd collected visiting three gas stations and emptying their ice vaults: you couldn't have too much ice, that's what DiGiacomo said, echoing the wise and sainted Lou who, once upon a time (and frequently), had said the same about sex.

The tables and tablecloths he'd ordered from Frannie DiGiacomo's Cater Council (the middle generation: they'd done his son's wedding twenty or more years previous, though not the poor kid's divorce) arrived right on time, and Frannie herself even helped him set everything up. No one from the Rocky Pond Summer Theater had turned up by noon, and Miller was glad. Frannie DiGiacomo left in a rush—she had a bat mitzvah to attend to. He got the bar set up—rows of DiGiacomo wineglasses, the twenty nice bottles of red wine he'd bought carefully arrayed, two corkscrews handy. He'd found a thick doormat at the hardware store and now he put it on the floor where he'd stand at his task. He'd even thought to bring his suit to change into while act 3 was in progress, crisp white shirt and bow tie. He'd have to hurry to lay out the food just at curtain, as the meats had to be kept cold till the last possible second: no one was going to get sick on his watch. He cut lemons, he cut limes, he dished olives, he put goldfish and jelly beans in bowls for kids. And then he lined up the liquor. Who knew what actors might drink? Patrón tequila, Hendrick's gin, Bulleit bourbon, old Macallan scotch, a big blue bottle of vodka DiGiacomo said was popular. And then the mixers, whatever they had, you name it. Lou would laugh, that boozy old lunkhead, she'd laugh and love him and hug his neck and kiss him silly.

No sign of the stage director.

But when the orchestra leader drove into the lot, Miller collared him, a white-haired guy who looked startled. His bio had included stints in Europe and Japan, and in winter he was concertmeister with the Bridgeport Philharmonic, not kidding around. "Sir, sir," Miller said. "Do you think some of your folks could put together a little dance ensemble for the party this evening? A thousand bucks?"

Done.

When Marcia turned up, she gasped, and Miller saw that he'd gone too far.

"We'll have to watch Jack," she said, pointing at the gin.

But then, that minor concern aside, she grinned and hugged his neck, kissed his cheek, pure warmth.

And in the end, what a party, all afternoon, all evening, way past midnight, Marcia beamingly pleased, the actors shouting with laughter, the music divine, Jack Dance holding forth heroically sober (Miller helped him by pretending not to hear his orders), Supergirl surrounded and doing impressions of the others, hilarious.

In the morning, still energized, Miller cleaned up solo, right down to the puke in the planters. Later, he helped the techies break the set and then Tuesday close the theater, another season done.

THE ROCKY POND SUMMER theater's winter headquarters was in a tiny office on Jane Street in Greenwich Village, New York City. There for generations a beleaguered directorship had done fund-raising and held auditions and won over playwrights, negotiated parsimonious royalties. They'd made many a deal to preview new work (once a minor

Neil Simon play, woot-toot, overrepresented among the many photos on the walls), rescued the languishing stars of old sitcoms, launched the careers of dozens of newcomers (one of the hobbits was theirs), seduced donors, sold season tickets, held on through thick and thin. But never quite this thin, the financial disaster of the late W years having left an arts desert only slowly growing back to dates and palms.

The actual troupe was constantly shifting, though two versatile old character actors, sober Jack Dance and perennially tipsy Lois Tremaine (stage names both), had been in the ranks for over twenty years, both of them squirrelly as hell, was Miller's instant take. He deployed his best compliments, however, and soon felt he had Lois at ease. She'd been in film and you could see why—enunciation, carriage, mane of auburn hair, narrow figure, the most soulful brown eyes. And yet her beauty had become a shell, something to be wrapped around whatever character was at hand, and perhaps whatever man. Miller Malloy remained formal with her, which wasn't hard—never a thing to talk about except the nearness of a martini bar or shoe store, and plenty of off-putting sexual insinuation, emotional quicksand. Jack Dance, by contrast, had given up alcohol and was no shell, and anything but messy: his characters roasted in the furnace of his psyche, emerged dazed and scorched, annealed: good stuff on stage, not so much in person, where he was bristly and cynical, touchy, trip wired, jagged. He was dashingly handsome face on, sharp featured in profile, intensely sagittal, a hand-forged axe to chop open scenes, relationships, too (or anyway rumors were rife).

Marcia Case, the woman Miller had met on his first day (Basket Case, as Jack invidiously called her), was the executive director, also the one full-time employee, just as cheerful in New York as on the shores of the actual Rocky Pond. Marcia was at home both places, and many more, spoke a half-dozen languages (which you only gathered as you attended parties with her, or heard her on the phone, she didn't flaunt it). She took pleasure in kindness, found power in persuasion, let what she thought show on her face plainly, then said it, plainly. With Marcia, you knew where you stood.

Miller lived up on East Seventh-Ninth Street in the brownstone he and Lou had owned forty years, best investment of their lives, and pretty soon was all but commuting down to the Village, keeping Marcia company if nothing else. She seemed to love having Miller around, but their interactions, hard as Miller tried (he adored her snuggly plumpness), were somehow never flirty, not even on the three occasions when she came to his home for dinner, not even after multiple bottles of wine. He was so old school, she told him, when he was surprised, even shocked, to learn she was gay. She'd only brought it up because he'd asked courtly for a kiss (strongest feeling of Lou watching on some kind of afterlife surveillance cam). Marcia had politely allowed just one, then explained that while being a lesbian might not mean she was entirely unavailable, her long-term relationship did.

"But I hope desire is not the reason you've been so helpful," she said.

"It is not," Miller said truly.

"You may love me from afar," she said.

He didn't even feel rueful. "I'll love you right up close," he said. "And not a thing will change!"

"Well, then. I suppose I won't have to report this drunken incident."

He'd hoped Lou laughed, too, wherever she might be.

HE STARTED BY ORGANIZING the office, which was a mess, even donating a couple of up-to-date computers—come on, Rocky Pond, get with the revolution!—and scrubbing everything down to the floors, bucket and sponge, soapy water. He'd never felt so good. And with the romantic angle entirely out of the way, he and Marcia became close indeed. She was huggy and kissy and confiding, and never had he had such a friend.

He worked on grants: National Endowment for the Arts, National

Endowment for the Humanities, New Hampshire Council on the Arts, various corporate outreach funds to which he had uncommon access, private foundations, banks. That freed Marcia to chase actors. And without being asked, he worked on gifts, hitting up a couple dozen sure old friends for the new Lou Dollwitz Molloy Summer Theater Fund. She'd been universally loved, and everyone he asked dropped money on the fund, which in turn dropped it on Rocky Pond. He set up a Rocky Pond foundation, all the proper bank accounts, legal legwork, all the proper tax forms—easy as pie for him, all his business years—went to work investing everything he'd collected in a freshly booming stock market. Altogether, by midwinter Miller Malloy had increased the troupe's endowment ten times over and counting.

And he and Marcia put on parties at his large yet intimate place, thoughtful dinners with Rocky Pond actors new and old, famous and unknown, meteors and has-beens, all of them meeting and putting the touch on donors mostly new—the one percent, all right—eating well, debating, dreaming, drinking hard, even dancing, even making out. But not Miller, who'd become Marcia's puppy. Marcia, in her capacity as executive director and sole full-time employee, regularly said she loved him, adored him, found him indispensible. That felt nice. Her wife, Deanne, an upscale veterinarian ("Poms, pekes, and poodles," she joked), seemed jealous—tough little lesbian lady, to put it old-school politely—but Miller won her over, too. And pretty soon they were three for dinner, three for a walk, three holding hands, three talking company finances. Marcia took him to a board meeting late in March. The members *applauded* him. "I've always dreamed of a life in the arts," Miller told them. "I can't believe it's come true." And, though he was a man who didn't believe in public display, he wept.

With Marcia's approval, Miller traveled up to New Hampshire, stayed happily in the lake house, frozen everything all around, there oversaw a few weeks of renovations on the theater company's main asset—its gorgeous barn theater. He'd sent out a questionnaire to everyone in the company and to their bigger donors and to the town of Rocky Pond asking what needed to be done. And the answer was *lots*, from new sound design to new stage surface to new curtains to better dressing rooms to air-conditioning in the box office to properly accessible bathrooms, also fire-code upgrades, big bucks. He enjoyed conversations with the contractor—a guy who'd built Lou's dream decks and docks and twin bunkhouses and who knew every tradesman in the area, and even donated ten percent of his projected profit to the new Rocky Pond Summer Theater Company endowment fund, a good guy who'd never seen a play in his life and wasn't going to start.

But at night, alone in their house, double-lot frontage on the shores of what could only be called Frozen Lake, Miller felt guilty to realize several days had gone by without mourning, that something like happiness was once again welling in him. It seemed too soon, this stage they'd told him about in grief group. Two years only since her sudden death from stroke! He made a point of remembering her, found her face fading in memory, worked through several photo albums, set a place for her the third Saturday night, kept up his end of the conversation. His seventieth birthday had passed without his noticing, he realized, so he sang himself the song, ended the night in puddles of tears. In the morning he figured out the problem: A house on a lake in the middle of winter is no place to be alone. He cut his trip short, left the theater renovation in the contractor's trusty hands, returned to New York City in his sensible Honda Civic: back to civilization.

LOU'S SISTER'S OLD ROOMMATE'S uncle was a very, *very* well-known old Shakespearian, the one and only Sir John Postlewaite. Miller felt no modesty approaching him for the role of King Lear in the company's yearly Shakespeare production. Rocky Pond had the money to pay a real star now, and in a phone conference with Marcia and Miller the stylish old eccentric bird astonishingly said yes. He just needed permission from the film he'd be working on come that time of year and certain guarantees: he'd have his own dressing room, he'd pick his own director, he'd be in on all further casting, he'd take a cut of the gate.

"You bet," Miller told him, though Marcia had not agreed to any of it and stiffened. "But in return for all that," Miller said carefully, full eye contact with Marcia, "we need a guarantee of full rehearsal and full run, also a donation to the endowment fund to match in its entirety the cut of the gate you'll take: tax write-off."

"I'll do but one night's rehearsal. Full run is fine," said the famous voice. "As for donations, doubtless I'll be returning more than any cut of the gate! It's my style, after all."

"Three weeks rehearsal," said Miller.

King Lear himself spoke: "My good man, push me and I fall off your carriage, no matter how elegant. I've been King Lear forever! I've been Lear longer than Lear was Lear. I could do King Lear in my sleep. You will rehearse the company with a stand-in. That's how it's done. I'll step in for three nights' dress."

"Two weeks," Miller said. "We need you to instruct the company, direct the director. But if it's only going to be two weeks' rehearsal, then you guarantee us a week more at the other end if we get held over."

And, Marcia's mouth agape, her pleasure rampant, it was agreed.

JACK DANCE BURST INTO the new company offices, a rough Tribeca loft Miller Malloy had organized and funded permanently through acquaintances at the Corcoran Group. The space was a former truck showroom, enormous elevators opening directly into the Rocky Pond Summer Theater New York City headquarters, room enough for full rehearsals if need be, even space for winter showcases.

"Goddamn," Jack shouted. "Goddamn, anyway!"

"What's the problem, Jack?" Marcia said, unperturbed: he was only enraged, not drunk.

"You know what the goddamn problem is. The goddamn problem is you hired John goddamn Postlewaite for goddamn *Lear*, and not a word to me, not a nod, not a grunt, not a moment's consideration after twenty-five years with the company, twenty-five!"

Marcia's cheeks had gone pink. Her mouth bowed down—a powerful woman—but very quietly she said, "*Sir* John Postlewaite, Jack. *John Postlewaite.* He *is* Lear. You've got to feel badly, I understand that you feel badly. But look at it this way: we've got Lear himself! Sir John Postlewaite knew Shakespeare in person, for pity's sake. What's good for the company is good for the players, Jack. And you'll be playing opposite God. How can that hurt?"

He drew himself up, spoke as Lear, or maybe Othello, anyway grand, and no trifling talent (but no Sir John, either): "I goddamn am supposed to be notified and given a goddamn audition."

"We thought of you for *The Odd Couple*," Marcia said. "You can audition for *The Odd Couple.* Auditions are in February."

"Well, wait," Miller said. "I don't see the need for any audition, Marcia. Seeing Jack angry like this. He's Felix all over."

Jack said, "And who the fuck do you think you are?"

"I understand you're pissed," Miller said. "But please don't say you don't want the part, all right? I am Miller Malloy. I'm the new development director. And please don't curse me out."

"I remember you. You're a fucking *intern.* You're a fucking *caterer.* You wouldn't fix me a goddamn drink!"

"For which you should thank him," Marcia said. Pregnant pause. "You want the part. Felix Unger. Believe me. You want it."

"I want Lear! Twenty-five years! I. Want. *Lear*!" He said Lear like the woman's name Leah, two Boston syllables.

Miller bit off a smile.

"It's Sir John Postlewaite we're talking about," Marcia said again. "Royal Shakespeare."

"And don't think I don't know it: *CSI Miami*, too, which is the real reason you've booked him, goddamn!"

"Was it Miami?" Marcia said. "I thought, like, Scranton."

Jack grinned despite himself, a small crack in the door.

Miller put his figurative foot in, said, "Jack, we've got two student matinees and no Postlewaite for those. How would that be? Lear for two student matinees during the run and of course understudy throughout. And I think everyone agrees you'll play Kent, no need for an audition there, either, one of the great roles, a dual identity. And Felix Unger—eyes on the prize—later in the summer. But Kent—I see in you his stalwart loyalty!"

"Well."

Miller kept up the pressure: "And this run may well be Postlewaite's last live performances. You're part of history, playing Kent opposite that kind of eminence!"

"Well."

"Theater *history*, Jack!"

"Well."

"You keep thinking on it," Marcia said doubtfully.

"No thinking," Miller said. "This is a beautiful offer, and we can cancel auditions for Felix if you say yes now, Felix in the summer comedy, and then put you up as Kent."

Jack carefully acted the role of a man making a decision. Finally, stealing a breath of epic proportion, he found his answer: "All right," he said bravely. And then he said it again, this time a hint of brio: "All right."

They shook hands all around, hugged as a group. And Jack left, a definite spring in his step. Kent was a plum, no matter how you stewed it.

"You're a genius," Miller said to Marcia.

"*I'm* a genius?" she said amused. "You and your reverse psychology. I'm a workhorse. You're the genius. And oh, by the way, we don't have student matinees."

"We do now. Plus, we've got our understudy for Lear."

"Jack once did time for injuring an ex-wife," Marcia said. "I think you should know. Very serious injuries."

"He does seem it," Miller said. "Just this side of control."

"So long as he doesn't drink."

"He's a hell of an actor. I'll keep him close."

"He could have been a Postlewaite. That's what I'm trying to say."

"He will be yet."

"No, never. And he knows it, too. He's a case study in self-destruction."

Suddenly the druid sun hit the daily slot between the neighboring buildings and filled the office with light. Shielding her eyes, Marcia came to Miller, put her cheek firmly against his, welcome touch, said very softly, "Miller Malloy, you're getting too big for your britches." She took his hands, and they shared a long moment affectionate as between any couple, all that Miller needed, he told himself, thirstily lapping every single drop.

JOHN POSTLEWAITE HAD DEMANDED the Royal Shakespeare's Tamara Keith for director and Tamara had consented, if expensively. Using the two names in tandem, Miller had presold every ticket to every show, added a week, and presold all of those tickets, too. And not only that, with his new price points they'd doubled the take while making two long rows of unprecedented five-dollar student seats available balcony rear, the area where lights had once been stored, made accessible by the new fire egress Miller had seen built. More important, he was pulling in grants they'd never before had a chance at. This year, all of the actors would be paid, and handsomely, even while the endowment continued to surge.

The start of rehearsals at Rocky Pond Theater was always a heady time, but more so this year. The renovations were complete, a dozen new professional actors had joined the company, the crew had arrived, the college interns, the groundskeepers, also a daily cohort of volunteers, and Sir John Postlewaite himself was due at any moment. Sir John! Already five days late, but never mind. Marcia had discovered that he was over eighty years old, perhaps perfect for Lear, but theirs was going to be an exhausting schedule for such an old fart—why begrudge him a few days? Tamara Keith, reputed dragon, was right on time and so cheery and kind and direct that even her most blunt criticisms came off as love. Miller got his widower's eye on her. She was sixty years old if a day but cute to him as a campus canary, and appealingly sly: "I see you've taken to dressing for me."

Which was true.

She took every single cast member, even the lowliest knights, off for walks and private discussions about their roles, ways to bring surprise and clarity to sometimes difficult lines, bring light to opaque meanings. She confided in Miller, bounced ideas off him ("Let's light the bloody castle scene with torches . . ." and "Let's take the entire thing outdoors for an act, scenes in the lake, the whole audience in silent procession to the beach . . ."), feigned hurt when he shot them down, but let him shoot, called him her producer, knew what she was doing: owning him.

As a group, they began to block scenes. Miller watched closely, drew maps and diagrams for future reference, studied Tam's management style, found he admired her more and more hopelessly, noticed the way her tongue traced her lips when she listened, noticed her long body, her dark chocolate skin, ran off on constant errands for her, whatever she needed (those torches he'd thought he'd nixed). Third day, the company gathered to work on staging the more complicated scenes. It was a given that everyone had their lines down. The action, though, that was the physical body of the play, constant movement to keep away from that kind of amateur stasis that ruins Shakespeare for everyone: flow was Tamara's specialty, her fame.

She grew testy, visibly unhappy with the sword fighting and knife play. "You look like you're in fencing class! Too polite! Kill him! Kill that fucker or die yourself! It's life and death! It's not just lines on a page! No, no, no! You look as if you're playing a childhood game! Clash! Clash! Clatter! Kill!"

But with the heavy wooden swords, no matter how hard the young actors tried, it remained a game.

Tamara knew a Hollywood violence choreographer (Miller wanted that title!), and as it happened the fellow was directing a martial arts movie in New York. A couple of phone calls and Miller had secured his services for the cost of travel: another guy who'd do anything for Tamara, and likely anything to get a break from his film, which had reached some kind of financial impasse. He was Park Ji-Hun, known as Honey, Korean, speaker of schematic English, full of cheerful, deadly advice as he took over rehearsal: "If you want to be assassin, push knife upward from belt and in under ribs, spin, then retract." Big grin. And of course he demonstrated, palming a big, very real knife just as his hand hit Miller's chest in an upward stroke, so convincingly that everyone screamed. Even Miller thought he'd been punctured, exhilarating relief to find he was not. Honey let everyone have a try. Jack Dance was extraordinary at it, stalked the stage killing everyone realistically to shouts and laughter.

Honey just kept grinning, moved on: "If your character is amateur killer? Fist around handle, so. Turn wrist down on impact, so! Loud grunt helps!" And he made a few *Psycho* plunges with his knife, accompanying shouts and groans, genuine horror in it. Late in the morning, he switched out the Rocky Pond prop swords for real ones he was willing to loan and coached Edmund and Edgar, who were already pretty good (years of fencing class and attendant delicacy—Tamara had been right—these dedicated pretty boys, not exactly street toughs). Honey offered a dozen simple tricks for making it all look real, even live and close-up. You caught the sword under your arm, sure, but it was all in how the victim snapped his head, the aggressor arched his back, all about the noises you made, the surprise you evinced at dying.

Honey suggested a siesta, that everyone take a rest, unheard of, but off to inns and the company dorm went one and all (Mr. Park with Tamara, as Miller sussed out: They were lovers! Damn!). Afterward, Honey gave an amazing class on using the motions and interactions of violence in scenes that weren't violent, very useful in Lear. Stabbing motions, feints, dodges, all weaponless, all while saying age-old lines, brilliant. And strong praise for Jack Dance: "Brutal." And then they all practiced dying and reacting to death. "Don't let go easy!" Honey kept saying. And, "Look him in the eye!" Death, he meant.

(Miller, observing, kept thinking of Lou's late lying in hospice—seventy pounds and fearless—then one morning a long whispered sentence, eye contact eternal, her last great scene.)

SIR JOHN POSTLEWAITE WAS, as it turned out, a very lovely gentleman, made his entrance as Honey Park made his exit. He rode in a limo from New York, using his own driver on his own schedule, swept onstage unannounced during the first read-through (clearly on intelligence from Tamara Keith), gaily interrupting everything. He shook each hand superciliously, already playing Lear. His presence was electric, pure magnetism. He greeted his favorite knights, snarled at the disfavored lords, disdained his youngest daughter, Cordelia (a beautiful, hurt Russian actress with very formal English), fatherly kissed Goneril (the estimable Emma Murdock), kissed Regan, too (Lois Tremaine, smelling of wine and swooning), cried, "Let's simply begin! I call for Kent!"

Someone had warned him about Jack Dance.

Who else but Tamara Keith? She called for silence, and sober Jack took the stage in the plain daylight streaming through the barn doors, act 1, scene 4. He was loyal Kent, come back to aid his addled Lord Lear, though Lear has by that time in the play banished him. Kent has disguised himself as Caius, and so Jack was a man playing a man playing another, famous lines—"If but as well I other accents borrow / That can my speech diffuse / my good intent / May . . ." Jack froze, forgetful in the face of Sir John, who glowered. "May . . . My good intent may . . . Goddamn, this isn't how it's done. With all you goddamn knights looming in the wings. Quiet back there!"

"Speech," said Tamara Keith bluntly.

Jack pulled himself up, got stuck in the same spot.

And here came Sir John Postlewaite, dressed as Lear (every rehearsal was full dress for him), trundling onstage and saying Jack's lines *for* him, suddenly an entirely different person: Sir John as Lear as Kent as Caius. When he finished, a flourish, he said, "That's how it's done. Now enter Lear!"

"Yes," said Tamara Keith. "That indeed is how it's done. Enter Lear!"

Jack flushed mightily, clenched his fists as the knights' positions backstage were resumed, gripped the invisible knives Honey had taught as Lear retreated. Jack made his entrance again, continued forward through the whole scene, gave the reading of his life opposite the best Lear he possibly ever could have imagined, Sir John's power flowing into him. The knights, twelve actors from around the English-speaking world, applauded when the scene was done.

Miller Malloy shouted, too. He was proud of his own manipulations, sometimes too proud, pride going before a fall, all that, and sorry, Lou (who hated secrets, machinations of any kind, the misuse of psychology, deliberate misdirection, what Miller thought of as business).

"Jack, that was screamingly beautiful," said Tamara. "You have invented a Kent I've never seen, steadfast but wounded as well, suppressing narcissistic injury. It's genius."

"Well," Jack said as the applause continued.

The (very expensive) Hendrick's gin, never opened at the party, was missing from the milking room pantry, Miller noticed. And then proceeded to think everything through as well, working from the signs. Jack was going to be great as Kent. But Jack would need extra love for the entire run. As much love as Miller could find in his heart, which was, Lou always said, a very great lot. Some efforts at containment for Jack, a good talking to, but primarily love and respect and kindness, a firm grip. And Jack would be great, and would ride the greatness into his role as Felix, and that was the big picture going forward. And all for the future of Rocky Pond.

Which Lou had loved.

MILLER MALLOY OBSERVED EVERY minute of every rehearsal, watched the unattainable Tamara give notes after, and (expressly invited by both) sat in on every session she had with Lear in his dressing room: acting lessons, basically, and nothing defensive about Sir John Postlewaite. He'd nod his head and think a moment. "Like this?" he'd say. And try her suggestion without prejudice, very impressive, also moving: the consummate pro, still growing.

And she'd say, "Yes, yes."

Jack Dance was more brittle, of course, but in the end he always came around, saw what Tamara was doing for him, always made a crack about Miller's presence. But with a man so difficult, Tam felt a witness made the discussions go better and helped make everyone's memory line up if later there were complaints or differences. Jack called her a snob, called her meddling, called her distant, called her worse than that, but only behind her back, and harmless.

Tamara, far from being aloof, took the whole company under her wing. They were various and many of them young, and they reacted to her, Miller noticed, in wildly divergent ways. The actors (all but Jack) thought her a special personal ally; each in turn told Miller that she favored him or her. The lady was frank, she was loving, she had a gift, praised the actors for what wasn't yet emerging and thereby made it emerge.

Management style, Miller had always called it, sexy as hell. He stuffed down his growing crush, redirected the energy, all for Rocky Pond!

Quickly it became apparent that Sir John Postlewaite was not all there. He didn't remember lines and, more upsetting, gave whole speeches from the *The Merchant of Venice* and *Macbeth.* He'd exit left when he was supposed to exit right. He'd sit when he was supposed to stand. He'd gather Lois in a clinch backstage and soul-kiss her in front of anyone. (Lois seemed to take it in stride—perhaps a great deal more was going on after hours.) He'd arrive from the elegant Inn of the Lakes still wearing pajama bottoms, his hair wildly uncombed. But despite all, he was Postlewaite, and Postlewaite was Lear!

Miller took up position in the wings and served as Sir John's personal prompter. The other actors compensated, too. Something so very likeable about the great man. If he faltered, just repeat the cue as if in reverie: give the old crumpet a chance.

Jack Dance was impatient, though. "Goddamn!" he'd shout. "Just say the goddamn line, Sir John!"

And Postlewaite would freeze him with a glance.

Miller took it upon himself to run lines with Sir John every morning, keep that memory fresh, enjoyed realizing that he was as off-book as the actors, knew all the lines by heart, every word of the play, made himself a further resource.

Betimes, the professional stagehands built the sets (earning scale!)—including a scary heath complete with real birch trees. At the second dress rehearsal, standing in the wrong place among them, Postlewaite drifted into lines from Hamlet, Hamlet talking to Yorick's skull: "I knew him, Horatio," very moving, brilliant in fact, wrong play. But Jack Dance had had it. He stormed off the scene, kicked a panel of the castle set out of his way, exited the theater by way of the milking parlor pantry, stormed out the barn doors at the back with two bottles of expensive red wine in each hand, total silence in his wake, perhaps his greatest performance ever, his car starting after some grinding, his tires spinning in the gravel lot.

"Sir John!" Tamara Keith pleaded. "This is *Lear*, you are *Lear*!"

"Indeed," Postlewaite said unperturbed.

"John," Miller called from the wings. "John, it's: 'Blow, winds, and crack your cheeks!' "

"We used to giggle at that line," John said happily.

"'Blow winds,'" Miller repeated.

John gazed at him with pity, found his place: "And crack your cheeks! Rage! Blow! / You cataracts and hurricanoes, spout / Till you have drenched our steeples, drowned the cocks!" He giggled expressively, seemed fourteen. "Drown your cocks and crack your cheeks! *Blow* winds!" He didn't notice that no one else laughed.

Or that then everyone laughed. And that then a great hubbub broke out. Tomorrow was opening night. John kept giggling.

"From 'Blow, winds,'" Tamara said gently when he had subsided. "And really great preparation, sir. The madness has *infected* you."

"Blow winds," John said again, but mightily, no trace of the sillies. And onward: "And crack your cheeks! Rage! Blow! / You cataracts and hurricanoes, spout / till you have drenched our steeples, drowned the cocks! / You sulphurous and thought-executing fires, / Vaunt-couriers to oak-cleaving thunderbolts, / Singe my white head! And thou, all-shaking thunder, / Strike flat the thick rotundity o' the world! / Crack nature's moulds, all germens spill at once / that make ingrateful man!"

The doomed fool, played by Mark Berryman, a real comedian (brilliant casting—thanks to Tamara), said his scorching lines, then Lear ranted further. Then Berryman, beautiful rhythm and energy between them.

And then, of course, everyone realized that Kent was not there to say his lines. Miller let but a beat pass and stepped out, a fair imitation of Jack's entrance, good enough.

And Lear said, "No, I will be the pattern of all patience; / I will say nothing."

"Who's there?" Miller Malloy said, a force he'd never felt before filling him, equal parts desire, sadness, ambition, despair, and the feeling, weird, of being another man, also sudden terror that was not entirely his own.

They finished the scene and Lear hastened away across the heath, mad soliloquy breaking every heart in the house, from soundman to intern to actor to director—certainly Miller's. To end, Sir John staggered forward to the edge of the stage, collapsed in desolation, truly a thing of beauty, searing, forceful, commanding. But it was out of place.

Miller tried an ad lib: "Come, my king. Up and to the hovel."

The king swayed to his feet and looked out over the empty seats of the theater. He roared, he shook his staff, he roared again. Then he cast Miller's or Kent's arm off him, spun and swept away, Lear's last proud moment. But, compass broken, Sir John had swept the wrong direction, swept in all his glory right off the stage and into the orchestra pit, where he crashed onto the kettle drums and crumpled like a bag of sticks and wet leaves, the drums making a sound like thunder, the great actor nothing now but an old man lying bleeding and unconscious on a cement floor.

JACK DANCE'S BIG OPPORTUNITY had come, but Jack Dance was nowhere to be found. Opening night was Thursday, a sold-out house, the Donor Dinner beforehand. And Thursday was day after tomorrow. Miller had accompanied Sir John to the hospital, confirmed that his injuries were not life threatening, contacted all of the great actor's people, assured he'd be in good hands, and then he called Jack, left three careful messages, each building on the last—logic, then pleading, then full supplication—all while driving back to the theater. There, he and Marcia huddled. She was devastated about Sir John but agreed Jack Dance was their only choice, tried a different tactic with him: unveiled threats. In the end, after they'd both left messages for the old shit all over New Hampshire and New York and even Los Angeles, they started on Florida, enlisting Jack's ex-wife Candy, but come morning, there was no Jack to be found. Lakes County Regional Hospital had confirmed that Sir John was out for the duration with a broken hip, broken jaw, and bruised ribs, about to be airlifted via private medical jet to England. At least he was only blaming himself.

The day's rehearsals started as usual at 10 a.m. Tamara Keith called the company together, no sign of panic. "Tomorrow is opening night," she said. "And tomorrow we go on." She pointed at one of the young knights of Lear's retinue. "You are now Gentleman." She pointed at the able fellow who'd been playing Gentleman, a kid from the Yale School of Drama. "You are now Kent."

The new Gentleman quailed, but the Yale kid said, "My pleasure," with comic flair, and everyone saw he could do it.

Tamara squashed down her afro, pulled it back high, squashed it down again, unconscious gestures of worry to which she finally gave voice: "You've both got some lines to learn. We'll run it three times today, run-through, off-book after lunch, dress after dinner. Tomorrow we're off till curtain. Stage doors open four o'clock. Be here no later than five."

"Tamara, wait. You're talking schedule?" Marcia said, unable to hide her own panic. "Who's going to play fucking Lear?"

"Lear is right in front of us," Tamara Keith said calmly and, unveiling her carefully planned surprise, pointed to Miller Malloy.

The company burst into agitated conversation.

"No thanks," Miller said, proper measures of wryness and respect, but firm: "No way."

But Tamara wasn't kidding. "Run-through," she shouted.

"But wait," Miller said.

"You know the lines," Tamara said. "You know them very well. Just say them, be Lear. Don't act. Muss that fabulous hair."

"Don't act?" Miller said.

"Don't act," Tamara said again.

"Holy shit," someone said.

"Jack will turn up," Miller said as the makeup woman tousled his hair and dirtied his face. The costumer threw John Postlewaite's ragged greatcoat around Miller's shoulders. And then Miller was onstage as King Lear, a stumbling performance. The new Kent, at least, was passable.

After lunch was not just off-book, it was full dress, props, and lights. After a hastily prepared and scarfed dinner, more so, including an audience: cast families, two college classes, and media in the house, reviewers for three local papers and the *Boston Globe*. The *Times* wouldn't come till opening night, thank goodness.

"Use real emotion," Tamara said to Miller Malloy, special session.

"Breathe," the stage manager said contemptuously.

And Miller realized he was not.

"Real despair," Tamara said again.

The stage manager clacked her tongue: Miller Malloy was no actor.

Miller breathed and recalled deeply the days after Lou had passed, recalled and replayed his own brush with madness.

"You're useless now," Tamara said. "A useless, powerless old man."

Useless! Powerless!

"Here's your last chance to have any control. Doubtful it will work. Some king you turned out to be."

Last chance!

Marcia appeared and patted his back, even she seeming to lack confidence in him. "I love you, Miller Malloy," she said.

Surely she was false.

The useless man recalled his lines flawlessly, but his Lear though much improved for the dress was too diffident, was too much like Miller: ingratiating, respectful. Tamara Keith sat him down and they talked past midnight. "It's all inside you," she said. "Every bit. These fuckers around you, they hate you, they have cursed you, they are plotting against you. Only Cordelia is true, and you've mucked that up, haven't you, you old fool. Kent, too, your one true friend. Banished? What were you thinking? Where does this awful abuse come from? You've ruined everything. Your kingdom is gone. Face it. Howl for me. Howl for me now." She gripped his shoulders and shook him.

Miller howled, howled from his feet, through his guts, up into his chest, out his open mouth. He pushed his coach away, howled louder yet, rage blotting his eyes.

"Break a leg," Tamara said. "Break everyone's leg. And for God's sake, sleep late."

CURTAIN CAME INEXORABLY. The stage manager called "Thirty minutes!" through the dressing room intercom and then, eternally later, "We've got a full house. Five minutes!"

Miller's heart was not exactly in his throat—as CEO of a large company he'd been on bigger stages any number of times and in hairier situations countless, speaking both scripted and unscripted. The difference now was that Lou was dead, and worse than that, he really was useless, mourning he'd never fully processed, self-abnegation he'd begun to feel and never articulated and never named: useless, a useless man. How he hated Tamara Keith! How he hated them all!

He made a grand but shuffling entrance, the weight of England upon him. He said, "Attend the Lords of France and Burgundy." Or Lear said it. Lear said it neither loud nor soft, and with a touch of anger that hadn't occurred to Miller before, and volumes of sadness, same, and shame, and helplessness. The house was dead silent as he explained the division of his kingdom, as his elder daughters gave their duplicitous speeches, and as Cordelia gave her fatal but honest one. Someone in the audience shouted "No!" when Lear disinherited her.

Miller, for his part, felt that a fog bank had drifted in and surrounded him, a fog that only slowly lifted, then cleared suddenly at the moment that Kent returned to the play. Loyal Kent, whom mad Lear had banished, returning disguised as Caius. But it wasn't the callow Yale kid playing the role. It was Jack Dance. Jack Dance was back, and Jack was Kent. He reeked of gin, of restless nights, of days in a car, of bad coffee, worse food, desultory rage. In his bleary eyes was adrenaline, and something more: white powder still dusted the edges of his nostrils. The dressers had slapped his face with mud makeup. His dress was Lear's, however, a bad sign: he'd dressed as Lear, the narcissistic fuck.

Miller found that he could breathe again, that he was firmly onstage, that he was both in his character and in the room with four hundred others, a task to perform, a person to take care of. Jack Dance as Kent as Caius was his ready servant, loving, warm, magnanimous, tinge of fury, and the scene went well. Backstage, however, Jack would communicate with no one, wary and unhappy and tense—his prep, Miller supposed, feeling thoroughly dissed. But it wasn't like Miller wanted any conversation either.

They stayed separate, worlds apart.

Onstage, Jack's tightly stuffed emotions rose in total control, and he was electric, absolute dynamite, everyone would later agree. Miller felt the power of what was between their characters—loyalty, love, misprision. Sir John's example, Jack's booze-fueled skill, Tamara's manipulations, all of it made Miller a great actor, too. He absorbed the power of what was between Jack and him, then breathed it out, unequal, undiscussed: competition, miscommunication, hatred even, hatred that it was hard to admit flowed both ways. The audience felt all of it, too—when Kent confessed that he was Caius, that same voice out there shouted, "Forgive!"

The evening proceeded, inexorably, Miller never so alive.

Credulous Edmund was killed duly by his duplicitous half brother, Edgar, even as Regan and Goneril died tangled in their own plots.

Then it was time for Lear's last entrance. Backstage, the busy (and now very respectful) stage manager and two burly stage hands arranged the tiny Russian playing Cordelia, arranged her dead on Lear's shoulder and held her weight for him till the moment of his entrance—there wasn't much to her, but it was plenty for Miller. When he stepped onstage that broad stagger was real.

And now for Lear's last lines, which seemed to reside somewhere down in Miller's boots, a deep reach, anyway. "Howl! Howl! Howl!" He'd learned how to say this by watching John Postlewaite, learned how to feel it from Tamara, believed in it now, a low, keening, measured howl contained in its own name, not quite allowed past the word, times three.

Cordelia was dead.

Miller felt it profoundly.

Loyal Kent picked up the knife that had taken her life, still dripping with pretend blood (those capsules were amazing), an old and ornate hunting knife Miller himself had found in a junk shop near Quechee, quite real. Jack as Kent contemplated the blade, weighed it in two hands, stage business they hadn't rehearsed ever, but of course they hadn't rehearsed together, Jack and Miller, and there was always room for improvisation, especially with the audience absolutely riveted, silent in their seats, not a cough, not a creak. Together, Jack and Miller added a few extra beats, a breathtaking moment that would be discussed for decades to come, and not only at Rocky Pond.

It was time for Lear to die. The company, of course, had often gotten this far in rehearsal, two full weeks. And Miller had watched them, coached them, helped John Postlewaite remember what play he was in. But Miller himself had never gotten this far as Lear. Thanks, however, to Honey Park, he knew how to die. Very much in the moment, in a different man's very different body, Miller coughed, dropped to his knees on the proscenium, then slumped sideways till his cheek hit the boards. He patted the stage forlornly (that would be discussed as well, the genius of that demonstration of the king's connection to his land), closed his eyes, rolled onto his back as Postlewaite had done.

"He faints!" cried the perfidious Edgar, a great young actor from Ireland.

Kent leapt to Lear, practically a martial arts move, Jack a very physical actor. He cried, "Break heart. I prithee, break!" And fell upon Lear, heart indeed broken, off-script, the entire cast taken by surprise.

Miller felt the tip of the hunting knife under his solar plexus, at first merely uncomfortable—what was Jack Dance doing?—then painful. And then worse, he thought he felt it slide into him, first a pressure, then a blinding pain and shock in all his organs, which convulsed inside him, a collapsing kind of sudden cramp, a piercing heat up under his ribs from below, an odd and final feeling of mortification, so many watching, the pounding weight of his heart giving way like an overwhelmed dam. Jack let Miller go, withdrew the weapon, and then, eye-to-eye, kissed him on the forehead, the scene as perhaps it should have been written.

The actor playing Edgar knew something had gone amiss but, unsure what, said his line: "Look up, my lord." He saw the blood then, the wound in Lear's thin gown, pulled Jack away from Miller Malloy in horror: he knew what capsule blood looked like, smelled like.

Even as Jack said his own line, exquisite desperation: "Vex not his ghost!"

"He is gone, indeed," Edgar said automatically, confused (later he'd mention the iron smell of Miller's blood), then, coming to his wits, cried, "A doctor!"

Albany, oblivious, finished his line, all the way to the "gor'd state," didn't understand why Edgar was tussling with Kent. But then he, too, got it—so much to understand in that split second—smelled the very real blood and the real smell of opened organs, leapt to Miller, his instinct to staunch the wound, got his own hands bathed in blood. Poor dead Cordelia caught on and opened an eye, then both, then leapt to her feet and screamed. From the audience it looked like a crazily interesting and surely controversial variation of the play was in progress till Albany shouted, "Nine-one-one! Someone call nine-one-one!"

Jack was the only one to keep his cool. He cheated toward the audience, fending Edgar off with one arm, and delivered the last line of his career: "I have a journey, sir, shortly to go; / My master calls me, I must not say no."

Then he shoved Edgar to the stage (that poor Irish kid, forever to be traumatized), bolted out of the back of the theater and into the blue rental car the police would later find on the verge of one of the dirt roads along the Canadian border—loyal Kent, never to be seen again, never to be caught, never to be punished, though the unidentified remains of men are often discovered in those woods, years, sometimes decades, after whatever violence has befallen them.

NO WORDS WOULD COME to Miller, though he moved his lips expressively, no cry of pain though he was nothing but pain, no further howling though he felt a bellowing inside him, a roaring that rose up from his very genius (as Shakespeare called the soul), only a feeble "Lou" emerging, and repeated, and then a vision: her face, her loving, deepening, all-consuming gaze, and finally a kiss, a juicy naked kiss, a kiss from those first heady days of love, something eternal lodged within it, the last tactile moment of Miller's life.

Some Should

A LAMB IS BORN. The mother is Cindy, a Katahdin hair sheep of some distinction, one of the older gals, not a nurture natural, never was. I believe in the Andean idea that women are better at lambing time, that being a woman myself there's a way I feel everything my ewes go through. Anyway, I don't judge Cindy. I just get to work. Which means rising at three thirty to try to help with the new one, lick it clean with a wet towel first rubbed on Cindy, then put its questing mouth to the teat. But still the ewe isn't into it, kicking the babe away repeatedly. In the end I tie the new mom to a section of fence so she can't get away. Only takes a dawn and a day to make a bond, and Cindy's always been like that, gets into it eventually, even turns fiercely protective, as if compensating for the late onset of instinct. So I have some confidence. My date will not have to be postponed:

A priest.

Or, anyway, in his profile pic he's wearing one of those white tabs in his collar. He says in his bio that he's a widower, says he's looking for a change. He loves to hike, a plus. He loves to travel, same. He's a gardener, plus ten. He speaks French fluently. (I speak Spanish—together we can go places.) He was on two dating sites, one snuggly, the other filthy, but then, so was I. His eyes are almost black in the photo, which looks official, the one you'd send to the newspaper, eyebrows heavy, salt-and-pepper hair. No way, I thought, first time I saw him, but later put my thumb over his neck, trying to see him without the collar. And then, worse, I cut a flannel shirt out of an Eddie Bauer catalog, intricate, teeny work with the scissors, and tried it on him: sexy.

And now I'm in my Toyota Tundra, heading down to Ann Arbor, more than an hour's drive, two bales of hay and a broken spreader in the back. My priest will have seen my snuggly photo, which is fairly honest: pretty-enough me with the skeptical look in my eyes, jeans and a sweater, hoe in hand, bare feet. He won't mind that I'm thirty-three (my year to be crucified), hopefully hasn't cut out a nun's habit and wimple to stick on me. Or maybe that's the Catholics. This one's Episcopalian—a little explanation right in the profile, both sites. I keep going back to look at his photo: he's kind and decent and strong, you can tell, or maybe you can't tell, not a pushover, anyway, not quite a goody-goody, something in his eyes. Also kindness. My own self-delusion, no doubt. Nothing to do with the fact that he's extremely handsome. But he's been so frank!

Well, I've been frank, too, the only farmer on HotLava as far as I can see, certainly the only one with a bikini shot: see what hard work can do for the abs? I'm a babe, let's face it. At least I think so when I don't think the opposite, which is pretty much all the time. Dirt under the nails, arms covered in barbed-wire scratches, sunburned cheeks, pale forehead. My bio isn't as complete as his, but I'll give him the rest tonight: after lambs and a fairly successful allium stand at the Saturday farmers' market way up in Traverse City (garlic, onions, shallots, leeks, ornamentals), my business is organic vegetable seeds in a pretty narrow range for the International Seed Project. I keep a very sweet pair of work mules (Butch and Jim), also a flock of layers. Another thing about me: I'll drive an hour and a half for a blind date.

With a priest.

HURON RIVER KITCHEN I haven't been to before, though I've heard of it—expensive, farm to table. I approve. Most of the dates I've met so far have picked, like, Applebee's, and those were the good ones. The way this web thing is done is you meet outside whatever restaurant or maybe at the bar (if the place *has* a bar, fucking teetotalers), chat a minute either way, car keys in hand, just to make sure there's a good bailout point.

My priest suggested a coffee shop at first, but some more daring part of me emailed back that we would want alcohol. He didn't mind a glass of wine, he said. Or didn't say, exactly—this was all email. You're supposed to go dutch, but he said if I couldn't afford the place he'd happily pay. I didn't know how I felt about his paying. I didn't know about the insistence on wine. In mind of his profession, I'd dressed modestly, but then, also in mind of his profession, I'd changed, a really good new bra under a short dress in bold fields of color, satiny breeze of a thing I'd found in Traverse just that last week, couple of dabs of my new perfume (Long-Term Relationship by Lanvin, ha) where some part of me hoped his nose would go.

The good father was waiting patiently near the hostess station, gorgeous. Just as in his photo. Like any layperson, he took in my legs first. But he was better than most at keeping my eye after that, didn't linger over the bra situation. I'd have to check on that.

He'd expected a farmer.

We shook hands. Mine was rough. His was soft. "You're wearing your *collar*?" I said.

"I wanted my cards on the table, is all," he said meekly. We were still shaking hands.

"You planned that line," I said.

He laughed: yes he had.

"But the collar actually hides your cards, doesn't it," I said.

Now he did look at my chest, leisurely. I mean my bra. I'm all freckles down in there and it makes a pretty attractive package, strong shoulders. *Titties first for the gold*, as Coach Sandra used to say, talking posture. Equestrian team. *Play to your strengths*, she also said. And did eventually teach me that I was a *package* of strengths. A counter to my mom, who focused on flaws, made me feel like a package of shit. And to my dad, barely present, yet my hero for life, just for being positive. The kind of stuff you do not under any circumstances talk about on dates. Did my priest like my bra or not?

"This place, it's a little overly beautiful," I said.

"I've made a reservation," he said. He'd missed a spot shaving and his beard was coming in grayer than the hair on his temples, which he'd barely combed, not a vain person, I surmised, and more than a little weary looking, no predator. The trendy dining room was crowded and already bustling, and on a Tuesday night. I'm tall but he was taller. I'm zaftig where he was more trim. It's not every Internet date that wants me the way he did. This kind of thing you can figure out in the first seconds of an interaction, of course. It lay behind his gentleness like a fire behind an ornate grate, flowers and hummingbirds in filigree, lovingly designed and cast but too hot to touch. He was very high scoring on the first-impression meter, is what I'm trying to say. Plus he'd gotten nervous, while I'd relaxed. He kept trying to stand up straighter; I cocked a satin hip and slouched. I mean, all of this in less than a minute. The hostess came our way, a pencil with breasts.

My priest turned quizzically to me, not so much as a hello for her. For him, I was the only woman in the room. More points for the Episcopalians. The hostess said she was Caroline and did we have reservations, a perfectly nice person who had come under my guns. Contrite,

I said, “Yes, we do. But we’ll sit at the bar here and have a drink first, okay?”

“Tremendous,” Caroline said, and pointed where to go.

I couldn’t stop thinking about what a strange answer that was, really, as if she’d said, “Very, very large.”

No one was at the bar, which was fancy and very, very clean in a wooden alcove built among big structural columns—a chilly, industrial space, tremendous in the actual sense. We took a private-looking spot between columns, just three barstools, one for our jackets, two for us, this close together, basically hip to hip the way you aren’t at a table. He ordered a manhattan on the rocks, whiskey where I’d been thinking maybe that glass of wine. I felt a flicker of mistrust. But part of me is a big believer in pairing drinks with dates.

“Manhattan,” I said. “Straight up.”

“Okay, straight up,” he said, satisfyingly following my lead.

Part of me couldn’t leave it alone: “You wear the collar because women want to conquer it.”

“No, I wear it because I’m an Episcopalian pastor.”

“You’re a challenge wearing that, and you know it.”

We sipped our drinks. Tears seemed to have come to his eyes. “I’m sorry, but you’re upsetting me,” he said. “I haven’t done this before. I have read all the tips, though. I understand I’m not to speak of my widowerhood, my loneliness, my worries, but in fact I *am* a widower, still missing my wife. I long for companionship. I long for a rather extensive change in my trajectory, which has peaked long since. This is abstract, I know, and as of yet has nothing to do with you.”

“ ‘As of yet.’ I like that.”

“You’ve been on a date or two, I gather.”

“How so?”

“Just your cynicism.”

“All this formal language. You sound like you’re giving a sermon. But

I like the idea of a priest who uses his mysterious church-given powers to seduce women."

"My goodness, this is a strong drink. I'd forgotten."

"Go slow, Father."

"My name is Paul," he said.

"You wrote those letters," part of me said. "To the Corinthians, the Ephesians."

He shook his head sadly: he'd heard that joke before. "Tell me yours."

"It's Jayden," I said, but that was made up.

"It's not that I'm lonely," he said.

"Just cruising HotLava," part of me wanted to say, and so said it, immediately regretful.

"Ours is not to judge," he said, significant flicker of the eyes: I was on HotLava, too, he meant. And what's more, I was @ProwlerPink. He sipped his drink, said, "May I tell you a story?"

"Make it a parable," Jayden said, irrepressible.

"It's a parable, all right." He sipped his drink, sipped again, gazed at me, eye-to-eye over the rim of the heavy glass. Those eyebrows, the abyss of his eyes, his hunger, all the stuff he knew about the greater life. Plus his beauty. He wasn't a guy who was going to go bald, all kinds of hairline, gray at the temples, otherwise mostly pepper, wavy, uncombed. He looked again very briefly at the freckles of my cleavage, said, "The story is about a minister doing pastoral counseling, a big part of his work. He goes into a home in which a teenager has been acting out—some serious bad behavior, very destructive—and the parents have called him in, parishioners he cares little for, though he has tried to apply God's love. They are heavy smokers and high achievers just coming to middle age and clearly very miserable in their new recovering-alcoholic lives. The house reeks of smoke and misery. But bless them. The daughter is seventeen yet only a sophomore in high school, having been held back twice over the years. She has been caught, this girl, shoplifting alcohol from a mom-and-pop store in town, and in her family's state-of-the-art minivan, the police found one thousand OxyContin pills, which are very powerful painkillers, Schedule I narcotics. Also one hundred twenty thousand dollars in cash, not enough for liquor, apparently. And a weapon, one of these enormous new handguns, a three-something-something, fully automatic something-something, armor-piercing bullets, if I'm getting it right, with a magazine that holds enough to kill everyone in Michigan. The men she was with ran off at sight of the cops, later that evening to be arrested in an actual shootout. They're in their twenties, two of them, a third in his late forties, my age. And the situation was that she was going to have to go off to a program in Arizona, a kind of boot camp for juvenile offenders, not a pretty picture, though (if we can get her to agree to it) there's another option: she can attend a rehabilitation facility right here in town and with a few promises avoid the year in what is basically prison and then, if she's good, avoid the adult-court date when she turns eighteen. The boyfriends got fifteen years each, by the way, and not in any boot camp—swastika tattoos, that kind of person, shaved heads and jackboots. The older gentleman in their cohort was able to post bail and skipped out of the country. I'm her pastor, as our parable opens, but I've never spoken to her, and these desperate, abandoning parents ask one of their maids to show me to the kid's room back in the barn wing of their house, which is a gargantuan old-money mansion set among the fields and orchards of a glorious estate—he's some kind of investment banker, the dad, these new-money people in their old-money house, but bless them, this neglected child alone and holed up alone among her designer shoes and electronics."

He saw that my drink was gone, so guzzled the other half of his, put a finger up, and the little sphinx bartending brought us two more in our silence, which had extended long enough for her to make them, my priest still leaning forward confidingly with his story, and I trying not to look at his face too much, this utterly handsome man, trouble. Think of the most handsome actor ever—that's who would play him, and me no Lauren Bacall or Katharine Hepburn. Someone smart, a very smart actor to play this guy, who was clearly my equal in guile, equal to that part of me, I mean. The bartender dropped our drinks with a kindly, reverent gaze for him and something else altogether for me, the oddest look, probably nothing at all in it but my own sense of being one of Paul's new-money people in an old-money house, dating-wise, I mean, what he no doubt referred to as God's house. Oh, how I liked that our priest didn't particularly look at the bartender. She was an eyeful, clothes like skin. But bless her.

In our column-bound alcove he just started in on his story again: "So this unfriendly housemaid lets me in the kid's room and walks off down the corridor, and here's this young woman, not a kid at all, lounging on her bed in a camisole and underpants and headphones. And I sit on the other bed. She's got two kings—her room's like a hotel suite—and try a calm gaze, try waiting her out or waiting out whatever song it is she's listening to. She doesn't so much as look up at me; I'm invisible, barely a presence, song after song."

I gave him a long look, said, "This started out as a story about some anonymous priest doing pastoral counseling, and now it seems to be about you."

He liked that, said, "And you, you gave me a false name. I'd feel better knowing the real one."

"Okay, it's Carol."

"And that's another fake."

"Daisy."

"You're quick at thinking of them. Disturbing."

"It's Frances. It's really Frances."

"Thank you, Frances."

"Your parable. It's about you. More a confession. Do you have confession in the Episcopal Church?"

" 'All may. Some should. None must.' "

"Which one is you?"

"Some should, I suppose."

"Continue, Father."

"Paul. And please, I don't regard this as confession, but an offer of friendship: the total person standing before you, totally vulnerable."

"You are sitting."

He looked wounded. I mean really.

I said, "Okay, I'm sorry. Continue. I'm listening."

"I know it seems bizarre, my talking about this other woman."

I didn't mind. I didn't mind at all. I said, " 'None must.' "

He smiled faintly, finally continued with the unburdening, if that's what it was: "Our priest wasn't good at waiting her out. Because although he is a dedicated man of the Lord, he is also a widower after a years-long ovarian cancer story and intensely lonely and sitting not knee's length from this young woman in her underpants, and her legs are long and attentively tanned and her camisole is short and worn and her belly is flat and glistening with lotion and her navel is taut and nothing short of darling, as is her face."

"Oh, Jesus."

"I'm sorry. Is it too much?

"It's like Court TV. Or the Victoria's Secret *Sports Illustrated* swimsuit special. I can't tear my eyes away."

He looked puzzled. Had he never watched TV? He said, "I'm just compelled to honesty."

"Well, go ahead, young George Washington."

He had such a nice smile, generous and self-deprecating at once. He said, "She well knows her pastor is due to visit, and this is how she has chosen to greet him. Her power excites her—not sexually, don't get me wrong—it excites her to simply be there in her underpants with her minister waiting her out on her other king bed."

I downed my drink in a gulp and said, "No, the minister was excited, and you do mean sexually, and you're projecting this on a mere child, or maybe projecting *through* her, trying to get your movie to play on me. Which might work. But I'm not some blank screen."

He finished his drink as fast as I had and it made him grimace. But he liked that I'd just basically declared my interest, the push-pull of my interior monologue like two paths to the same barn. "No," he said, "I'm not trying anything like that. Because, in fact, this minister didn't know it, didn't see her power, no idea; you see, he thinks he's just waiting out the young woman and that he will eventually prevail. He can clearly hear whatever music it is she's listening to, profane hip-hop by the sound of it, and her foot tapping just enough that a cord in her inner thigh is flexing and unflexing and a gape in her underpants is opening and closing and there are these unholy glimpses of her most intimate self."

"Unholy glimpses! You *are* a minister. And by the way? She knows exactly what she's doing. Poor old goat with his appetites. And now he's going to suppress them all saintlike and do God's labor. Yes?"

The little bartender dropped more drinks. She was outrageously pretty, now that I looked at her. My date gave her no notice, not the slightest twink. When our drops of moisture were wiped up and our fresh napkins laid and our drinks plopped down and she was gone, he looked a little crestfallen, said, "Should I go on?"

I nodded: he should.

"All right, then. Our minister kept staring, and when the young lady's playlist was suddenly done she caught him, and their eye contact then was very rich. In the old days you'd insert something here about the devil in her, some glint of evil in her eye, but none of that, she was just well adjusted to a certain kind of life and a certain kind of attention and a certain kind of control and power which she knew must be used at best discretion, plus she'd been kept in what amounted to solitary confinement. She held my gaze and all languid took those five-hundred-dollar headphones off and said, 'Are you here to save me?' And I said, 'That's not really my job.' And she said, 'I've been marooned here in this house six weeks.' 'That is the judge's order,' I said. 'And you've got quite a long while to go.' You try to keep your tone neutral. But *marooned*, that was a good word. And suddenly I got this whole complete shimmering idea in my head. So I said, all neutral, something about how if we could just get her to agree to pastoral counseling, that would get her off the hook for both juvenile boot camp and adult sentencing and maybe even rehab (her lawyers had recommended voluntary rehab), just a little something I could arrange, the judge and I being old friends, I told her, true enough, old tennis pals. And she said she didn't care much for counseling, sultry gaze, this seventeen-year-old. And she lifts her leg just so. And absolutely I'm looking. It's obvious that I'm looking and it's obvious that I'm supposed to. And she says, 'Marooned,' again. And that was my moment, the moment I could do right or do wrong. And I did wrong. I said, 'Marooned.' Something about the old-fashioned word in that context. And she said, 'There's a lock on the bathroom door. If you're chicken. No one's going to think.' "

"And you're telling me you went in the bathroom with her?"

"I am. I did." He kept his tone neutral, I noticed, no shame or self-judgment, no pride either: "She sat on the counter in there, two sinks and very fancy fixtures, sat right on the granite, and we barely had to shift clothing. Very urgent on both ends of the equation."

"And God didn't strike you with a lightning bolt?"

"In a manner of speaking, yes, He did. *Coup de foudre.*"

"One of your hobbies."

"Hm?"

"French. You listed French on your HotLava profile. Under hobbies."

"Ah."

The bartender slunk past like some exotic cat. Had she been listening? My minister gave a subtle nod and soon she was making us two more drinks.

"We'd better eat," I said. "We'd better eat a lot."

THE FOOD WAS TERRIFIC, that's what I remember, right at the bar, though no particular dish comes to mind, haze of whiskey. Oh—miniature swordfish burgers on a bed of caramelized shallots with roasted cherry tomatoes. Like tapas, only they didn't call them that, little sexy plates of everything. A cheese selection. An olive selection. Bottle of wine with a pig on the label, everything calculated for the farmgirl. These splayed scallops barely cooked and with pink candied rose petals dropped in the crease.

"Like little cunts," my increasingly inebriated date says. He's testing me: Can I handle a vulgar priest?

Of course I can, the drinker in me: "Too bad no bratwurst."

Then he's putting bites in my mouth. And more surprising, I'm putting bites in his. His lips are soft, kind of overly full. His teeth are okay, crooked and white. I love his nose, it's got various planes and angles. I want to put my tongue in his nostrils, so clean. He nips my fingers and I more or less kiss his, getting every flavor. There are these chickpeas in some kind of yogurt and cucumber sauce on bread rounds. And his hand's in my lap, and mine's in his, very close to the hot center of things, little squeezes back and forth. I accept that he's playing me. Probably he's not even a priest. Probably he just goes to a costume shop.

But no: "These manhattans are disinhibiting," says my definitely, really priest, dizzy nod of his head. He's scooting the hem of my dress up and then he's got a finger under my panties, and not just any panties but La Perla, in case he thinks he's got himself hold of a hillbilly.

"I haven't many inhibitions in any case," Jayden tells him, increasingly her own being. But I cross my legs, capture his digits, which keep wriggling in place, not quite home, he didn't get. Lovely.

And suddenly we're kissing in our little alcove at the bar, lung kissing, a gross high-school girlfriend used to call it, breath and tongues involved, exchange of fluids down to the very molecules and atoms and even muons, but also that rhythm, excited breath, some of the flavors of our food and the whiskey, sweet manhattans. Also, another secret no doubt, he's had a cigarette in the last several hours, I can taste it, something a little cloying and chemical and off back there in the far corners of our kiss. And we're eating, and our little bartender is walking back and forth past us with a pleased smile on her pretty face and a second then a third button open on her shirt. But not for us: in the next alcove a foursome of noisy young men in suits has arrived. My date withdraws his mangled fingers from the hot grasp of my mule-wrangling thighs. I wish I were pretty as the little bartender, and unlike my other self, who considers herself supreme, I'm sure my minister wishes the same. But Jayden knows we're beautiful, in this moment we're so fucking beautiful, and the knowing crosses over to me, and for once I am complete. His last name is Gerald, of all names. At some point I've asked him and he's told me: Gerald. Paul Gerald. Pronounced kind of Frenchily. For a joke I'm calling him P.G., and he says his mother used to call him that.

The bartender. His eyes do not follow her, not a second look. She can't get enough of him, though. The boys have been buying her shots. Another button and her shirt will fall off. He's ordering cognac, I think, something French, and in long French sentences. How did that girl learn to speak French? Anyway, the old brandy comes in snifters. He's either the most honest man we've ever met or an excellent liar. Either way, we'll take him.

P.G. AND I ARE RIDING the forty-one country miles to my little farm in the back of a taxi and kissing comfortably and there's the infidel's brown eyes pleased in the mirror, everyone pleased to see us kissing. I'm sorry I said infidel—he's just an elderly Iraqi guy, very pleasant, a lot of Muslim faith around here, huge mosque in Flint, several other mosques in the countryside around me. "You two kids, you're in *love*," he says reverently and a little thickly, and turns up the music, another kind man in the world.

Paul plays his fingers nicely among the candied rose petals and I've made a bun of my hand for him and the thing is we're still talking, talking, like our words don't care what our actions are up to, or like we can each be two at once.

"You tell *me* a story now," he says.

I know just which one and I place it in his ear with only a break now and again for gasping and panting and so forth. "We had an intern at the farm."

"What's the name of your farm, by the way?"

"Lakeview. I'm not the one who named it. Mmm."

"You can see the lake."

"No, it's sixty fucking miles."

"We'll rename it, then. Something like . . . Lovestruck Acres."

"Are we getting ahead of ourselves?"

" 'Lovestruck Acres. More a state of being than a farm.' Can't you see it on the egg cartons?"

"I can see it on the tax bill."

"I see a 503c."

Way ahead of me. But bless him. "Anyway, there's a little college a couple towns north, this Christian outfit but pretty well respected."

"Alma College."

"Yes, exactly, Alma. Unh. And they have a farm program of some kind and the kids need to find internships and out of the blue this dork drives up and he can barely talk he's so nervous and he needs to eat more he's so skinny and someone needs to show him how to shave and his

Adam's apple is like a little fist in his throat and his first word and last word is 'like.' 'Like, do you need, I mean, I'm out at Alma, and like.' I knew what he meant, of course. So I said, 'Like, sure.' I happened to be planting onion sets that afternoon, two thousand of them, roughly, ten pounds of Georgian whites and it was wonderful to have him."

Kisses. Hmn. County Road 77, straight as a javelin. And P.G. and I are trying to pull back a little on the basically hand jobs going on—I've got several beds at home. We part slightly in deference to my story, not to our driver, who whistles Arabian scales, oblivious.

I continue: "My husband, who's at work in Grand Rapids and wants nothing to do with the work of the farm and who's not interested in the idea of kids, has been coming home at eleven and midnight, one of these lawyers who works till all hours. Admirably, I mean. He just really loves the law and loves the clients he serves, don't get me wrong, a good guy with a quarter of his accounts pro bono for good causes. One of them's the Seed Project, always these lawsuits from Monsanto and the others, patents on the fucking building blocks of life, you know?"

"And your intern?"

"He's like you, long legs and no butt to speak of and his pants are falling down and his glasses are falling off in the dirt and he's got smudges on his face and he's getting sunburned and I'm expecting him to, like, die of exhaustion at any moment, but he doesn't, he just keeps plugging those onion sets in, a great eye for the bed, the onion bed, I mean, great sense of spacing, just a natural. You know onion sets? They're just these, like, baby onions I've grown from seed the year before and brought to maybe marble size."

With his fingers he finds the marble of me, a little something I've been hiding. I wriggle by way of saying stop, and he does, man of intuition. More kisses, about three miles of kisses till Avon, which is not much more than a Tastee Freez and a gas pump. P.G. traces a couple of constellations in the freckles of my cleavage with his me-damp and fragrant fingers, not that he can see, but I know the constellations well and he traces them all before discretion kicks in. I've got all sorts of wine at home, also coffee, also food. I'm going to keep this guy awake all night.

"To make a long story short," I say.

"I'm all for the idea of kids," P.G. says. "I've longed for kids."

The conversation moves to three levels. Ignoring all that, I say, "We get the sets in, very tiring, and I'm happy with him, delighted with him. He's gotten over his shyness and he's been talking a blue streak about some invention he's working on, and gradually I'm realizing he's brilliant and kind of funny, too, and he's got this idea for a squash-beetle trap that just listening you realize is going to work perfectly and that he's going to be rich from it, everyone in the organic produce world sick and weary of squash beetles." And P.G. is listening to me, listening very closely, deeply aware of both sides of my coin: true fascination with squash beetles; the fear that the idea out of nowhere of kids has wrought. But he's an integrating force, our P.G., and my halves cross into one another at his touch, which resumes. What hands.

"I've got dreams for my place," I'm telling his ear, "A greenhouse there, an asparagus gully here." And he's listening, listening, clearly enjoying the music of the very instrument he's playing. I say, "You'll see the place in the light of the morning—it's come such a long way. These interns, they have really helped me. I've got four this spring, it's beautiful, all women, per my request."

His fingers find my hot center again.

My single center, and I'm getting off in a wave that hits the shore and keeps on going, drowning the villages, uprooting the palm trees. I keep the story afloat by force: "I invite him in for, hmn, dinner and of course a shower and he says, 'Lady, you should, hmn, go first,' but the kid yanks open the curtain and, hmn, climbs in the shower with me halfway through, hmn, and he's naked and, well, we were on the bathroom floor when my husband came home, hours later, beginning of the end."

THE RIDE IS ONE HOUR and twenty-five minutes, and after my story there is a feeling of the tide going out. Mudflats, earthy smells, tidal pools, breakers distant, islands out there, all beautiful in their own way, I suppose. My priest looking out his window at the night, I from mine, the driver's whistling increasingly pleasant, those Arabic half-tones, a studied oblivion. That starts a train of thought, and eventually out of nowhere, like Father Paul with the children thing, I say, "I mean, how can you believe in that church stuff? The Holy Trinity—that's a big part of Episcopalianism, right? How can you believe in it? I mean faith, okay, that's the easy answer, but believing in all this patently false and crazy church stuff, it just puzzles me."

And P.G. is very patient—this kind of thing he's heard before. He wriggles away from me a touch and with a quick motion of his good, long hands zips his pants back up. Only then he says, "Well, this is a big topic. And I may actually agree with you. But as far as the Trinity goes—Father, Son, Holy Ghost being all one? It's like water: you might see it in the form of steam, ice, or liquid, but it's still water."

I'm not buying it. I straighten my own clothes, say, "That's the best you can do? It's like water? That old saw? I'm sorry, but it's not like water. It's nothing like water. Water you can drink, you can see. You can put it in an ice tray, you can boil it in the teapot, you can walk on it. And it keeps you alive literally."

"You don't drink God? See God in everything? God doesn't keep you alive? Literally inspire?"

"I drink a collection of natural forces all acting upon one another in wonderful ways. And I keep *myself* alive, I keep a collection of molecules together in a certain shape and form, later to be some other form when my electrical impulses cease."

"A miracle in itself."

"Okay, sure."

"Call it God, then, why not?"

"Because then the morons will pray to it?"

"Your hostility is fascinating."

"I'm losing my buzz."

"What is your name really?"

Something in me is anxious to change the subject and whispers, "I haven't come that hard in like five years." And P.G. likes that, big warm grin. We slide close again, watch the high prairie go by in half moonlight, really enormous farms planted in corn and soy and not much else, alfalfa, one small field of milo, maybe some potatoes across the tracks there.

He says, "Your name."

"It's Ellen."

"Ellen."

"Okay. Yes. I like it. My name. In your mouth."

He's a little angry: "Your real name at last."

Several miles go by, the home territory, straightest possible road, a partial moon rising. I say, "So what ended up happening with you and that girl?"

And a little angrier yet, he says, "Oh, I see. You're jealous. And you were jealous of the bartender, too. Also the hostess. As for me, I don't like your intern. And I don't like your husband, I don't care he's your ex." He's not very scary.

I give him a squeeze, and he's still hard as a cross on a hill.

That's it for irritation. "Let's save it for home," he says softly.

"You have not saved me for home."

"But you, unlike I, are a bottomless well."

He's right about that.

We sit up. Eyes front. The driver's GPS glows, speaks directions in Arabic. I know exactly what it's saying: my road is only two miles, a nice square intersection, turn right.

P.G. says, "Okay. At her hearing I went back to chambers with the judge, my tennis friend, and I suggested that in some cases the best course of action might be pastoral counseling. Daily counseling. After school. At her home. I was willing to do it—to make a project of her, keep her off the streets, keep her in mind of morals, teach her those things she'd never been taught by her coarse parents, bless them, keep her away from the Aryan Nation, the methamphetamine nation, the cult nation, the inner Michigan, the weapons."

I say, "And the judge agreed, and then you fucked her every day."

"Yes. Every day for a year, which was her sentence. The year of pastoral counseling, I mean. Not the lovemaking. Which I would like to believe she enjoyed."

"And then you got caught."

"No. Nothing like that. Not at all. Just that we got to be very close. I would say we had fallen in love. She read the books I suggested. She was wise far beyond her peers. But before the year was even up she and I agreed there was no place for the relationship to go, a matter of our ages more than propriety. She'd gotten interested in college. In fact, she'd been accepted into the Residential College at the University of Michigan."

"Go Blue."

"It's an elite admission, the RC. She's done very well. Environmental studies. Also soccer, a big deal."

"Her parents must be glad."

"Her father is in jail. Financial fraud."

"Which is where you belong. Jail. I mean, she was underage, P.G. Or are you making all this up?"

"No, sadly true. And note that seventeen is not underage in Michigan."

"If you say so."

"Ellen, you're right. I'm skirting the issue."

"Which is: How can you stay in the church?"

"In fact, I have resigned."

He'd been shown another path.

THE TAXI DRIVER DROPPED us; we tipped him vastly. He was another of the angels that surrounded P.G., I thought, and realized the bartender had been one as well, certainly that teenage girl in the old-money house who went to college and became a success. And maybe me.

I said, "Am I really your first Internet date?"

"My first of any kind."

"Since . . ."

"Well, that's correct, exactly. Since . . ." Since his wife died.

In the barn ewe and lamb were asleep together, nicely nestled.

In the house I made P.G. put his little collar-tab thing in the woodstove, and we watched it burn, then built up the fire. We ate a plate of eggs and toast that we made together and then we drank more whiskey (you could about bite his breath, delicious) and the moon rose and our sexual tide came in high and we finished what we had started, made love while talking, just the two of us, only two of us, only him and me, these completed adults, and then we slept an indeterminate time and woke and slept and woke, very powerful, only partly alcoholic.

AND THEN UNDER FAINT sun it was a tour of the farm and honestly several days of lovemaking and eating and talk and even some actual farmwork (more lambs, everyone dropping at once) and pretty serious discussions of what he could add to the mix ("Jism," I said, and he knew what I meant, not the slightest backing away: "I've always wanted to be a father." "I believe you, Father," said I in the chicken house, always the clown, but deliquescing: kids were on my agenda, too.)

He'd wanted to do more with his gardening as well, and that's why he'd answered my ad. "I want to grow huge zucchini," he said. "And eggplants and cucumbers and carrots and what are those things called? Butternut squash."

"We grow alliums here, not dildos."

"We can grow *both*."

Funny priest!

Four days of this little honeymoon of an Internet date before we even got ourselves a ride into town to retrieve our two cars from the parking garage they both happened to be in (and more freakily, parked exactly next to each other—I mean, please) and then to the rectory at St. Marks to gather his things and leave the Prius, which was owned by the diocese. He owned practically nothing, in fact, one load in the Tundra, a big vehicle, granted—mostly books, one box of knickknacks, two suitcases of useless fine clothes alongside my bales of hay, the broken spreader—and home to the farm, happily ever after, ha.

Dung Beetle

MY FELLOWSHIP, FROM AN American foundation, included a modest stipend toward room and board. Word was that this was best spent on a flat rather than on university housing: in summer, every flat in Oxford was available on sublease for ha'pennies on the pound. That would leave some extra for my bad habits: cigarettes, ale, used books, and just maybe, if luck were with me, a girlfriend. This was 1975, remember, and England to me was all miniskirts and rock and roll and Bond, James Bond—Britt Ekland in her bikini, *The Man with the Golden Gun*.

First hours in town, my brain boiling with excitement, also jet lag, I found the bulletin board my mentor in the Public Policy program at Georgetown had described: boarder wanted, flatmate wanted, sublease available. Holding sheaves of notes and tear-offs in my teeth, I struggled with an enormous red pay phone. In those days, long before answering machines, before e-anything, the first nine or eleven numbers I dialed only rang a double-toned foreign signal that made my heart sink. The tenth or twelfth was answered on a half ring: thickly accented English, neither British nor American, a man named

Sileshi Silboumi. His offering was "near enough" the university, rent of "fourteen pounds the month." We made an appointment for "an hour's time hence." He'd have to "hurtle homeward" from his office at the university to meet me.

The image of a perfect dwelling with a perfect flatmate named Sileshi Silboumi overtook me, and I walked a crooked couple of miles to the address he'd given me in Motherly Street. There was no ringer. "One must bellow up," he'd instructed.

I did, and shortly his broad black face appeared over the balustrade four floors up. He sang down: "Will it do?"

I shouted back, "So far!"

Upstairs (many stairs), the flimsy door to the flat opened directly into a bedroom. Puffing, I attempted to shake his hand, but Sileshi wouldn't take mine, only half-bowed and tilted his head, frank gaze, no words between us. His cheeks and forehead were decorated with a star-shaped cicatrix. He was a small man, short and thin, with large front teeth, something athletic expressed in his broad-striped rugby shirt. His face was wide open, beautiful really, cheerful, accepting, intelligent. His skin was very dark, truly black. Mine was truly white, pink when drinking, freckles either way. His hair was buzzed off close. Mine was long, in proto-hippie curls.

At last Sileshi tilted his head almost to his shoulder. He said, "You are most agreeable."

I tilted my head the same and said, "Could you show me around?"

He straightened. "I have subleased this citadel from a graduate student in physics." All his accents were original and landed on last syllables: cita*del*, stu*dent*, phys*ics*. "It has a mathematical air, don't you agree?"

That was a joke and I laughed. The place had a drooping air, nothing mathemati*cal* about it, and a moldy air, and was fiercely hot that late afternoon. We could "scarce breathe," as Sileshi put it. We kept laughing, though, and suddenly he pulled me to him, hugged me sweatily, comradely, sweet smell of incense behind his ear.

"All right, then, mate," he said too loudly. "We have found each other."

I wanted to say, Not so fast, but his enthusiasm charmed me to silence.

I followed him through the flat, which was a simple dumbbell, rudimentary kitchen lined up in the center. My prospective room was at the far end, piled tidily with books, a thin mattress on the floor, no door of its own. The toilet, said he, was on the first floor, two floors down, "actually." I asked after the shower, drew a blank look, described the concept with hand gestures over my head.

"Ah, the bath," Sileshi said, with his own gesture, that of turning a low knob. I think it was then I first saw that he was missing fingers on his left hand, all but thumb and pinkie. And he saw that I noticed, opened the hand sub rosa to show me, even as his face continued the conversation. "No bath for the filthy. We use the public baths—a pleasant walk."

"All this for fourteen pounds monthly," I said, hard to believe my luck.

"Yes. Seven pounds in division."

Even better.

MOVING IN WAS A MATTER of retrieving my suitcase, canceling my horrid hotel, and returning to Sileshi's that very afternoon. I handed over seven pounds in coins and notes, accepted yet more kisses on both cheeks. My new flatmate and I gazed upon one another at length, contemplated the summer ahead. A ray of late-afternoon light pierced the motes of the kitchen, was as quickly gone: sunset in Oxford.

"Settle in," Sileshi said, pointing me at my room. Then he excused himself with a bow and a flourish. Soon—there were no doors to close—I heard him drumming at the floor and muttering. Prayer of some kind, I surmised.

Nonplussed, exhausted, I lay on the narrow mattress that would be my bed, closed my eyes, and prayed, too, via profound sleep, my only religion even then.

In darkness I awoke to Sileshi serving a meal on the floor of my room. At first I tried to beg off, embarrassed by his largesse, his intimate presence, also befuddled from the snooze. But he took no notice, handed me a napkin of rough linen. I struggled up, and the two of us sat cross-legged in silence and ate a kind of meat stew, using torn pieces of gummy flatbread as our only implements, sharing the bowl. The spice in the food burned my mouth pleasantly. After, we ate strange fruits and talked, leaning at one another. Sileshi was finishing his PhD dissertation in economics, meanwhile teaching two classes in the summer session. His father was an important king or chieftain in an area of central Africa he refused to call a country, an area upon which the Belgians and several other European powers had long imposed borders and were now instituting "native" parliaments before departing per treaty after generations of brutal occupation.

I was no tribal prince, but I had an interest in politics, with a goal of elective office (why did this amuse my new flatmate so?). And my father was no important chieftain but a well-paid and vitriolic cowhide stretch-and-cut operator at a tanning plant in Kansas City, Missouri.

My first week as a rent-paying denizen of Oxford was filled with new impressions, dozens of near-fatal steps into left-hand traffic, bangers and mash for breakfast, and the start of my summer Government program at Oxford, which was thrilling and absurdly demanding: seminars and tutorials and caucuses, stacks of books to read, position papers and analyses to write, and, of course, robust socializing to attend to each evening. I got home close after ten most nights—pub closing—and every night found Sileshi asleep. I learned to open the stairwell door quietly into his room and make my way quietly to my own. I read stirring, sobering course texts by candlelight (there was no lamp or electrical outlet in my room, an insignificant defect, I thought), read until one or two in the morning. When I woke at eight—leaving barely time to dress and make the first caucus each day—Sileshi was always already gone. For two weeks we didn't exchange a syllable, though he was firmly part of my life. His incense sweetened the flat. He left exotic stews for me in stone bowls, fruits cut open and arrayed on beautiful woven cloths, strange nuts, sour candies. It didn't occur to me to reciprocate or that the place was so clean because he cleaned it.

In that second week I took an interest in an Irish student nicknamed Baby, real name of Colleen, not one of the formidable minds from my program but a waitress from the Pig and Prudence Pub, which we all frequented. She was formidable in her way, too, don't get me wrong; it's just that for her there were other subjects besides Marxism. Callow boy, I was surprised to learn she was a top student, a rising senior like me but reading in history, and unconflicted about taking the summer to make some cash far away from her Irish parents. I found out her day off and one evening drank enough to ask her out on an American picnic. She was charmed by Sileshi's spare blanket and the park he'd suggested, charmed by the great empty lawn over the river, charmed by the bread and cheeses, the three bottles of wine, and especially charmed by Sileshi's well-worn soccer ball, which I'd borrowed in a fit of inspiration, having told him I was going out with a few of the boys. After some hilariously physical one-on-one against a rubbish-bin goal, Baby and I ate lunch, then got ourselves quite smashed, serious talk of novels and dog breeds and airplanes (her pa a dead pilot) and finally the loneliness of the foreign student, and soon we were kissing and soon again packing up the picnic to go to my place where she said there'd best be no funny business. That with her hand in my front trousers pocket, where no girl's hand had gone before. Sileshi wasn't home, thankfully, and we fell on my slim mattress and soon it was all funny business, drunken declarations, and even tears of love around such salacious acts as I had never taken part in, all powered by Baby's instructive gusto.

"We've soaked your sheets," she said memorably, merrily. At least some part of the moisture was a Rhinelander wine she'd bought on the walk home, bottle four, and which we'd spilled in our naked enthusiasm.

Tangled together we embarked on still more peculiar business, followed by a plummet into sleep. I woke in the night to the sound of dishes in the apartment's tiny kitchen, the swish of a broom, pounding headache, the girl naked half atop me. I noted with chagrin that the clothes we'd shed were folded in two neat piles. The wine bottle was gone, the glasses we'd drunk from missing. I smelled Sileshi's evening food preparation (breakfast little different from dinner), garlic and cardamom and meat, heard him eating the meal bite by bite at the tiny kitchen table. Baby didn't stir, breathed heavily, all of her pressed into me, lovely luck. I heard my flatmate's prayers then, and shortly the lights went out. An hour later Baby woke and gave me squeezes.

She whispered, "What's the stench?" Sileshi's dinner, of course, and incense. The funny business resumed. In fact, quietly as possible, we snogged and shagged and shimmied till dawn, my vocabulary growing. Then Baby had to go. Her flatmates would be "dilly bothered" at her absence, she said, six of them, all girls from the home country.

IN THE MORNING I was surprised to find Sileshi at the kitchen table. He was a statue, gazed at me ruefully as I made my daily peanut butter jelly sandwich. His cicatricial array formed a greater frown, made him fearsome.

"Unclean," he said finally.

"I'm sorry," I said.

"To ferry a whore here!"

"A whore? No, no. She's a friend."

"Some kind of friend!"

"A *girl*friend."

"And intoxicants," he said, voice rising. "This is wrong. And to leave it to me to tidy the mess. Do you have servants at home?"

I thought of my mother's kindly face. I thought of my diplomacy seminar, in which I'd already learned much. I framed his argument per instruction: "You don't want women here in the apartment, and you want me to do my share of the cleaning."

"Quite," he said.

I offered honest apologies and promises I could keep, spoke formally as he had, kept his eye as he kept mine: "I've been remiss. I will clean daily to catch up with you. I noticed you've been making my bed, folding my clothes. I've had no chance to thank you for your kindness in this as in all things. The problem, I think, is that you get to it before I am able. Perhaps our standards are slightly different. Please leave my mess and I will get to it. Leave your own from here on in and I will clean for you, too."

We held a long silence. I didn't even dare bite my PBJ.

Finally his face softened. His head made the slightest tilt, progress for diplomacy. He said, "You speak well. Your proposal is just. Though one can't just 'leave a mess,' as you put it. A mess must be seen to."

I took on the next issue: "Were Colleen and I too loud for you?"

Sileshi hardened again. "It's hardly a matter of volume," he said.

It's a matter of envy, I thought, but I said, "You don't approve of sex?"

He gasped, cried out, said, "I have never said the word! These are marital relations, and you, little brother, are not married!"

My emotion rose: "But I think I am in love, and I think she is—her name is Colleen—and in our two cultures, which are not absolutely the same, but quite different from your own, our relations are our own business."

"In my house, not."

"This is my house too."

"You sully your house."

"We'll leave before you're home," I said.

"Whether I am here or not, you are *seen*."

I pulled him into a hug, that gesture I'd learned from him, spoke into his ear. "Flatmate. You and I should spend time together, get to know one another."

Sileshi's head tilted sidewise on its own volition. He pushed me away to gauge my seriousness. His brow unknit itself. "I am home today," he said.

I was full of the magnanimity of my night with Baby, and still half-drunk. I declared that I would be home, too. Sileshi went cheerfully to his room, dressed himself in a long cotton gown, dull white with a geometric pattern in green and gold sewn into the hem and sleeves. We took a long walk to Derrydown Castle, which he'd read about, passing through neighborhoods of growing opulence, and Sileshi gave a disquisition along the way on the fluid meaning of wealth across societies and continents. It wasn't an argument I entirely followed, but Sileshi swayed me with his passion, also big gestures, those missing fingers the very ghosts of emphasis. His conclusion arrived like the end of an aria, the music of ideas, and a group of our fellow pedestrians turned to stare: in his world, at least, the only solution was going to be a period of extreme militant anarchism, then in the ashes a return to tribal ways and lands.

"Isn't that unlikely?" I said after a silence.

Sileshi's passion was spent. He only shrugged, said, "Even the highest coconut finds its way down." He took my hand, and we walked holding hands till—American boy—I was decently able to let go, feigning the need to point.

At the castle we took the tour, lingering over the dungeons and a horrifying display of the machines and implements of medieval torture.

Sileshi sighed mightily. He said, "I know why they made these things."

"I guess we all do," I said.

"I guess we all don't," he said.

I was content to leave it at that.

On the walk home he pulled up suddenly, stopped me, took my hands, gazed into my eyes in his unsettling way. His grip trembled, his eyes grew liquid. I awaited a political query.

"How much did you pay her?" he said.

"She's a friend," I said, taken aback. "I didn't pay her, and she didn't pay me. A person doesn't have to pay."

"I know so little," he said.

THE NEXT MORNING, AS I rushed along the old streets to campus, books stacked architecturally under my arm, I became aware that someone was dogging me, following closer and then further behind. I looked over my shoulder, not much to see, just a businessman, as I read him, brown suit, black tie, buzz cut, clearly the enemy. I took a medieval alleyway, and the man took it, too. If he was following me, he wasn't trying to hide the fact. Under an ivied archway at the university I pulled up short, cocky kid, and waited for him. I knew a policeman when I saw one. And he didn't break stride, just marched right up to me.

Unperturbed, I said, "May I help you?"

He hissed, "How do you know Silboumi?"

"Barely," I said, wise guy.

He grabbed my throat in one hand, smashed me up against the stone wall silently, sending my books flying. He then proceeded to knock my head repeatedly against the masonry. I kicked—all I could do in my position—and that earned me an expert knee in the groin. The thug held my throat till I thought I would pass out, then knocked my head again, hard, let me fall to the ground where I lay groaning and gagging among my tumbled books.

BABY THOUGHT MY ROOMMATE A HUNK, and she told him so repeatedly, as if his problem with women and sex were one of self-esteem. He'd slowly accepted Baby's presence in our kitchen and seemed to linger longer in the mornings. Buh-*bee*, as he called her, was a great toucher of hands and faces. Wrapped less than modestly in my bedsheets, she'd lean to him over one of his breakfast presentations and touch his decorated cheeks, tell him she thought her flatmate Shelagh would "spin" over him. Sileshi didn't know what a date was, much less a blind date, and to spin was surely a sin, but he grinned and tilted his head every time Shelagh's name came up.

He wouldn't say yes to a date, so Baby took it into her own hands, arranging a dinner to surprise them both, against my more cautious instincts. But I was the shill and Sileshi and I waited in the little restaurant she'd picked, nervously eyeing the prices. And then the young women came in. We gentlemen rose, bowed courtly. Shelagh was nearly six inches taller than my chaste flatmate, thin and sincere, a beanpole, not a beauty like Baby but handsome, her lofty intelligence clear in her face and green eyes. She gave a commanding curtsy as Baby introduced her.

Sileshi gave a short cry at the name Shelagh, looked up at her in obvious panic.

"You've been touched by God's hands," she said, and boldly put her own mortal fingers on my roommate's facial welts, thumbs on the off-welts over his eyes. I'd never realized the significance of the array till that moment.

Sileshi closed his eyes. Beads of sweat appeared on his brow. "Precisely," he said.

"Ach, Shelagh, you're not to handle my young man," Baby said. She patted my roommate's bottom, gave it a squeeze.

Sileshi surprised me by letting out a high giggle. And the giggle didn't stop—he stood there in his normal stiff posture *giggling*. The giggling got the girls going, too, and there he was, hands all over him, a puddle of glee.

Shelagh let her fingers rest on his face till she'd felt his soul, finally let go.

"She's got some bumps of her own to show you," Baby said salaciously, and winked at me.

I just wanted the girls to stop.

We took our seats around a tiny table. The bargirl came by, a gum-snapping acquaintance of Baby's, and after some banter Baby ordered wine. Sileshi drew himself up. "I cannot."

"Scotch, then," Shelagh said.

Sileshi sweated and tilted his head and grinned unstoppably and drank Scotch one to one with our glasses of wine, quite as if he were familiar with alcohol. By dessert he'd relaxed somewhat, his attention focused on Shelagh like a ray, and it was clear Baby had been right: the two of them were a match. They were black and white as a newspaper, but I was apparently the only one thinking that way, American boy. Sileshi found his tongue, though, found words somewhere deep inside him, began to make his gentle jokes, told a long story of a lion he'd encountered in his youth, used his mysterious metaphors ("angry as a man with nutshells 'round his lodge"). Shelagh leaned at him, clutched his arm at every laugh, suddenly asked after his missing fingers, something I'd not brought myself to do in all the weeks I'd known my prince.

"Fortunately I am right handed," he said.

"But how did it happen?" said Baby.

"That very lion," said Sileshi, tilting his head, pinching his thumb and pinky together repeatedly, an unconscious gesture.

"Bosh," said Shelagh.

Sileshi sat up very straight, thought for some moments, looked at each of us in turn, patted Shelagh's arm with the deformed hand. He said, "It was an explosive device. When I had but five years." He'd say no more, though we quizzed him. Gradually then, he shifted the conversation to my home country (how had I felt when the Kennedys were killed?) and that of the young women (deadly Ireland). His part of the world had no monopoly on political violence, was his point.

BY THE END OF the evening, all four of us were back in the little apartment, Sileshi having made no protests. The girls were already calling him Boom-Boom, which would stick. In the kitchen dear Baby said, "Here's the way to do it," and began to kiss me. I held back in embarrassment, but Shelagh took Sileshi's face in her hands, kissed his lips gently. He hadn't shown signs of much intoxication, but at the touch of her tongue dropped instantly to the floor in an unrousable faint.

The next several dates went better, and before long hardly a night passed by when both girls weren't in our rooms. Sileshi took to hanging the hallway carpet over his door to muffle her prodigious moaning—he himself was always utterly silent. His little clay figures turned their backs on the room when the girl was there, I noted.

I held off telling them about the man who'd attacked me. Baby would hit the roof, I knew, demand action. I had no clue what to make of the event, in any case. Plus, Sileshi was so nervous to start with, always looking around the pub if we were out, always asking where the nearest exit was, wearing English clothing by night, hiding his face under his umbrella, rain or no. His private face—when reading a book, for example—was hard and pensive, knit brows, deep frown. He sighed frequently, even groaned at times. In any case it was obvious, also thrilling: Sileshi, our prince, was under the eye of British intelligence.

Baby thought him merely shy.

Shelagh became the unofficial leader of our little group. She found us all pathetically philistine when it came to matters of her subject, which was art and art history. Under her wing, we went to the museums, even taking the Saturday train into London several weeks running. She pored over paintings in a way that had never occurred to me, standing close and then far, even touching the painted surface when the guards were elsewhere, constantly setting off alarms. She hugged a statue of David, grasping his buttocks, not kidding, not in the slightest: this was true love. She liked to read to us from her textbooks and from her art magazines, even at pub. And at pub she grilled Sileshi about the art of his world: she was disdainful that he knew so little. He tried hard to please her, began to study his own culture, neglected his students, his writing.

She was disdainful in other ways, too, just subtly, just enough to keep a friend off balance and a lover slightly desperate. I don't think she did it on purpose, it was just her way: you should know what she knew, value what she valued, and if you didn't, you could piss off. Sileshi changed his syllabus under her eye, did a section on economies of art, undertook studies of African art as it was collected in the British Isles. We visited some tiny galleries and vest-pocket museums with Shelagh: the stuff was everywhere. Soon enough I was talking the politics of art in my government caucus, always parroting Shelagh, and found to my delight that I'd finally interested my chief don and his terrifying acolytes. Even as the summer waned I became the spokesman for art and culture at school, desperately quizzing Shelagh every night to get my points lined up for the following day's arguments, wedding my new pet subject to our ongoing discussions of imperialism, nationalism, capitalism, socialism, continentalism, Marxism, and of course (with no proper nod to Sileshi), tribalism.

Our little crowd's last Saturday train was to the west side of London. Through her father, a top aide to a top MP, Shelagh had gotten tickets to the opening of an exhibit of Polynesian art gathered from museums all over the world. We four huddled, holding glasses of free wine, eating free caviar on points of toast, lingering over each work in the show, taking two hours, studying weave and stroke and whittle, provenance, ownership, a universe complete unto ourselves. As the party roaring around us grew even louder, the laughter yet more hilarious, we found ourselves circum-ogling an amazing outrigger canoe loaned with some fanfare by the Natural History Museum in New York. Sileshi gazed at it with us, pulled himself up in a way that was becoming familiar to me. He began to move his head side to side with a waggle, the opposite of the tilt, I knew.

He spat, "Why is nothing in this exhibit from Polynesia?"

The sudden emotion surprised the girls.

"What are you saying, Boom-Boom?" Shelagh said.

"Every piece, stolen! Whom, for example, did this Unnatural Museum in New York City pay for this boat?" He grew more agitated yet, pointed around the sumptuous galleries, including in his indictment all the museum goers, all the catering staff, the very columns and lintels of the fine old building, fumbled his English uncharacteristically: "Who was remunerated for totems there? Those weavings? That group of figurines, so beautiful? Whose ancestors are without their history and on which island so richly and unknowingly represented here? Why is the curator having the name Fitzherbert and not something more like, yes, Taramanini? This is no exhibit of art, it is exhibit of the *booty of conquest*!" He had begun to shout. Shelagh put a hand on his arm, not a little proud. The crowd around us moved back, stared, champagne flutes aimed delicately at us. Baby stood with her mouth agape: sweet Sileshi! Two guards came into the room, approached warily. Sileshi addressed them, commanded them, paralyzed them in their marble tracks, and we all of us stood frozen with guilt, if that's the right word, frozen anyway by the enormous, rippling force of his emotion. Flinging his arms, pointing at one wonderful object and then the next, he roared, "Where are represented the people who made these things?"

A FEW NIGHTS LATER—a school night, but Baby's birthday—we got Sileshi to the Pig and Prudence one last time. Having figured out how to get his nose past the foam, Sileshi ordered ales with the rest of us. We spoke in excitement about his new dream for his people: a museum of the culture, where there was none. A museum that would bring back the stolen and collect the forgotten, return the soul of the tribes to the land such that a museum was no longer needed.

Outside afterward, we shouted with laughter and linked arms four across, marched down the middle of narrow streets toward home. Baby pointed to a statue atop a fountain, four sprites holding up a nymph, shouted: "Where are represented the people who made this!" We chanted that for a mile or more, pointing at this cornice and that hitching post—solidarity, not irony—and then we sang the dung beetle song, something our prince had taught us in his natal language, the theme of his people as they'd risen up against the colonial power: the dung beetle keeps on trying, rolls his ball of shit, obstacles or no, unto death.

"Dung beetle!" we cried out in tongue-popping dialect. "Dung beetle! Roll your ball of shit past thorn and promontory!"

At the head of our street, two large men stepped out from the hedges and into the road ahead of us. The smaller of them was the violent fellow I'd already met. We froze.

He said, "You are seen."

I made fists.

Sileshi claimed us boldly, said, "These are but my friends."

Baby spat on the sidewalk at their feet. "Get moving, you," she said. "We're not afraid of the likes of you!"

The men looked at one another and, miraculously, turned, walked away, made the corner by a pharmacy, and disappeared.

Sileshi was defiant, put on a show for those Irish girls, who were on fire with indignation. He called the men "agents of the Crown." He said, "I'll show those blokes if they dare come back!" We all continued on to the flat, covering our fear with a hard-marching Gaelic football song Shelagh knew, "Stomp the Fairies."

In the morning, though, Sileshi was clearly depressed, subdued, nervous, even scared. Over breakfast, I confessed I'd encountered the secret agent before, and his face grew taut. He went out twice to make phone calls. Later, after we'd eaten, he drew Shelagh into his room, and we heard her protesting, heard his even tones, heard the stairway door locks snap open, heard the door, heard Sileshi leave. Shelagh came to Baby and me in tears.

"I'm not to come back," she said, and then, imitating him exactly: "I've played a useful role in his life that here and henceforth is finished."

Sileshi went missing, day by day till it was a week. I couldn't go to the police—what if Interpol were looking for him? I began to check the street before leaving the flat, as Sileshi had always done. The summer session was over but for exams. Sileshi's absence was devastating, terrifying. Baby was furious with him, Shelagh distraught. And now Baby was furious with me, too, in frequent tears, as perhaps I should have been, but as frequently loving: my flight home was six days off, then five, then only four. We made promises. We wrapped ourselves in one another. I jeopardized my grades, even missed an exam by oversleeping beneath her. She jeopardized her job, calling in sick evening after evening. I cared for nothing in the world but her; even my missing flatmate slipped my mind, long guilty stretches. Baby and I arrived back at the flat on our very last afternoon in a state of concupiscent confusion and sorrow—I was to fly the next morning—burst from the stairwell into Sileshi's room ready for some valedictory ravishment, likely tears.

But on my flatmate's bed two round women lounged in ornate gowns, their arms covered in bracelets. They looked our way, absolutely aloof, unsurprised. Only slowly I noticed a pair of teenage boys, gangly and embarrassed in formal gowns and headgear sparkling with metal and cut glass, both trying to see Baby whole while looking at the floor. Sileshi heard Baby's cry of frustration, leapt into the room. "My aunts," he said, and gave names I couldn't retain. The women on his bed nodded unsmiling. "My nephews." The boys looked up, tilted their heads, looked away. A grand, serious couple glided stately into the little room from the even smaller kitchen: Sileshi's parents. He introduced Baby and me as flatmate and tutor, I noticed. The apartment was broiling, a closet full of ceremonial clothes in motion, strong scents.

A fat man in a blue gown squeezed into the room, Sileshi's younger brother, whom I knew to be Siltii, nodding and grinning. The children who followed were his, three little girls in jewels and aqua gowns, hair woven with dyed ribbons of coarse cloth and ceramic beads, very beautiful. They pressed up against Baby, who was only reluctantly charmed. There were more people in the kitchen, and yet more back in my room. Sileshi tilted his head at me, drew me in, kissed me. "My family," he said formally, proudly, no acknowledgment that he'd been missing nearly a week. He said, "My departmental ceremony is this evening." Then he leaned to me and hissed, "Send Baby away."

I whispered to her and she whispered back, and it must have been clear she wasn't my tutor. She gave a great false smile to all the company, pulled at my arm to get me into the stairwell. Still angry over Sileshi's treatment of Shelagh, she was little inclined to come to his aid.

"Ten minutes," I said. "I mayn't see him ever again."

"You mayn't ever see me again," she said, and leapt down the stairs three at a time. Later it would take an agonized hour to find her, another hour to make up, but we would.

"So kind of your tutor to walk you home," Sileshi said loudly as I came back in.

I made my way to my room (the condoms I needed were in there), relative by relative, only to come face-to-face with the grim-faced white man who'd assaulted me. He was in an inferior position, kneeling among rolls of brown shipping tape, caught in the servile act of placing Sileshi's books in boxes. So my cop was merely the employee of overprotective parents. A withered factotum stood over him and wrote each title in an account book, a slow process. I changed into my pubbing clothes as if the two of them weren't there, deliberately stepped on my assailant's ankle without apology—satisfying crunch—dropped my dirty clothes over his head.

In the kitchen, Sileshi introduced me to the king of their ancient family nation, his father. The ethereal man tilted his head, smiled briefly, waves of power like I'd never felt before. I couldn't speak, impossible to think in his presence. He made a throne room of our little kitchen, a palace of our flat. I found myself bowing and scraping, kissed his hand. The mother was slightly more mortal, took both my hands in hers, kissed me the way Sileshi always did: cheek, cheek, forehead. She tilted her head, said, "So you are the bad influence."

"No, it's your son," I said, jocular.

But she frowned and that was the end of my audience with her.

"Never mind the puritans," Sileshi's brother said jovially. He pulled me to him, gave me kisses. "Today we celebrate our educated men."

"Dung beetle!" cried the little girls in their language, and the song rose up.

LATER IN LIFE I took up with the Senate campaign of a former Black Panther who garnered three percent of the vote across Missouri, hard to cast as victory. He continued to be a fixture in Kansas City politics, however, and tapped me to run his ingenious inner-city arts program, a plum. During one of our long campaign bus rides, I'd briefly expressed an interest in art, and so the world had turned. The pay was modest, the job frustrating, but it was a life in government. I wore a suit, called meetings, wrote grants, negotiated resource and faculty exchanges with well-heeled suburban schools, curried favor frankly.

I thought of my time in England fondly all those years, thought of Baby too often, less so after I was married, but yes, still. She'd gotten work at the Tate after graduation, brilliant young woman. The two of us had written feverishly back and forth across prairie and ocean for more than a year, but my Irish lass was too poor to travel, and I too foolish to pay her way, too foolish to go to her.

After the letters stopped—an Australian curator named Buddy—I pined and moped but carried on, finished school, took a master's degree in government, volunteered in the soup kitchens, met the leaders of the community, met the Black Panther, met Nancy Darling, fellow volunteer and idealist. Nancy was a tall, troubled woman with deep eyes and excellent hygiene. And it was she who introduced me to the senator who got me the position at the Kansas City Museum of Fine Art, which led via lucky breaks to my taking the directorship in 1990.

Politicos without end, unhappily childless, Nancy and I read ten newspapers closely each day and watched the news on TV each night, consecutive cable shows till bedtime—we missed little—so it was no surprise in the early eighties that I happened to see a half-minute story about the upheaval in a certain freehold somewhere deep in central Africa, a skirmish in a destroyed capital city, dozens of members of a new parliament assassinated along with a new prime minister. There was dramatic footage (visual drama the reason such an obscure story had made the news at all); the scene was a state occasion, long outdoor dais festooned with flowers and banners, politicians waving to a large, happy crowd, a limo pulling up, the prime minister climbing out, the prime minister helping his wife out, the two of them turning to the camera beaming. With a shock I realized who the couple was: Sileshi's parents. Just then shots were heard off-camera and the once-royal couple crumpled to the ground like exhausted marionettes. Their driver pulled a large handgun out from under his jacket but was shot, too, fell back over them. The cameraman, bless his departed soul, turned in the direction of the fire, still shooting video, and into the frame came masked men peppering the parliamentary dais with submachine guns, people diving in all directions, people falling, shouting, crying out—pandemonium—and then the camera's view spun and fell, too, and all went black, famous footage.

The *New York Times* ran a short article the next day—not much information. *Time* and *Newsweek* both had very small articles the following week, mostly because a dramatic photo was available. The insurgents, it seemed, had retreated to a suburb. The trusted general who'd taken over for the dead prime minister promised they would meet their fates "like so many snakes under forked sticks." That was it, all three articles illustrated with the same image: masked men firing their weapons into the dais. I stuck the *Newsweek* photo on my fridge. And only after weeks of seeing it there did I notice the deformed left hand of one of the shooters—just a pinky finger and empty knuckles, abandoned thumb gripping the weapon's steel stock: Sileshi.

I THOUGHT OF HIM often during the decade after, a decade in which I rose in importance in the art world, joining the boards of over a dozen museums and foundations—constant travel, inveterate schmoozing, friend to artist and congressperson alike, confidant of businessman and philanthropist, conduit to gallery owner, agent, collector. And, face it, thugs—the kind of money that makes that world spin is not always perfectly clean and might on occasion need a reputable museum to wash it off. You played one person off against another, surfed shifting loyalties, symbolically killed your countrymen, killed them over and over, even assassinated your parents. I thought of Sileshi, all right, but had no way of finding him, no wish to find him, really, only a wish to go back to pub days, pathetic. Likely he was dead, or hiding in the deep rain forest, a miserable life for the once-great man.

Nancy left me on the grounds of incompatibility—we called it all amicable in public. But the real grounds were what she saw as my degraded character, that I skulked in high places, the very places she'd introduced me to, that I'd damaged her reputation by my dealings, humiliated her among her friends. Something about Sileshi's story had infected me, was her theory, which in my distress I came to believe. I'd become an insurgent like him, the thinking went, hiding out in a jungle of my own making. Or, anyway, she divorced me, a long, expensive story, better left untold. After, I fell into an extended depression.

During the course of which I received a handwritten letter on official stationery: Office of the Prime Minister (country not to be named, not here). Just a note to ask after my days. A note to say hello. And give good news: The People had prevailed. Really, it was pretty impersonal, but it woke me up. Suddenly I could see the world again, hear music, taste food. I vowed to clean up my own act, to prevail in my own war, to live up to my ideals, or at least remember them.

Prime Minister! How Sileshi had railed against such titles! And not the first time in history a patricidal radical had taken his father's place, become the thing he hated. I kept my reply reserved, simply congratulating him, a little of my news, sad as it was, all on my museum letterhead and using my title, keeping it all very formal in case there was a trick—perhaps his enemies fishing for information, perhaps he himself talking in code toward an undisclosed purpose—anyway, quite insecure about addressing such a great personage and thinking the vellum envelope would get the missive past his screeners, who were no doubt vigorous in such a place. In the morning I opened the envelope back up, read what I'd written, added a PS: I was planning a trip to Ireland to see Baby on her birthday, upcoming. But this was a fantasy. In fact, I hadn't even so much as written or called her since our brief communication by phone in the month after we'd parted, all those years before. I didn't mention Shelagh, who had moved to Texas last I'd heard, and was no longer the woman we'd known.

Months later, after a week of mere domestic travel, I found amid my office mail a fibrous, bright orange envelope, blocky handwriting: Sileshi, of course, writing privately, a pleasant little note of thanks on a card of hard handmade paper, fulsome congratulations on my position, and the proposal that we meet in Ireland "on or proximate 19 August," which he remembered (with perfect accuracy) as Baby's birthday. "Our unruly lion," he called her, referring to astrology. He wasn't allowed in the States and that might be our only opportunity "to breathe each other's air." The coda seemed surreptitious: "In truth, cousin, I regard such a meeting with utmost urgency."

And so Colleen and I came together on August 17, ages almost forty-four and still forty-three, planets colliding, or suns, such was the heat. Our simple kiss hello at the Belfast airport—neither of us expecting it—unleashed every repressed emotional anything and streams of tears, simultaneous professions of undying love, this in front of her glowering, rightly embarrassed daughter, Gail-Lynn, age sixteen, who'd just arrived from Australia, where she'd lived with her father growing up. After some trouble with an older boy, and prescription drugs, she was now to live with Colleen.

I had honestly forgotten about real love-powered sex, but in their pleasant tiny house near Rosemary Street (Gail-Lynn off at a cousin sleepover, hastily arranged), I was made to remember quite a great deal. We soaked the sheets, quite so, even spilling our wine, like time had resumed, and my observation to that effect rocked us with laughter that echoed down the years. Her body had changed, as mine had, but thickened and somewhat padded, we were only more enticing to one another. Her calves had retained their perfection, the slope of her back its allure, and what was new was beautiful, too.

At our first breakfast, however—which we cooked together side by side—we had a moody half hour, something awkward passing between us, perhaps guilt uncommunicated (where to start the lists?), certainly regret, but all that was quickly waved away in favor of more lovemaking, rather on the rough side, violence dispelling anger. I left reluctantly (Gail-Lynn due home), floated through the old streets to finally check into my hotel for an afternoon nap before dinner with Prime Minister Sileshi Silesh Silboumi Silboumi.

He came into Belfast by train from London, alone and wearing a plain suit, hiding himself under a large English hat. He had changed little, no additional fat, just a brushing of close-cropped gray at his temples. But his eyes were more wary, and he was slower to tilt his head, took my hands emotionally, kissed my cheeks, my forehead, did it all again by way of emphasis. We walked in a misty rain to his hotel, which he said was close. No one stared at us, though I, for one, felt conspicuous.

"Well, old man," he said.

"Your Excellency," I said wryly.

"My people call me simply Father," he said with surprising heat.

The anger gave me pause and I fumbled for words, finally muttering, then repeating myself: "I'd expected bodyguards."

At last, he grinned a little. "The coffers are empty."

"Do countries still have coffers?"

"Not mine. Certainly not mine."

We walked in silence several blocks. I cast about in my head for conversation, feeling timid, losing the ease of our old friendship. My normal gambit, to ask questions, wasn't working either. What does one ask a head of state? A man who has assassinated his own parents? Lamely, gamely, I said, "How are things going for your administration?"

He answered with stately seriousness: "Since the fall of the Soviet Union we are without funds. Spain offers loans. In London I have been petitioning for grants. The Norwegians may intercede on our behalf with the World Bank—I address their parliament Tuesday next. But the outlook, cousin, is bleak. The army ant gobbles the lodge!" We walked in his subsequent dark silence up a long hill into a neighborhood of large homes. At the top of the climb Sileshi cleared his throat elaborately. "But you run a great museum," he said. "You know what sorts of things can go wrong."

"I don't have an army," I said lightly.

"You are blessed," he said heavily.

We walked in a deeply awkward silence, and I began to wonder why either of us might have considered this meeting a good idea. I longed to get back to my beloved Colleen. Passing alongside Singe Park, we paused in the rain to admire a crabbed old cherry tree. Sileshi patted one of the low-slung branches, gave it a shake, sniffed the bark, pinched the leaves between thumb and pinkie, exotic flora. His posture changed utterly, everything about him softened. He sighed in a manner familiar to me from the old days, enunciated gently, slowly: "Have you had reason to speak with Baby about our art lover?"

He couldn't even say her name. I said, "Shelagh lives in Texas," and with a shrug I let him know the whole story—she was lost to us, lost to him, married rich, "born again," Americanized, mother of three, the only one of our gang to have come to no relation with art.

"No matter. I have heard that they are bad to Blacks in Texas," Sileshi said with some of the old humor.

We tilted our heads properly at one another and grinned, a full minute of rich but silent communication, old friendship returning, then we carried on, strolled to the Old Belfast Hotel, the nicest in town, where Sileshi had a standard room, taken under the name of one of his secretaries. He went up to "wash his ears," which gave me the opportunity to call Colleen.

Gail-Lynn answered, "Yar," and said her mum was out. I tried a few friendly phrases, but the girl was having none of it, this sulky Australian teenager who, if the urgent promises of the previous night between her mother and me were kept, would be my stepdaughter within the month.

And that's what I was thinking when Sileshi appeared in the hotel bar in his gowns. We didn't talk, only drank Scotch glass by glass at his pace, which was no longer amateur. I wanted to know him, recalled that I never really had, asked him directly, for starters, if he'd ever married.

"Four times," he said. "A fifth on the way. They get along well. Twenty-one children."

"Wuruju!" I cried. Dung beetle.

He tilted his head with pride.

I asked what he regarded as his principal accomplishment as a leader of his people (I knew not to say nation; nationhood was not his goal).

"It's what Shelagh taught us," he said. "With the help of my ministers I've gathered the art of our people wherever we could find it, built an object-repatriation campaign to shame world collectors, sometimes successfully." The old grin. "And finally, just a few years gone, we turned the old Belgian governor's mansion into a museum of the life of our people, imperishable."

"Shelagh brought me to art, too," I said, tilting my head. "And brought Colleen to it, as well—she's involved in galleries."

"Let us talk about Colleen," Sileshi said sadly. But after that he became abstracted. I kept a hand on his arm to keep him listening, talked for the sake of filling the abyss in front of us, told him all about what Colleen and I had planned in the midst of our passion, that Gail-Lynn would come with us to Kansas City. "Apparently," I said with some forced cheer, "the girl is miserable in Ireland in any case, and loves Coca-Cola and Talking Heads. Aside from my presence the deal should be an easy sell. Colleen says we'll promise her Brad Pitt and American football, and stand back, mate. The kid'll be packing her room in a frenzy."

Sileshi didn't laugh. "One should honor one's parents," he said lugubriously. He caught my eye at that, and we held a long, profound look, staring across the void of multiple marriages, murderous regimes, divorce, imminent elopement, daughters not one's own.

All of which, along with strong spirits, gave me courage to say the one true thing: "Sileshi, you *killed* your parents."

He continued to stare into my eyes, but the look hardened, congealed, the lie he must have been telling himself for so long about to come to his lips. I thought if he spoke he would shout. I took his thumb and pinkie, held them. "I saw this hand on that gun, I saw it in a wire-service photo."

We regarded each other, frozen. He could have said that there were many such hands in his world; he could have made me believe him. But he said, "I have mounted and framed that picture at some expense and hung it in the old palace." His head bowed just perceptibly, his body sagged so. The truth was the truth. He touched my arm with that hand, pinched my sleeve, pulled me close, tilted his head, no grin, whispered, boast or lament I couldn't tell: "My beloved parents were collusionists. They were killing our people. They were destroying our culture. I saved them from their folly. I saved us all. Our lands will be a kingdom once again. We will return home by refusing ever to leave."

"Wuruju," I intoned.

"You must help," he said.

"Help how?"

He couldn't hold my eye. At length, he said, "We have art treasures to sell."

"You would let them leave your country? Your kingdom, I mean? After all you've done to gather them?"

"If I do not, there will be no kingdom."

"Wuruju," I said yet again, sadly.

"Dung beetle," Sileshi said. Then, together, both of us starting to tears, we sang the phrase in his language as the maître d' looked on, moved. Then, holding hands, we sang the whole song, lovely, surprised at the end when our fellow diners applauded.

■ ■ ■

IN MISSOURI, COLLEEN FLOURISHED, starting an art imports business, three points of trade: Ireland, Australia, the United States. Gail-Lynn became a high-school soccer star, made the All-Kansas team, never happier, then on to university, more sports, a fraternity boyfriend, finally a degree in engineering, of all things, strong interest in bridges.

I opened the Wuruju Wing at the KCMFA, the finest collection of African art in the world, a ten-year project, our acquisition stream routed through London and Montreal, I'm ashamed to say, Sileshi silent behind the deals we'd made, dozens of shady middlemen, Byzantine paperwork, dozens of other museums unwittingly party to illegal transfers, a long story, but no matter: my old friend had funded the continued success of his revolution.

It seems just the other day that, along with the rest of the world, Colleen and I saw Sileshi on television. He'd united three colonial states as tribal lands without borders, erased the names of three countries, disbanded three parliaments, funded and consolidated three ragtag armies, armed and dressed them in the traditional way, disenfranchised everyone else, kicked out foreign business, left hundreds of thousands dead, horrible. And then, of course, he'd taken the title of king.

There was a scandal when the method of acquisition of our treasures hit the news in the wake of the final revolution, as it was called. I spent a year in and out of congressional hearings and testifying at special board meetings at dozens of museums, too often found myself in front of news cameras attempting to explain how KCMFA had gotten involved in an African war. My ouster from the museum was national news, my censure by Congress humiliating, but I avoided prison, just an ankle monitor and a year at home, more time with Colleen, who found it all heroic and remains the solid center of my life.

As king, Sileshi stood up to international pressure, stood up to his detractors at home, stood up to the neighboring states pressing at his borders, the funds I'd procured for him dwindling. I've got a video of the results via an acquaintance who was then an intern at CNN, not something I'll ever watch again: Wearing traditional dress, King Sileshi Silesh Silboumi Silboumi turns to the camera, tilts his head, gives a winning grin, ceremonially bends to retrieve an ornate crossbow as tall as he, then bends again to retrieve an exquisitely woven quiver of long arrows. He takes a broad stance, notches a lethal-looking shaft, fires it out of the frame of the film, notches another, fires it, keeps firing arrows as the French-made tank rumbles into the frame, Sileshi posing there calmly, firing arrows right up to the moment the huge machine rolls over him on its way to restoring order.

The Girl of the Lake

CHICK FLEXHARDT HAD NEVER arrived at the lake in a cab, not once in his seventeen years. So he asked the cabbie to drop him at the top of the lane—at least he'd arrive walking. The woods were as dense as ever, the two-tracked lane as grassy, and the dark thoughts that had gripped him on the plane trip seemed to float up among the leaves of the trees and disappear.

Glimpses of the lake through the dense foliage, too. And then coming over the familiar rise he couldn't help but drop his enormous suitcase and run. As the old house came into view below he gave the family whistle, something between a loon and a lost coyote, grinned at the banner Grandma and he and his cousins and siblings had made a decade past—1959—all whacked up from felt scraps and home-boiled glue, a dozen colors—WELCOME TO THE LAKE—and nicely draped across the front of the house. Now how had Grandma managed that? He himself had cut and glued the last childish *e*, tall and narrow. He whistled again, ran faster.

The screen door banged and here was Grandma herself, undiminished at eighty-two (born 1887!), bustling up the steps to hug him. Her face was speckled and pale and full of expression, and family history, his mother's smile exactly, his brother's nose, her own eyes bright and blue, liquid at sight of him. She smelled of cookies and lotion and wood smoke and patted at his back as he patted at hers, hugged him longer than he'd been hugged since he was five, pushed him away to look at him, drew him back in. He fell into her willingly and hugged her back willingly, fragrance of powder, something flowery. Poor Grandma, all alone now.

She knew what he was thinking, as always. Cheerily, she said, "This place is a little quiet for just one of me!" She wouldn't make any more direct reference to Grandpa's death, Chick knew, and so Chick would say nothing, either. All that could be said about the old man's death, sadness and grief and abiding love and anger, had been in the hug.

In the cabin, everything was in place as it had been. Old-fashioned toys, some from Grandpa's childhood, the building blocks *Great-*Grandfather had made, chewed by a storied dog named Frisky, dead eighty years now.

"If you'll open some windows, I'll serve cookies and milk."

She'd been here a week with the shutters closed! Chick remembered the drill, could hear Grandpa as he carefully flicked the eyehook latches and pushed the shutters open, letting in light plane by plane till the years of dust sailed in it, swirled by the new breeze. The mildew tang left the living room, left the dining room, left the sunroom built out over the retaining wall to the very edge of the water. From the sunroom windows he watched the lake: whitecaps, which, as Grandpa had taught him, meant at least a fourteen-knot breeze. Straight out one mile away was Conflagration Island, then another mile to the far shore. Off along this shore to the east was the Gilman place on Abenaki Point, twenty-five rooms seldom occupied, and it didn't look as if anyone were there now. Then the DuPont place, almost hidden in the bassing cove, huge pines unmolested. Next there was the Mulvaney's more modest place with its half mile of shorefront looking somehow raw, Chick thought, then realized that most of its large old trees were missing. Further, there were signs of construction, plywood gleaming in yellow intervals along the shore where thick forest had always prevailed. Chick recalled all those dozen or more Mulvaney kids Grandpa had made such fun of—they'd been teenagers when Chick was small. They'd be grown-ups now, lots of babies in their arms, not a chance to find a person his own age or even close. Grandpa had predicted this: new cabins being built in choice spots on the land old man Mulvaney had bought so presciently when he'd become rich from ball bearings.

To the west, a long bight of untouched shoreline called Grandpa's Mile among the family. His money had come from the small-town insurance business Great-Grandpa had started and Grandpa had expanded into national prominence, then sold at peak value (such were the terms of the family story), only to fare poorly in subsequent ventures. But faring poorly was all relative—here still was the summer cottage Great-Grandpa had built, here still was the contiguous land Grandpa had later purchased outright from a logging outfit, unbroken for, in fact, 1.6 miles, all the way to the rocky point where the cluster of regular houses started, their rear windows facing the lake blandly, as if the water—so glorious—were just a wet back yard, nothing to put a dock in. *Working people,* Great-Grandpa had liked to repeat: *short on imagination.* The man himself was short on compassion. Born 1867! His grumpy face came vague to Chick's mind, the awful things he could say, the disappointment always in his ancient eyes, the sadness back there that a kid could see but not name, only avoid, the claws to grip your shoulder. Well, Great-Grandpa had been dead a long time.

Chick was very fond of working people and in fact meant to be a working person himself, despite the family prejudice. He was an excellent carpenter and mechanic, skills he'd learned from Grandpa, who'd bucked the old man and worked for a time in the trades.

Outside, Chick hooked each shutter faithfully open, tapping the eyehooks into spiderwebbed eyes, tight to the bend as Grandpa always insisted, opened the huge basement doors to air the dripping granite blocks of the walls in there, just another step of the familiar "house-up" routine, in Grandpa's phrase. In the basement Chick patted the canoes each in turn—red, white, and blue—*the fleet*, Grandpa always called them, three old wooden rigs built in another era by the last of the "wild" Abenaki Indians for Great-Grandpa, price of five dollars each, still in good shape these eighty years of maintenance later.

Chick heard his grandmother upstairs creaking the kitchen floorboards: safe. From his shirt pocket he quickly whipped his tight little bag of pot, plucked out the joint he'd rolled in the bathroom of the Greyhound, lit it quickly, flash of matchlight in the dank dark, two puffs, three, a fourth. Those cookies would taste good. He tucked it all back in his pocket, waved at the small cloud of smoke he'd made, then commenced to tugging at the blue canoe, brought it out into the light, the wings of his ears beginning to burn—how funny to have ears. He grinned and pulled the canoe out onto the grass, wanted to remember something. The paddles. He recalled the paddles and where they were and Grandpa clearly and he welled with such stoned sadness and such a profound feeling of being alone that tears started to his eyes.

He looked out across the lake. A whole summer! He'd been sacrificed for Grandma's happiness while his New York cousins all got to spend the summer in France. The Seattle cousins were safely in Seattle, little creeps, playing tennis indoors and out. The somewhat older Texas cousins remained in Houston doing their oil-industry and state-government internships, square as blocks. Dad had made it sound as if Chick had volunteered for a Grandma internship. Meanwhile, brother Frank got to stay on in his college town. Meanwhile, both his sisters got to go to greenhorn camp in Wyoming for two whole months. Meanwhile, his parents had started their six-week Kenyan adventure. And maybe come to think of it he *had* volunteered in a moment of warmth. But *Jumpin' Jehosaphat*. To quote an old man.

The summers of cousins were over.

Grandma's cookies were antidote to all that. Chocolate chip–peanut butter, a recipe Chick and she and a couple of cousins had invented for themselves in this very kitchen many years past. The woman was a genius of food, even here with no resources. Chick thought of the long drive to town. Twelve miles and all you got was tiny little Beemis Corners, with its meat shop and wooden grocery, its old-timey, one-pump gas station, tiny post office, busy feed store, one white church. He said, "Can you drive the jeep okay?"

"Mr. Parmenter has been driving us."

Chick grinned. He loved Mr. Parmenter, that jack-of-all-trades, bent and wizened but strong and sudden as a tractor transmission, too, almost as old as Grandma, loved him so much, in fact, that he had since kindergarten faithfully answered "caretaker" when asked what he'd like to be when grown up. The picture of Grandma and gruff Mr. Parmenter driving to town in Mr. Parmenter's old dump truck was too funny. Chick said, "Because I have learned to drive a shift."

Grandma fixed him in her patented firm gaze, formidable: "I'm told your permit isn't valid outside Connecticut."

Chick grinned, caught. "But I can practice? Just up and down the driveway?"

"You'll have to get that old thing to start first."

Chick took another cookie, bit it grinning. He'd fix that car all right. He said, "And I want to paddle to the island."

Grandma said, "We'll see about that!"

"I'm old enough," said Chick, the tones of a child invading his voice.

Grandma stared off, suddenly wistful. She said, "You all used to blueberry out there, didn't you."

Chick struggled to be adult, to think of Grandma and all she must be going through, just the words his mother had used admonishing him during good-byes. Quietly he said, "And the night before we went Grandpa would always tell the story."

"Well," said Grandma, drawing the syllable out fondly, Grandpa suddenly in her head and in the room around them.

Chick thought she'd like to tell the story. He primed the pump: "How there was once a house out there to rival the Gilman place . . ."

Again: "Well."

"And how it burned down."

"So he called it Conflagration Island, yes." She sounded irritable, suddenly. "But, of course, that's not the name. It's just Spruce Island. Such picnics you had, all of you." Her irritation seemed to give way to sadness. Grandma had never accompanied them out there, claiming "canoe aversion" in a comical, seasick way that yet seemed to hide something.

He prompted her again: "Grandpa said the family had to leave in guide boats."

"Total loss, yes. I wasn't in the picture at that time, of course." Sadder yet again, her soul shutters closing, the little clicks of the eyehooks all but audible: "'Twas a long, long time ago."

"And someone was killed?" This in a whisper. Chick knew just who was killed, but he fished for the secret he knew was lurking. When Grandpa would tell the story (all the cousins close around him at the fireplace), he'd grow sober and somber, not like him at all, and Grandma would sit away from him or even leave the room, such that as a kid with kid powers, you knew forcefully that something adult was going unsaid. Chick served himself a cookie, ate it in small bites, very patient, very polite.

Grandma thought a while, perfectly still, her head bowed. Suddenly she shifted, seemed to have made a decision. She said, "The daughter was killed, yes. Seventeen years old. And the dog, who they say went back into the house for her." She looked up quickly, said, "Your grandfather knew her, Chick." She held his eye. "He knew her rather well."

"She was his *girlfriend*," Chick blurted. Why else such emotion around the story for all these years? Grandma's tone, her reluctance, it was *jealousy*.

"I'm not sure they saw it like that," Grandma said slowly. "They were friends. Very good friends indeed."

"Very good friends indeed," said Chick. He saw Grandpa and the girl holding hands on an extensive dock, out of sight of the great house on the island, Grandpa seventeen (like Chick!), the girl lovely beside him. Grandpa he could picture perfectly. The girl—she was harder to conjure up, sepia tones, tight curls, sailor outfit. But no, that was an old photo of Grandma.

Who said pointedly, "Oh, it was all very proper, I think."

Clearly not! Chick pinched another cookie, munched it in excitement.

Grandma, eighty-two years old, *flushed*. Her voice grew hard. "The father, the girl's father, Chick, was a *bootlegger*. What we'd think of now as an organized-crime boss, something of a hero, perversely. One knew him from the newspapers: very dapper, very Irish. All his sons became politicians, all the daughters, well! *Tout ingénues*, you know, all very innocent, despite rife rumors. This one, the one who died, the youngest, she was called Aine, spelled in the Irish way." Grandma spelled it out, pronounced it *Anya*. "The fire, they say, was caused by a whiskey still or alternately by an explosion in the storage cellars: *spirits*." She stage-whispered that last word, loving a conspiracy of two.

"Spirits!" Chick gasped for her benefit.

"Meaning alcohol, young man, *with* which I'm certain you have no relation and *of* which no knowledge!"

Chick smiled innocently for her. "But you guys liked to drink! Martinis, every day at five."

"Darling, it's true, we did like a cocktail."

"And the people on the island never came back?"

"No, no, I suppose they couldn't bring themselves to do so. But in fact Shaunesseys still own Spruce Island. The children of Aine's siblings. They've let it all go back to nature, an agreeable tribute to her, even if it's an accident of finances. But something terrible is happening, Chick, now that we're speaking of it." She gave him a long, unhappy look.

Chick kept his face composed, gazed back at her soberly, hoping for something juicy. He'd be a receptacle for her secrets!

At length she coughed, all her sentences ready in her head. She said, "Mr. Parmenter says the island—well, he says it's up for sale."

That was what was so terrible? Chick's face must have given him away. Grandma's voice took on an injured tone he'd heard her use considerably but only with real adults. She said, "In the last four years nearly all the big parcels of land on the lake have changed hands, Chick. That Mulvaney boy is determined to turn this lake into a Levittown. Your uncle Bob is with him."

Chick swallowed his grin, which was a Flexhardt grin, the very one that plagued his grandpa and his father and his uncles and his brother, a show of teeth in the face of emotion. He knew what a Levittown was—vast tracts of houses packed together. Well, that wouldn't happen here.

Grandma rose, collected their plates and napkins and glasses, dropped them by the sink, returned for the cookie platter, which she pulled out from under Chick's nose pointedly and emptied into the cookie jar, off limits. She looked out the window over the sink for a long time, suddenly sagged into grief, much as she had at Grandpa's funeral, a sudden folding of the fortress, sorrow no grandmotherly courage could hide. Chick went to her, held her, planted his feet for strength. If he was all she had, then he would have to be enough.

HE WOKE TO THE smell of bacon frying, of course. Bacon was daily at the lake. Grandma seemed happy again, cheerfully whistling complete arias from Bellini's *I Puritani*, something she'd done so much over the years that Chick could whistle along. The day was brilliant again, a strong wind in the pine trees. After he'd eaten double what he wanted, and only then, he tripped outside and straight to the old jeep. His head was fuzzy from the pot he'd slipped out to smoke at midnight. Under the hood—that familiar, simple old engine—he found the battery freshly missing, that was all. Mr. Parmenter would have it in his shop on a charger, no doubt, no doubt would deliver it this afternoon with the newspaper and tonight's pork chops; that's how Grandma operated, three steps ahead of you, no matter what.

So next it was a walk up through the butterfly meadow, which was also the stargazing meadow and also the firefly meadow and sometimes the football field, or a Capture the Flag base, all depending, and quite a bit of making out—not Chick but those older cousins and their steadies, probably his parents as well back in their day. Up there he felt too alone, ran back down the lane to the lake, stared out at Spruce Island, conjuring not so much Grandpa and his colorful past and not so much the girl who had burned up as the idea of girls, girls in general, and love in general, loss in general, a sad feeling in his breast. He'd had such awful dates in the past year since Ginnie had handed him back his I.D. bracelet, dates crowned by the horror of his junior prom. When you had no steady girl, you had to ask someone cold. And Kelly Twiningham was cold, all right. First was her undisguised disgust when she learned he had no driver's license. No credit for having been grounded for the Southern Comfort incident at the homecoming game and therefore delayed a year. And then, just when she'd loosened up ever so slightly (he was an enthusiastic dancer), his dad had arrived to pick them up, brainlessly walking in on the last dance.

And to the boathouse. The wind was too strong, but Chick dragged the blue canoe across the lawn to the rudimentary beach. A loud knocking caught his attention, and there, suddenly, Grandma stood in the window of the house, plucking at the front of her smock: Don't forget your life vest. Well, a life vest was nice to sit on. He found an old one, dull orange, and two paddles, waved to her, shaking the vest for her to see, launched the heavy boat, made his way hugging the shore against the wind, all the way to Mulvaney's. Down there, yes, a number of houses had been built in the four years since Grandpa's crippling first heart attack. Chick waved to Patrick Mulvaney and two little girls, and they all waved back. The grand old family house reminded him of a mother hen, suddenly, all those littler houses growing up around it. He saw Mary Margaret Mulvaney (now named Carlson) down at their beach and waved. She was with four little boys. Once she'd been such a great beauty that even Chick at six had been smitten. She sat heavily on the stern of a rowboat, her chin cradled in her hands, oblivious of Chick in his canoe.

He turned and the wind scooted him along, sun in his face. He felt great, suddenly. Bad Patrick Mulvaney might have a beer for him one of these nights, at least that. Home, he tugged the canoe up onto the sand, lifting it high as Grandpa always commanded, saving that paint. Mr. Parmenter was there, big truck in the driveway. The jeep hood was up, battery going in. "Yes, and which one are you?" Mr. Parmenter said, avoiding eye contact, his ears flopping under his oily cap.

"I'm Charles Flexhardt," said Chick.

"Yup, yup. After your grandpa, you. He loved those old canoes, too, he did."

"I was just up the lake looking at the Mulvaney's."

"Oh, that Ronald Mulvaney. All them houses new, too, yup. You watch, next seasons several. There won't be a lot left on the shore here. Do you know Mulvaney himself has a bill in the state legislature to lift the motor ban? And for all his blither-blather about it the reason ain't boating, nope. The reason ain't fishing, nossuh! The reason is *opportunism*, going by the name of 'development,' going by the name of 'growth,' going by the name of 'jobs.' And much as I hate to say it, Charles, your uncle Bob is in on it, shortsighted of him, but there it is. Your uncle Bob and your aunt Lauren. Before—back when they was teens like you are now—it was always a *motorboat.* Now they've found a way to combine desecrations."

"People like to water ski," said Chick equably. He was familiar with Uncle Bob's arguments, Aunt Lauren's, all the fights they'd had with Grandpa. His own dad went along with the older siblings, generally, but with no great conviction. Uncle Philip, well, he wanted the house and land to stay forever as it was, but he was the baby of the family, a beatnik in New York with troubled daughters, what clout did he have?

Mr. Parmenter's fire had ignited. "You been to Lake Winnipesaukee lately? All the hell-roaring and gasoline fumes?"

"Well," Chick said. He pictured pretty two-piece girls in motorboats waving and wasn't entirely against the idea.

Mr. Parmenter didn't pause. He tapped the connector on the hot terminal, tightened the nut with his wrench, talked fast, thick accent as from another century: "You know the stripe of calm water as follows a motorboat? Those two-cycle engines put *one-third* of their gasoline unburned into the water, did you know that? A gallon for every three. These flatlanders will lift the motor ban, increase the property value, break everything up into lots, sell the shoreline dear, take the money and run. Your uncle Bob, he's one of them. What does he care for this place from far away in Houston?"

"He wouldn't break up Grandpa's Mile!"

"Oh, ho. You ask your grandmother what line Mr. Bob's been talking! You should read the letter of support he sent the *august* New Hampshire State Legislature! An out-of-stater, he! If they can change a few inconvenient laws and buy it all up! Well, then! Mulvaney's, DePew's, Gilman's, the railroad bed, your Grandpa's mile, Spruce Island—it all starts with motorboats."

"Then I don't want motorboats!"

"We'll see about that. Plenty of you kids to occupy plenty of new houses, and taxes to pay. You think your uncle Bob is going to watch a million dollars sit on its hairy fundament by water?"

Chick laughed. He loved Mr. Parmenter. Now he remembered Grandpa's banter with the sharp little man, tried it on: "Oh, come on, you old fat! It's not worth a million!" *Fat* meant "fart." It was Grandpa-talk.

"Soon be," said Mr. Parmenter, grinning briefly and infinitesimally as he had for the old man, very nearly looking directly at Chick. "Now clamp your fangs you little shite and let me show you the clutch on this old girl."

And soon Chick was on his own in the jeep, roaring up the quarter mile of lane, turning around in the meadow, stalling, turning the key, double clutching as instructed, pretending the twin boulders were cars to park between, K-turn, back down the hill, reverse cautiously into the car shed, then forward out, race up the driveway and back down, up and back, forward and reverse, pumping that clutch, shifting up, shifting down. Life was good.

BACON DAILY, CHORES ALSO, Sundays to town for church in Mr. Parmenter's truck, the old caretaker dressed in a white shirt of the thinnest imaginable cloth, washed weekly for forty years Chick guessed, the shiniest black jacket, ragged tie, same old work pants and boots. How Chick admired the man. At church—Congregationalist—Mr. Parmenter stood at the back. Chick and his grandmother sat in the third pew left, same as always, Grandma listening fervently, Chick scanning the crowd surreptitiously for girls during hymns, hallelujah.

That first Sunday a button-tight summer girl all in white captured his attention, but she wasn't about to return his gaze.

Toward the end of the interminable service, he managed to look behind him. In one of the side-facing pews under the windows, the gas-station girl caught his eye. She was a redhead with palest skin and freckles, her dress a homemade blue thing with ruffles at the collar. She'd outgrown it pretty thoroughly and it was short as a play dress, rode up her thighs, stretched taut across her tomboy's chest, gaped at the buttons, showing an underblouse of some kind. She caught Chick staring and blushed hard. Next hymn he looked back again and she stuck out her tongue. Next she crossed her eyes. Next time he craned, her father was the one looking, and she'd sat up straight, her hands on her knees.

She and her father were well known to live alone above the garage in town. Her mother had died of something years ago. The girl's name was old fashioned, Chick remembered, and she was called Mena. He'd been aware of her for some years—since childhood, really—as someone friendly and nice. Philomena. But now there was this, too: her legs were long and bare in church. He caught sight of her one more time during the recessional. In the old days you'd go to town for gas and groceries with Dad and see her, make kid jokes. White socks and saddle shoes in church, crossed ankles. Mechanic and daughter didn't attend the coffee circle after service, so that was about it for her. Still, now there was a reason to go to church.

Chick split all the wood Mr. Parmenter brought, raced him secretly load for load, did pretty well at it, too, small splits for the kitchen stove, larger for the living room stove, which they'd likely use but once or twice all summer, larger yet for the fireplace, which they'd use more, though not these days: the weather stayed hot. "Summah," Mr. Parmenter said with distaste. He came every day at three, brought ice, brought mail, brought the paper, brought meat, did a chore or two. Grandma cooked. That was her idea of a great day. She cooked and swept and worked in the gardens and took a swim and read thick books from the cabin shelves in one of the old leather chairs. Chick got bored with the driveway but resisted the temptation to pull the jeep out on Race Road and finally get to shift properly to third. That's something maybe you would do early on a Sunday morning, when the sheriff was still in bed, not that you ever saw the sheriff out here. He paddled to Patrick Mulvaney's one late afternoon, but Patrick had found Jesus and was no longer bad: no beer. Brenda Mulvaney, named DeCastro now, was up visiting—she was pretty nice but busy on the newest of all the houses going up. Her little brother Mark would be here later in the summer, she said. Whoop-dee-doo. Mark Mulvaney was youngest of that generation, only twenty-three, but his idea of a party had always been chess. He was an accountant now, had landed some kind of big-time tie-and-jacket job straight out of college.

The wind stayed high, but the little old sailboat was in poor shape, the sails rotted, so there was no fun to be had in wind. Chick got it in his mind to paddle one of the canoes out to Conflagration Island soon as the weather came calm. And a few weeks into his stay, it did. Grandma had never let any of the kids paddle out across the open water, so Chick waited till midmorning when she took her clockwork nap, telling her he'd go see Mark Mulvaney, of whom she hugely approved: Mark, boring or no, had vowed publicly to keep his section of the Mulvaney shore forever wild.

Grandma had spent her morning making Chick a lunch for the trip, insisted he provide for his conservation-minded friend, too. The ancient picnic basket weighed a ton: one whole roast chicken, the first three cucumbers from her garden, four thick slices of her raisin bread, a large bag of potato chips, great piles of chocolate cookies, and as if all of that weren't enough, fruit, too, all the grapes Mr. Parmenter had brought, three oranges, a pear.

The basket rode in the center of the canoe, shaded with an extra life preserver. Fishing rod, just in case. Grandpa's homemade wind keel, too, just in case—but the water was glass. Two extra paddles, just in case. Grandma saw to all that and saw him off with fond waves and brave smiles as if he were crossing into another life. Chick paddled in silence toward Mulvaney's, made the point of land at Gilman's, and figuring Grandma safely in her bed, made a sweeping turn to port and Conflagration Island. At first, he seemed to make no progress, and a vague fear touched at his chest, but soon enough the island grew perceptibly bigger, the trees perceptibly more individual, the gray mass of rocky shore differentiated into all its tumbled rocks. Chick could make out several little beaches, picked one of the middle ones. Halfway there, he got out of the lee of Mocassabontee Mountain and the breezes pushed at his bow, turning him, slowing him. J-stroke, pull hard, keep the bow straight. That was Grandpa's voice. Even with the wind and the diversion to Mulvaney's, the whole trip didn't take an hour.

The little landing he'd spotted was all sand, fine and white, like nothing on Grandpa's shore. He beached the canoe, tucked the picnic basket in the cold shade of a thicket of sheep laurel hard on the water. A faint path led into the spruce forest and then along the crest of a rise along the water toward the southern tip of the island. Okay. He'd make a perimeter hike before lunch. When the path petered, he kept going, just pushed his way through the thick woods, clambered down to the lake wherever a little beach presented itself, pleased at the lack of footprints in the varying types of sand. He made a cup with his two hands, drank deeply from the clarity of the lake, carried on. Warblers sang and blue jays called and chickadees twittered, rattling the twigs above him. A red squirrel scolded. How had the first one gotten out here? This was olden woods—not a place a house might have stood. Chick remembered Grandpa's gait, those sloped shoulders. The old man would never say where the mansion had been, only grew private when pressed, his face closing like a gate.

At length, already famished, Chick reached the northern tip of the island, a rock promontory he'd often seen from the sailboat, granite in tumbled slabs and cubes, nothing rounded, all of it gripped by lichens in several colors and shapes, the rock faces fissured and laced with quartz, lovely stuff. He sat. Why hadn't he thought to bring along just one single leg from that chicken? The breeze had freshened nicely. He sat on the rock, enjoying the air in his face, pulled out his pot, put it back, pulled it out again—hell, why not?—rolled an expert joint, thinking of his friends at home: Chris Zucco, Tim Collins, Merriweather Peters. Merriweather had his queer name but he also had Martha Linborn, most beautiful girl in school, and they made no secret of their love life, which was torrid and which Chick enjoyed vicariously and envied viciously. Chick struck a match, struck another, lit the joint. His summer's worth of marijuana, an amount carefully calculated during an hour's discussion with Chris and Tim to last three months, was more than a quarter gone, and summer barely underway. He wondered, puffing, if Mr. Parmenter would bring out a case of beer if he asked, or a bottle of gin more likely, since that is what Grandpa had drunk and wouldn't Grandma like a little? He still had one of the twenty-dollar bills Dad had pressed into his hand at the bus station. The other had gone for the long cab ride from Keene.

The breeze was heavenly in his face. What would it take to restore the sailboat? A sail, for starters. He carefully saved two-thirds of his joint, placed it in the pot bag, jammed this in his pocket. Merriweather and Martha, wow. He'd seen her with her shirt up once, what might have been an embarrassing moment but wasn't. Just that glimpse of her two breasts like fourteen-knot gusts and whitecaps before Merriweather's hand had blocked the view and Chick, having burst in through the screen door excited with some news or other, retreated from the gazebo in Merriweather's vast yard.

All alone on the perfect rocks of a perfect island, and nothing to eat, besides! He challenged himself to walk the perimeter of the island anyway, not retrace his steps for mere sustenance. He vaulted boulders, scurrying happily till the shore turned impossible, trotted up then into the spruce woods and ran on the soft duff, slapping branches away from his face, taking cuts on his legs. He dove out of the woods, raced down the length of a long sand beach that had only then gotten the morning sun, heavenly bright heat, sprinted till the beach ended at thick brush and boulders. He leapt back up into the woods, hot into his lone competition, noted the shift to white pines, tall, thick-boled trees, plenty of space in among them for a Spartan messenger to run full speed from his pursuers, then sunlight and a large meadow, well overgrown and blown with dandelion seed and dozens of tiny blue butterflies tumbling in pairs, rattling poplar trees taking over the far corner, crowding like Mulvaneys. He stopped to breathe it all in, pulled up a fistful of daisies—Grandma loved daisies—made a leaping pirouette, now a dancer, heard a steel jingle, turned in time to see a large black lab bounding toward him.

His breath caught, his heart started in his chest. This huge dog, racing silently at him. But it pulled up short ten feet away, still silent, dog grin, intelligent dog face, warm dog eyes gazing at him. Chick gazed back, a long locking of eyes, the sort even trusting dogs will only sometimes allow. Heavy golden chain for a collar. Golden tags, hanging. No wag of the tail. Just the gaze, the seeming smile. And then the creature bounded off the way it had come.

So someone else was here. Chick breathed. He stood watching the way the dog had gone. The scare dropped down through his legs and left him slowly. The thing was to simply continue on his way, and maybe he'd run into them, whoever they were. Plenty of people must paddle out here. Chick crossed the meadow into blueberry scruff. Maybe this was where he and his cousins and siblings had come with Grandpa. What else to do but continue his perimeter march, clear to the southern point of the island, rough going through blueberry bushes knee and thigh high, the berries so close to ripe but not, no handfuls to ease his hunger. All along the way he inspected the shore, visited every beach, but no boat, no footprints of dog or man. Quickly he made the south point, which was a sandy spit that drew itself out under water, a place he'd often grounded his sailboat in order to swim awhile, sunbathe.

No footprints. No boat. The dog bounded in Chick's mind. Lunch beckoned. The western shore was difficult walking, his stomach rumbling, but he kept up the pace, crossed into the far end of the meadow in which he'd encountered the dog, hurrying.

And fell into a basement hole.

HE STOOD SLOWLY WHERE he'd landed, found himself shoulder deep in the ground, happy to be unhurt. He knew where he was immediately: the ruins of the Shaunessey mansion. The wall visible in front of him wasn't just glacial granite but blasted blocks of great dimension, placed for the ages. The soil at his feet, grown in with weeds and the feeble shoots of crowded and ill-fed birch trees, would be old beams, burned and fallen in, long rotted. He climbed out easily, paced off the rest of the foundation, gradually picked out the dimensions of the house. He'd come right back here after lunch. And he vowed he'd come back daily and do some digging!

He ran, starved, excited. Come to think of it, his knee was sore from the fall. He checked out a little cove—no boats. He barreled through a hemlock grove and into a stand of old beeches—lovely, open forest on a high bluff. Then back into spruces, thick. He spotted his beach, but it wasn't his beach—it was another, its shape a mirror image of the first. He froze. A young woman was just then wading in from a swim, and she was naked. The dog leapt beside her, bounding from the water, seemed to catch scent of Chick, pulled up short. The girl looked where the dog was pointing and caught Chick's eye. He thought she'd shriek, but she only grinned and waved and kept coming, the lake dripping from her hair, her pale skin, her black diamond of pubic hair. She cocked her head and twisted her dark hair and wrung the water from it and kept Chick's eye, kept her grin. There was no boat. She walked to him much as the dog had done earlier, not bounding like the dog but walking purposefully, strode right to him across the little beach in a fond hurry as if she'd grab him and hug him and kiss him but stopped suddenly several yards away and only looked at him grinning, yes, much as the dog had done. Her face, wet in the bright shade, was somehow incandescent. Chick broke her gaze, looked lakeward so as not to look at her bare self: Where was her boat? Where was her bathing suit? But she kept staring. Chick looked back, quickest sweep of her body, then carefully into her eye, her unchanged, enamored expression.

"Hi," he said, heart pounding.

The young woman held his gaze just a moment more, said nothing, motioned with her head for him to follow, and darted prettily up into the spruces the way Chick had just come, the dog at her heels. Chick lingered a moment—where was her boat?—then followed. But in the vast openness of the woods the young woman and her dog were simply gone.

GRANDMA HAD MADE DINNER, of course. She was so thin, yet ate so much. They were quiet during the salty bean soup, and quiet during the main course, which was a pork roast with potatoes, but during Mr. Parmenter's garden asparagus, Grandma said, "I saw you paddling back from Spruce Island."

Chick just nodded.

Grandma gave him a long look. "What did you find out there?"

"Blueberries aren't ready."

"I've never been."

"Well, at the north end there are rocks. South end is sand. Lots of big trees—really big trees."

"It was Charles's favorite place," Grandma said.

"He took us every summer."

"Grandpa, I mean. I'm glad you like it, too."

"I like it very much."

Grandma got up, cleared the plates for the salad course, greens and radishes and some very tiny carrots from her own garden, with a dressing of her herbs in vinegar. Dessert was still to come.

Chick got up, too, cleared the table. There wouldn't be another word till every dish was done and dried and put away and dessert on the table. And soon enough, there it was, a raspberry tart fresh from the wood-fired oven.

They sat and briefly prayed once again, then dug in. Grandma with whipped cream on her nose said, "Chick, I burden you."

He shook his head—no, no—she couldn't possibly. He thought of the young woman on the island, thought better of telling Grandma.

"Grandma, the trees out there are the biggest ones I've seen anyplace."

"Oh, they'll cut those for lumber first thing."

"There were no footprints in the sand anywhere."

"Then there will be a cable sunk for power, and lights all night. Eventually a motor-ferry service, I imagine."

GRANDMA DRESSED HERSELF FOR an hour—prim blouse, hint of scent, rustling skirts, stockings, who knew how many layers of heavy cloth and unguents on the hot morning. Chick walked her up to wait by the jeep for Mr. Parmenter, who arrived punctually. Chick helped him pull the new sail in its canvas bag from the back of the truck. Grandma had banking to do, and some visiting, even an appointment at the hospital all the way down in Keene to certify her mental health for some changes in her will, and a stop at the lawyers to discuss that document and strategies in the fight against Uncle Bob and Aunt

Lauren. Grandpa's wishes were to be preserved! "Would you like to come along?"

Chick took his chin in hand comically, making a show of having to think very hard, which was not altogether an act. It was so windy there'd be no way to paddle to Spruce Island. Then again, there was nothing whatever to do in town. Except maybe talk with Philomena at the gas station. Her father, Mr. Hardy, was not only a mechanic but also first selectman of Beemis Corners (Mr. Parmenter had let it be known in response to Chick's discreet inquiry) and was famous for having memorized the entire text of Ralph Waldo Emerson's long essay *Nature*, which he'd declaim with some drama at town meeting. Chick saw himself just sort of sauntering up to the pumps while Grandma did her errands, saw himself making easy conversation with the gas girl, despite his personality. Her father was nice—he wouldn't mind. Mr. Parmenter, on the other hand, was impatient. Chick would need to comb his hair. He'd need to change into long pants. "No, no thanks," he said.

He lugged the new sail down to the boathouse, pulled out the J-boat's mast, puzzled over how to proceed, went to work. For a break he drove the jeep: roar up the hill, turn around, roar back down, turn around, roar up the hill to the very crest of Race Road. There he looked both ways a dozen times, worked the clutch expertly, and pulled out. The jeep had to climb through deep potholes to make it, popped onto the pavement with a lurch, and stalled broadside across the entire road. Chick pumped the gas pedal several times before he fully realized what had happened; when he tried to restart the engine, of course, the carburetor was flooded. In fact, it seemed to him that the whole forest smelled of gasoline. His stomach lurched, his heart raced. Mindful of the license plates four years out of date, he leapt out the door, opened the hood, waved at the gas fumes. You had to wait. He paced on the road. No car came, but what if one did? At length, he remembered a trick Grandpa had taught him, leapt back in, pushed the gas pedal to the floor. When he turned the key again the engine caught with an explosion, ran smoothly. Chastened, Chick reversed straight back into the sanctuary of the driveway, kept backing, right down the hill, left the jeep in its place, trotted to the cabin, made himself a king's luncheon of leftovers.

And then back to the sailboat. He finished lacing the new sail onto the mast and boom, then rigged the boat. It was dirty from years of disuse. He pulled it into the lake, found the big sponge, washed the hull and cockpit for an hour at least, every crevice, Grandpa's voice in his head: a clean boat wins. The tiller would need a sanding and varnish, the centerboard, too, but with the new sail and the wash, the J-boat looked pretty yar to Chick's eye. He set out for a test run but soon found himself sailing to the island, a slow process into a stiff breeze, long tacks north and south, gains upwater of a hundred yards at most, a couple of hours before he made the southern sandbar and pulled up.

He looked at the huge trees in front of him, the disarray of boulders. Quickly he tied up, waded ashore, walked inland. He made the meadow quickly, found the basement hole, looked into it, looked around. No sign of a dog. No sign of the young woman. He made his way in a froth to the place he'd seen her, pushed his way out of the forest. Her beach was empty. His footprints were there, just where he'd stood, somewhat faded.

She and the dog had left none, no trace.

AND SUMMER WORE ON. Chick sailed daily, and made a daily stop on Conflagration Island, never another sign of the island girl or her dog. He dug fervently for a few afternoons around the foundation of the Shaunessey mansion and found a tiny silver spoon, but that was all. This, he kept in his pocket. And one afternoon as he pulled up he spotted a canoe beached—he investigated in some excitement but found only a father and two young boys setting up a tent, getting ready to camp a few days. "We saw your dog," the father said warily.

Chick gazed at him long.

The man said, "Scared us half to death!"

The boys nodded.

Chick turned and walked into the woods, sprinted silently across the duff and to her end of the island. He waited at the foundation of Aine's house. He waited longer at her beach. He felt that she was near no longer.

CHICK PULLED WEEDS WHILE Grandma harvested radishes and spinach and two kinds of kale and pole beans. She took frequent breaks, sat on the large rock Mr. Parmenter had hauled and positioned as a bench so long ago. Chick thought of Grandpa, of Aine. He'd never been that near a grown girl naked before, for one thing; he'd never expected his pure response to such a sight, for another. It wouldn't be like that with a living girl.

The conversation with Grandma continued in starts. "Something to tell you," she said abruptly. Clearly she'd been saving whatever was coming, rehearsing her lines. She and Mr. Parmenter had made two more trips to town, and from each one she'd come back more beatific, all but glowing, charged with a secret cheer, but characteristically tight lipped.

"About time," Chick said wryly. They'd gotten awfully comfortable with one another in six weeks.

"Well, in a way it's rather simple. Let me just come right out with it." But she waited, beaming at him.

"What?" Chick said.

"Well, dear, you've bought an island."

"Me?" Chick said.

"Yourself," said Grandma.

"How on Earth?"

"I've got some papers for you to sign in Mr. Parmenter's presence."

"You mean Conflagration Island?"

"I mean *Spruce* Island. I have made you a gift of funds from my estate, such as it is, a gift that will doubtless make my children unhappy, since it leaves me impoverished. But my first allegiance is to Grandpa, and you are his only hope. Listen closely, would you? As your trustee, I've arranged to invest your newfound money in a certain well-defined piece of New Hampshire land. Yes, Spruce Island! Don't blink so! Are you with me? It's not so complicated as it seems. The island is yours, to do with as you wish. It seems I can also make you an outright gift of our land—not more than your share, of course, just exactly one-sixteenth the old Northern Paper tract, five hundred acres more or less. But your share will be the five hundred acres on the lake: Grandpa's Mile." She smiled again, couldn't help herself.

Chick grinned, but it was the Flexhardt grin, a shield to hide his surprise and his fear.

Grandma said, "We've arranged to set you up with a reasonable legal fund, too, just in case, although Mr. Milligan, Esquire, has revised my last will and testament so as to disinherit anyone implementing a lawsuit against the arrangements I'm outlining. Your grandpa's will was far too loose, would have left the land to everyone in a block. Mine was the same. My new will divides it precisely. Your uncle Bob will get his half a thousand acres, and surely he'll not want to jeopardize his ownership! It's the land up there along both sides of Highway Four, which begs for development. The rest of your kin too, everyone gets a share in large tracts behind yours—your parents, your siblings, your cousins and aunts and uncles—fair portions of deepest woods, beautiful cabin sites abounding. They might persuade the, um . . . the *lakefront owner* . . ." And here Grandma folded her hands dramatically and faintly bowed her head as if to a great lord. "They might persuade *such a man* to grant easements for footpaths to the water, nothing more. But, Chick, only he who loves it will get the lake."

AT BREAKFAST ON ONE of the perfect days of mid-August, still no notion in the wind that the season might ever end, Grandma asked Chick if he wanted ee-coff.

Chick laughed. "Ee-coff?" he said.

"Ee-coff," said Grandma.

"I don't drink ee-coff, Grandma."

She grinned sheepishly, charmingly, laughed at herself, and that had been that.

At lunch she said, "Look at me, Charles," and Chick looked a long while. She looked so beautiful, so square and strong and happy.

After dinner—which was one of Mr. Parmenter's chickens, roasted perfectly, tiny potatoes, string beans with almonds, chocolate cake, a delicate discussion about her favorite music versus Chick's (Italian opera not so different from Miles Davis, they decided, at least in its effects on the soul)—she said she had a *drumming* headache.

The next morning she stood vacantly in the kitchen, simply stared at Chick, a block of raw bacon in her hand.

"Grandma?"

She grinned sheepishly, said nothing.

"Grandma?"

Chick accepted the bacon from her, put it back on ice, gathered her up in his arms—surprisingly heavy for such a little bird—enveloped her and heaved her up the walk to the jeep, sat her in the passenger seat, where she retained her posture. One time his sister had gotten stitches from a doctor somewhere near, but he had no idea where, or who. Of course there was no phone. He drove carefully up the humped driveway to Race Road, pulled out over the potholes at the proper speed to beat them, drove stiffly twelve miles to Beemis Corners, twenty-five long minutes without conversation. At the gas station he pulled in and honked long and loud. Mena flounced out, annoyed at the honking till she saw Chick and blushed. He asked politely where he might find a hospital. She looked at him closely, then at Grandma. "Oh my," she said. "The hospital is in Keene. It's twenty miles. Mrs. Flexhardt?"

"Is there a doctor?"

"In Keene, I said."

Chick began to panic. He said, "How do I find it?"

"Oh dear," Philomena said. She patted his arm, eyes sparkling with care. In a rush, she said, "I'll go with you!" She called to her father, who hurried from the garage at her tone, wrenches in hand. The girl quickly explained: Mrs. Flexhardt was ill. Her father was as urgent as she, tears starting to his eyes. Everyone loved Grandma. Philomena climbed in the back seat and gave directions. Chick had never driven on a highway but found it easy once he got used to all the cars passing him, all the honking.

Mena leaned forward, held Grandma's shoulder, said, "Speed up a little," but it was hard for Chick to go over the speed limit Mr. Parmenter had told him for Race Road, thirty miles an hour. The girl smelled of gasoline. She put a hand on Chick's shoulder, too. Her hair was red in the mirror, her cheeks streaked with engine grease. He used the mirror to catch her bright green eye for reassurance. Grandma sat very still. Thinking of other disasters and with no preamble, Chick unburdened himself, said, "I saw the Shaunessey girl out there."

"I've seen her, too," Mena said matter of fact, knowing what he meant by "out there": Spruce Island, of course. She said, "Aine Shaunessey. She's so very beautiful, isn't she? Wasn't she? And her dog! I was frightened of them, though. Purely silent. That loverly dress. I dropped my bucket and ran back to the boat. No one believed me." She tightened her grip on his shoulder.

The trip took forty minutes, but they made Keene, Grandma's

posture perfect the whole ride. She was silent and unblinking, but she breathed well and Chick knew she'd be okay.

At the emergency-room entrance he pulled up perfectly, set the parking brake. He and Mena went to help Grandma out, but despite the straight spine and high chin, the open eyes, she was unmoving. Boy and girl hefted the old woman, carried her into the emergency-room lobby. Two nurses scurried to their sides as they lay their burden on the floor. A doctor rushed in, and then a couple of orderlies in blue scrubs who lifted Grandma onto their gurney in a calm hurry. But after a busy few minutes the doctor just stopped. He set his chin, looked at Chick. The orderlies relaxed.

"I'm sorry," one of the nurses said.

Philomena burst into hot tears. Chick, then, too. Shocked and weeping, standing among strangers, it was only natural that he and Mena caught one another in a tight embrace, the nurse then folding them both in her own arms, then an orderly joining in, then the doctor, a long group hug, protocol abandoned, all of them in their humanity.

Mena's father arrived with Mr. Parmenter in short order. Chick had never seen a man cry like Mr. Parmenter cried when he heard the news. The old bird dropped to his knees, held his face, sobbed and gulped inconsolably, so devastated that even an hour later he couldn't drive the jeep home but had to ride with Mr. Hardy, Mena and Chick in the broad back seat of the mechanic's ancient woodie, her foot hooked stealthily round Chick's calf, their fingers tightly interlaced, sweaty after a while, almost painful, too—didn't matter, they weren't going to let go.

CHICK'S PARENTS WERE SO far unreachable in Kenya, though Grandma's lawyer sent off a telegram. Uncle Philip, deeply saddened, said he'd find the next flight, a long phone conversation originated at Chick's end from the lawyer's office. The jeep had been Uncle Philip's, and he said he knew it well—he'd fly into Keene tomorrow first thing, get a cab to the hospital, deal with any bills, simply drive himself up to Beemis Corners and to the funeral home to make arrangements, and then head out to camp.

Uncle Bob, disturbed at work in Houston, asked after Grandma's will first thing, and the lawyer, quick and direct and mighty as a twelve-man rowing shell, told him of the changes, read from the document at length. "It's ironclad," he said to each query. "Witnessed by the probate judge here, as it happens." After a while, Chick could hear Uncle Bob shouting, but the lawyer kept his professional demeanor, finally said, "Why don't you call when you're feeling better, Mr. Flexhardt," hung up in the midst of the next fulmination.

So they wouldn't be seeing Uncle Bob until the funeral, if then. The lawyer had already put it in motion, and the minister was on board—they both knew Grandma's wishes—service to be that coming Saturday at the Congregational church, burial in the olden churchyard beside Grandpa, the last two people, as it happened, who would ever be buried there.

Chick was to stay with Mr. Parmenter overnight, and it was like staying in a tool museum, grilled cheese sandwiches cooked directly on the old man's smithy forge, Chick's bed nothing but a cot in the warm workshop, Mr. Parmenter's not much fancier, upstairs, those great, gulping sobs in the night.

MENA'S DAD DROPPED CHICK and Mena at the lake the next morning. He'd given his daughter the day off, but the station had to stay open, not a word about behaving: Mena lived in a world of trust.

Alone at the cabin, hot day, they were shy with one another, new friendship in the newly bereft setting, oddly sweet. Chick showed her around a little, then they made a lunch to bring in the sailboat, hardly had to say where they were going. She had a one-piece suit that didn't fit anymore, just like her church dress. Chick's heart leapt to her, how bare she looked, so pale. They launched the boat—she knew just what to do—sat shoulder-to-shoulder and hip-to-hip sailing, not much to say, though her fingers found his. There was little wind, just desultory breezes, and it was going to take forever to get out there.

"I always liked when you came to the shop with your grandpa," she said.

"We'd play in your sandbox."

"Yeah, and I'd see you in church."

They ate one of their bacon and tomato sandwiches. Grandma had been holding the bacon when she froze, Chick recalled. He'd had to take it from her hands.

Mena's hair was so red in the sun. She had freckles—a lot of freckles. She looked about half-mischievous, half-studious, all a little sad in the moment, studied him, some kind of plan back there behind those green eyes. "I had a dream we were married," she said after a long time.

Chick didn't know what to say to that.

"We were married and lived on Spruce Island," she said. "We had a big golden retriever, the sweetest dog."

He squeezed her hand. She picked his up and kissed it. He held the tiller and turned to her and tried to kiss her cheek but instead as the boat pitched bumped her eyebrow with his lips. No matter, she turned her mouth up to his and after a couple of tries they were kissing and the boat fell into irons and they kissed a long time. He hadn't done it much, just tried his best. It felt nice. It felt really nice. That she liked it, too. That it was new to her, too.

On the island there was no ghostly dog, no sign of anyone. They walked to the big meadow, crossed it in Queen Anne's lace. At the other end, Chick showed Mena the foundation of the Shaunessey mansion, showed her where he'd dug up the spoon. They dug a little more, didn't find anything. But it was her territory, too, and she showed him the giant, broken swimming pool—he'd never seen or heard of that—all grown in, filled with leaves and sticks and a deep layer of mud, a beautiful cement fountain at the far end. "You have to imagine," she said, and together they closed their eyes.

"She was naked," he said. That seemed too bold. So: "Skinny-dipping, I mean."

"In a sundress," Mena said. "And carrying a book. When I saw her." And then they opened their eyes and walked and she showed him where—the remains of an outbuilding, maybe a carriage house, a big building, anyway, or must have been.

He told her about the island. That he was the owner now. She seemed to know it already. She seemed to know a lot, and they chatted, walking. Back at the little beach they ate more, and then swam—increasingly sweltering day—and then as a breeze came up they stood face to face and neck deep in the lapping wavelets. She took his face in her hands and kissed him. And then she let him kiss her. And then they kissed and shared a full embrace, the water so nice. But after a while Chick fell into tears.

"I'm sorry," Mena said, not shushing him, just holding on. "Your grandma was really, really nice," she said, tears of her own.

Chick was okay. Chick was fine. So was Mena. They pressed up against one another, as close as two people could get, kissing. After a long time they started laughing, and then splashed one another, then spontaneously fell into an awkward, splattering race back to shore, Chick surprised to find himself far in the lead. But when they got to the beach he saw why: Mena was holding her suit in her hands, stood there naked as Aine.

"I just wanted you to see," she said, and he saw. She walked back into the water, neither slow nor fast, turned and walked toward him one more time, stood in her innocence neither close nor far.

"Later we'll do more," she said. "But let's not be too fast."

"Okay," Chick said, not even embarrassed, his bathing suit standing out. She was just that nice, easy to be with, not surprised by the truth of him, like they'd known each other a hundred years.

"We'll build a house over there," he said as she put her suit back on.

"And we'll have three children," she said.

And they said a lot more, fomenting a plan for Chick to attend high school there, fomenting all sorts of plans, lay on the beach and predicted a whole life in Beemis Corners and on the lake, the two of them and then a growing family caretaking all of Chick's land and Mena's father's acreage, too, not nearly so much but an important piece down by town, caretaking the lake and their property for all their years, which would be uncommonly long, caretaking for conservation, caretaking for increasing use, a detailed conversation, a subject they'd both thought about a great deal, and something new they were only feeling now, that they were in love and that their love would be part of the whole process, dreamy talk, not knowing, of course, that everything they said would come true but believing it truly. And they kissed all the while, the sun crossing the sky, and then when it seemed a danger that they'd go too far—an ache for the ages, and they with all the time in the world—they straightened up their suits, rolled up their towels, launched the little sailboat, and Mena at the tiller, sailed back to the storied old Flexhardt cabin, where Uncle Philip had arrived in the jeep, expansive wave, their ally for all the days to come.

Acknowledgments

THESE STORIES HAVE FOUND form over many years and continued to grow even as they came together here. I thank all the editors who touched them along the way, but especially Kathy Pories, my editor at Algonquin, who touched them last, and is a treasure. "Harbinger Hall" first appeared in the *Atlantic Monthly*. "Kiva" appeared under the title "Investigation" in *Iron Horse*. "The Fall" first appeared in *Playboy*. "Princesa" appeared in the *Missouri Review* and is offered in homage to the Elizabeth Bowen story "Contessa." "Broadax, Inc." and "The Girl of the Lake" first appeared in *Ecotone*. "Some Should" appeared as "Confession" as part of the *Ploughshares Solos* series, where it is still available. I thank my beautiful cadre of first readers, especially Katherine Heiny, Nina DeGramont, David Gessner, Melissa Falcon, and Debra Spark. Thanks to everyone at Algonquin, still my favorite publisher—it takes not only a village but a small army to make a book happen, and they are the very best at what they do, from acquisition to edit to design to cover to publicity to marketing to management, and just plain humanity overall. And finally, of course, thanks to Juliet and Elysia, the main characters every day of my life. Here's to the short story, long may it live!

About the Author

BILL ROORBACH'S PREVIOUS BOOKS from Algonquin are *The Remedy for Love*, one of six finalists for the 2015 Kirkus Fiction Prize, and the bestselling *Life Among Giants*, which won the Maine Literary Award for fiction in 2012. His story "Big Bend" won an O. Henry Award, and his collection by the same name won the Flannery O'Connor Award, both in 2000. His trio of memoirs in nature, *Temple Stream*, *Into Woods*, and *Summers with Juliet*, have been released in new paperback editions, and his craft book, *Writing Life Stories*, is used in writing programs around the world. Roorbach has been named a 2018 Civitella Ranieri Foundation fellow. He lives in Maine, where he writes full time. More at www.billroorbach.com.